The Oracle of Ur Book 2
TEMPLE OF LIES

Penny Barron

© 2024 by Penny Barron

All rights reserved. No part of this book, in part or in whole, may be reproduced, transmitted or utilized in any form or by any means, electronic, photographic or mechanical, including photocopying, recording, or by any information storage and retrieval system without permission in writing from Ozark Mountain Publishing, Inc. except for brief quotations embodied in literary articles and reviews.

For permission, serialization, condensation, adaptions, or for our catalog of other publications, write to Ozark Mountain Publishing, Inc., P.O. Box 754, Huntsville, AR 72740, ATTN: Permissions Department.

Library of Congress Cataloging-in-Publication Data
Penny Barron - 1972 -
The Oracle of Ur Book 2: Temple of Lies by Penny Barron
    Sequel to *The Oracle of Ur*, Ancient Sumer 3800 BC. The continuation of the life of Girl/Saoirse in the life as a seer.

1. Prehistory 2. Dreams 3. Visions 4. Oracles
I. Barron, Penny -1972- II. Metaphysical III. Prehistory IV. Title
Library of Congress Catalog Card Number: 2024947174
ISBN: 978-1-950639-43-4

Cover Art and Layout: Victoria Cooper Art
Book set in: Multiple Fonts
Book Design: Summer Garr
Published by:

PO Box 754, Huntsville, AR 72740
800-935-0045 or 479-738-2348; fax 479-738-2448
WWW.OZARKMT.COM
Printed in the United States of America

Treat your enemy like a crying baby
Imre Vallyon

ACKNOWLEDGMENTS

I'd like to thank Ozark Mountain Publishing from the bottom of my heart for taking a chance on me and having faith in my books. I'd also like to thank my Aunty Cathy who has steadfastly been there to beta-read and give me so much encouragement and support. And to my kids Chloe, Will and Toby - you light up my life! Finally, Imre Vallyon and the Foundation for Higher Learning have supported me, given me endless inspiration and learning, and have allowed me to have the understanding and awareness to work toward being my undiluted Self in this life.

CONTENTS

Chapter 1: *Sumer 3800 BC*	1
Chapter 2	12
Chapter 3	17
Chapter 4	24
Chapter 5	35
Chapter 6	42
Chapter 7	47
Chapter 8	55
Chapter 9	61
Chapter 10	71
Chapter 11	76
Chapter 12	79
Chapter 13	83
Chapter 14	88
Chatper 15	92
Chapter 16	94
Chapter 17	96
Chapter 18	97
Chapter 19	98
Chapter 20	101
Chapter 21	104
Chapter 22	112
Chapter 23	118
Chapter 24	127
Chapter 25	140
Chapter 26	149
Chatper 27	162
Chapter 28	179
Chapter 29	188
Chapter 30	193
Chapter 31	207
Chapter 32	222
Chapter 33	227
About the Author	233

CHAPTER 1
Sumer 3800 BC

Feeling suddenly faint, Girl, who must now after eight long years of slavery reaccustom herself to her birth name, Saoirse, turned away from the crowds below. They were still cheering her name and celebrating the discovery of their new Oracle. She didn't feel like an Oracle; more like a giant fraud. She suppressed a wave of vertigo to be so exposed, so high up, and so close to the sacred top-most Sanctum of the great Temple of Ur. It was only a few steps higher than she currently stood. Could she maybe even feel the breath of the gods emanating from its cool depths from where she was? Or was it just the breeze?

One thing she did know for sure was that the people wouldn't be cheering for long. Once they understood that they had somehow mistaken her for an Oracle, instead of the prostitute that she had only yesterday been, they would probably throw her from the top of the Temple. Even worse, when they understood that their lives were the only thing saved by her dream warning of the flood, their jubilation would change to despair.

Their homes, their possessions, and any wealth they previously owned would all be lost in the stinking mud left behind after the flood finally deigned to recede. They would all face the oncoming winter with nothing. Surely the people could see what the endless, shining waters that now surrounded them so far below would mean for their continued survival. For now, though, she had somehow, against so many odds, bought them all a measure of safety, however dubious.

Little would the people looking up at her so lovingly know about what that safety had truly cost. She wondered how she would be received if they ever found out that their esteemed Temple leaders were all addicts of the opium poppy. This little detail had turned out to be a blessing, allowing her to survive because she had used her gifts to seek out some previously hidden stashes of it around the Temple. She alone knew where to find them, which had prevented Anan, the great leader of the Temple, from quietly murdering her and Kaylem, her only friend in the known world.

It was far from the most ideal start to her new profession as Oracle of Ur, the highest position a woman could hold in the known world. The irony was not lost on her, of just how far she had accidentally progressed in the hierarchy of society in one mere night.

At the thought of Anan and his threats, she pictured the unspeakable beings who, she had recently discovered, somehow infested most of the Temple elite. Possessing their wills, the Ushum were parasites who forced their hosts into actions that made her own past misdeeds as a prostitute seem charming in comparison. She did her best not to shudder at the thought of their terrifying presence.

This was a chance at a new beginning for all of them, after all. It was a slim chance, at best, that things might become better, but still a chance. Not to mention, apparently, that she had the gods behind her who had sent her the dream warning of the flood in the first place.

The waters sparkled in the distance, blinding her and making her squint. Saoirse would have thought them beautiful had she not known of the carnage that lay beneath the calm, dazzling surface. Surely, Saoirse thought to herself, this must be the greatest flood since Enki came down from *D'ingir*, the home of the gods, and visited the legendary Ziusudra. All knew the story of Ziusudra, who had built a boat to save himself and his family, as well as many animals, from the Seven Day Flood. Saoirse shivered at the thought of the evil which must have brought about the end of most of humanity so long ago.

Unfortunately, the very same evil was enmeshed in the Temple elite standing around her, safe and well, as a result of her prophetic dream. Most of those very same people would

CHAPTER 1

have laughed at her message from the gods warning of the flood only the day before. It seemed like an age and she suppressed a yawn, wincing at the sting of her throat. Standing at the top of the Temple, she struggled to breathe with all the staring eyes and gaping mouths around her. These so-called upstanding elite of the Temple would not hesitate to be rid of her and Kaylem if it meant ensuring their continued stranglehold on the riches of Ur.

Kaylem stood solid and tall beside her, the only one to have believed her enough to put his life at risk to help her spread her message from the gods about the flood. Now he looked at her with concern, and he nodded to the guards waiting alongside them. Much to her surprise, they were escorted up to the warren of chambers neighboring the Sanctum. Even these rooms were considered so holy they should have been reserved only for the highest worship of the gods, but Saoirse couldn't bring herself to think of that now. Ears ringing, she swallowed down an uprising of guilt at her relief to be escaping, for the moment, into silence and solitude.

Allowing the guards to usher them through one of the ornately decorated doorways, Saoirse and Kaylem stood for a moment in the dim coolness. In the sacred teachings, this particular alcove would have an important purpose, but today it was dedicated to shelter. Most wonderfully of all, it was empty of people. Saoirse forced herself not to think of who might have been so rudely evacuated only moments before.

Stone statues of a pair of gods stared imposingly from their position on the far wall. One of them had flames boiling from his body and mouth. The other was a slit-eyed creature which reminded her too much of the Ushum, the beings who had fed from the evil inherent in the Temple leaders and whose presence she glimpsed now and then in all of them. She tried not to cringe away from its reptilian glare and decided it would be best if she blocked that one out of her consciousness for now. She didn't know the gods names, but some innate part of her recognized them immediately.

"Gibil and Kusu," Kaylem murmured. Saoirse looked at him, a question in her eyes. "Gibil is the fire god. He works with the other elemental gods in the Dance of Creation which happened when life on Mother Earth came to be. Kusu is his consort. She lives in the underworld and judges the dead when they pass out of their bodies. I suppose you'll have to learn about the gods and goddesses now that you're Oracle."

The Dance of Creation. Saoirse had seen it being performed in her dream. The Temple dancers would have practiced it over and over for many hours. Now, as a result of that dream, she was at the top of the great Temple of Ur, staring up at a couple of gods who looked as though they would be at home in her nightmares. The dream had seen her entire life transformed in a mere day, from despised prostitute to Oracle, and she wondered how long it would take for her to become accustomed to the changes it would bring.

As for the wondrous Dance of Creation, it hadn't been performed last night on the eve of Akitu, Harvest New Year, because the entire population of Ur was currently squeezed onto the upper levels of the Temple. There would have been no room for it. The dance would likely not be performed for many moons, if ever again, given how much work there would need to be done once the waters went down.

A pang of sadness filled her that the beauty of the dance would go unappreciated by any but her, and yet she shuddered to think of the consequences had the performance gone ahead without her warning of the flood. The entire population of Ur would have been by the treacherous river, instead of having taken shelter at the top of the Temple. Then, there would have been nothing but the Temple to slowly crumble into ruins.

Kaylem brought her out of her reverie with a touch on her shoulder. "Is there anything you need? I am certain we could ask for some food or ale? A healer maybe?"

"There's nothing that will fix my ailment but rest," she said with as much of a smile as she could muster.

Kaylem nodded. "Here's my shawl. We can both fit." He bustled around trying to make her comfortable and she smiled up at him gratefully as she lay back and shut her eyes.

Desperate for the escape sleep offered, Saoirse instead jerked awake to every noise that sounded outside, terrified that Anan would change his mind and follow up on his threat to have them both murdered. It would be so easy for anyone to sneak in and perform the deed. Even though nobody bothered them, she could not allow herself to trust that they were truly safe. Despite the guards posted outside to fend people away, and even though she

CHAPTER 1

could hardly remain standing either, her eyes remained stubbornly open, and her body was so tense it was uncomfortable to lie so still.

She forced herself to stop her restless twitching, but all that did was hurt her neck and she blinked up at the ceiling for what seemed like forever. After what seemed like an age, she gave up as her legs twitched and jumped all over the place. She could feel Gibil and Kusu staring balefully at her, their eyes unnervingly alive with a malevolent intelligence which reminded her too much of the beast she had seen within Anan. With a sigh, she pushed herself to standing and tiptoed quietly past Kaylem, who was deeply asleep, his arm thrown out beside him with abandon.

The heat, light, and noise of the people hit her like a wall as she emerged, blinking and disoriented. As they noticed her, everyone nearby fell silent and stared at her. She almost turned and ran back to the alcove.

"The Oracle..."

"Hail to the new Oracle..."

"Our savior..."

The whispers increased as they drew back to make a path for her to tread in whatever direction she wanted. At the same time, she could hear underlying cynicism in many of their voices, see the suspicion in their eyes, as well as cold knowing and calculation. For this was the level of the Temple reserved for the elite. As far as the elite were concerned, Saoirse had somehow manipulated events to end up as Oracle. A heaviness settled over her as she realized that it would never occur to these people that she, a former prostitute, might be the only relatively honest one among them.

Their attitude was a far cry from the townspeople who sat crammed together on the level below, unaware of the dubious past of their savior. Many of the elite already knew her true identity, and now their whispers rang scornfully in her ears, as though they were words of ridicule rather than accolades. Unsure of the polite protocol for acknowledging them, well intended or not, Saoirse bobbed her head at them and turned in the direction of the outer wall. The people made way for her until she reached the outer barrier and she stared, haunted, at the endless desolation.

Saoirse and the others around her fell still as they watched, hypnotized. Pockets of steaming mud and destruction now showed through the watery wastes. Below, the bowed heads of the town's people were also mostly silent, waiting patiently for the opening of the great gates that would allow them to walk among the desolation that had once been the great city of Ur. Eyes squinting painfully, she moved her gaze upward, away from the mire and into the endless blue of the sky. The birds wheeled and swooped as though it were just another day, as though the thousands of people below had not just lost everything.

I am Saoirse, the Oracle of Ur, she told herself for the thousandth time. *I have my name back. I'm not Girl, I'm Saoirse. I am the Oracle. I'm Saoirse… Saoirse the Oracle… the Oracle of Ur…*

By saying it so many times in her mind, she hoped it would eventually sit more comfortably. Yet the more she told it silently to herself, the more the sounds knocked against each other jaggedly, as though they'd never comfortably fit together. She wasn't Saoirse. She wasn't an Oracle. Nor was she a prostitute any longer, although she was certain those who knew of her past would never allow her to forget it. A string of coincidences had led her to this position, and all of the elite knew that she wasn't deserving of it. To hear her birth name uttered in the same sentence as the word Oracle made her want to cringe and hide.

"Saoirse," she whispered to herself, forcing the word quietly past her lips. "Saoirse," she said a little louder as her tongue formed the strange syllables that she had never associated with herself. For so long she had been called Girl.

The whispers behind her, which had faded for a moment as she was preoccupied with her thoughts, returned to the forefront of her awareness. In her mind's eye she saw the people of the Temple standing behind her with looks of contempt on their faces. A presence approached and she closed her eyes against the glare, pulling herself together to prepare to face this potential new threat.

"Saoirse, the Oracle," she whispered to herself again, vainly hoping that the words might build up around her like a shield, rather than cut her down further.

"There you are! I woke up and worried you'd been…" She sighed in relief to see Kaylem beside her. "Were you talking to someone just then?"

"Only to myself. They're all whispering, Kaylem…" Saoirse

CHAPTER 1

looked up at him and subtly moved her head in the direction of the people. Being close to him made her feel safe enough to turn away from the wall.

"Don't pay attention to them, Saoirse. Mostly they're in awe of how you achieved it. And they might resent you a little, but you can't blame them. They were born into this and here you've appeared from nowhere…"

Kaylem broke off as he noticed her cringe. "What's wrong?"

"I can't…" She sighed. "Kaylem, it just sounds wrong."

"What sounds wrong?"

"For you to call me that…"

"Saoirse?"

She nodded.

"What do you prefer me to call you?"

"Girl will do for now."

Kaylem was silent for a moment, his face unreadable. She turned back to the sky and found a new flock of birds to squint at.

"No," he said.

"What?"

"I'm not calling you Girl. I always knew it was what my mother named you instead of your true name. If you don't want Saoirse, what about something else?"

She blinked at him and shrugged. He reached out and held her gently by the shoulders.

"All I can see before me is a woman of courage and bravery. You protected those girls at the brothel against the owner who would have been more than happy to murder you all. You guided them safely to Ur where you managed to negotiate a somewhat safe place to stay."

She tried to turn away, but he held her firm and turned her back toward him.

"You stood up to one of the most terrifying men of the Temple and not only survived, but somehow also bought Anan's blessing… yes, I know it wasn't ideal, but you worked with what you had at the time."

Saoirse made to interrupt but he held firm.

"And, of course, you saved thousands of lives because you believed in the message you received from the gods and wouldn't stop until that message got through."

Kaylem stopped to peer deeply into her eyes and she wanted

only to look down at her feet. He was twisting a very complicated situation around to make her look like a hero, and all she had ever done to bring it about was to complain and hide against his chest, which, she recalled, was a very nice chest to hide against. She forced herself not to curve her mouth into a rueful smile.

"So, dear one, if you don't want me to call you Saoirse, I have no choice but to call you…" He looked at the birds again for a moment, blinking his eyes rapidly, "…Shaji."

"Shaji? That's not a name or a word."

"It's short for shajaea."

"Courage? But during all those things I did, I was ready to empty my bladder in terror and wanted nothing but to run away. That's not courage."

"You have more courage than anyone I've ever met. That's exactly what it means."

Thankfully, a quaking, knock-kneed servant appeared, releasing Saoirse from the intensity of Kaylem's gaze. The servant was holding a bladder of ale and a pouch of nuts, dates, and bread. He squeaked as he dropped the parcel into Kaylem's outstretched hands and then backed away, tripping over one of the reclining guards nearby. The guard growled like a dog and gave the servant boy a shove, sending him sprawling out among the group of other bored guards. They began to throw him around like a boar-skin ball.

Saoirse made a sound in her throat like a snarl and tensed. Kaylem laid a hand on her arm.

"It might be prudent to stay quiet."

"Kaylem, whether I'm a prostitute or an Oracle—"

"Girl…" He winced as he realized his error. "…Saoirse… I mean… Shaji…" Saoirse suppressed the hysterical laugh that tried to explode out of her. Now was not the time to be quibbling over names. "…they're growing tired of their game now, see? And the boy will only be more afraid if you approach."

It was true. As though he'd heard their conversation, the servant boy glanced back over at Saoirse, and she saw the whites of his eyes as they rolled around in their sockets in superstitious terror. He was more afraid of her than he was of the soldiers who meant him true harm, she saw with dismay. Eventually, the guards lost interest and the boy disappeared into the crowd.

"Here!" Kaylem held an open pouch of food and a mug

CHAPTER 1

of ale in front of her, and in response her stomach growled ravenously. She couldn't remember the last time she had eaten, and she grabbed a handful of nuts and dried dates, washing them down almost whole with a gulp of ale. She was vaguely aware of Kaylem's relief at distracting her from the potential conflict.

"Such gluttony is not acceptable behavior for the great Oracle!" mumbled Kaylem through his own mouthful, cheeks puffed to almost bursting and eyes glinting mischievously. His humor was a surprise, but very welcome. Saoirse choked on her laugh and coughed a spray of ale, marred with chunks of half-chewed nuts, out over the wall. Wide eyed, she watched it fall onto the people below, a rainbow forming in an instant as it caught the sun's rays. A couple of the people below looked upward and she pulled back guiltily, unintentionally leaning into Kaylem.

She caught a trace of his smell. Sweaty but not unpleasantly so, mixed with an echo of fragrant oil that reminded her of something. It might have been myrtle and clove.

It was still a surprise that she could be so comfortable even standing so close to a man, given what she had been forced to endure in the previous moons. Saoirse wondered whether that sense of comfort might extend to the act of what was supposed to be love between a man and a woman, not that it had ever been that way for her. A very uncharacteristic blush spread all over her skin at the thought, and Saoirse stared back up at the birds for a moment, unable to speak. Kaylem, she noticed, stood blinking silently as well. For want of something better to do they both watched the birds as they wheeled and swooped in the sky.

Myrtle and clove, her mind yammered at her. It must be myrtle and clove… Or was he wealthy enough to afford myrrh? The under-scent of him, mixed with the fragrant oils, made her feel heady. She couldn't bring herself to look up at him for a long moment, choosing instead to sense his breathing beside her.

"An almond for your thoughts," Kaylem murmured, holding it up for her to see with that same twinkle in his eyes.

Breathing in a sigh, she tore her gaze from the birds and looked at him. "I wish I could say I'd been pondering the mysteries of the heavens, but alas, my thoughts are much more mundane. Where will we go, Kaylem? Your dwelling would have been that way, if I'm not mistaken?"

He nodded in the direction of Saoirse's gesture. "Where

would you see us, then?"

"Aren't you upset to see the ruin of all you've worked for? Your home?"

Kaylem turned to her and put his hands on her shoulders, his face close to hers. "All I ever cared about is standing right before me." The tenderness of his voice sent warm shivers snaking up and down her body, and she shook herself to gather her thoughts.

"There's no place for us in Ur until it can be rebuilt. With winter approaching, how will anyone survive till spring? Why would the gods see fit to save the people for this?" As she spoke the words, the truth of them made her feel hollow and lost.

"We can't know the minds of the gods. An uncle of mine lives in Erech. We could go there. Let's hope it was untouched by the flood."

Saoirse wrenched her body away from him and scowled out at the expanse. "Kaylem, I'd rather die a thousand deaths than set one foot in that stinking dung hole of filth ever again!"

Kaylem moved to stand beside her at what she noticed was a safe distance. "Girl! I mean… Shaji… That's the sacred home of Inanna!"

Erech was also the city where she was taken against her will after Kaylem's mother sold her to a brothel, run by a man named Salik, who she had ended up stabbing to death. She shuddered, a full body tremble that made Kaylem go wide-eyed.

"There are many stories to tell, Kaylem… or maybe not, as some should never be put into words," she whispered by way of apology, haunted with the mere mention of the place. She turned her thoughts away from the blood-stained memories. Kaylem nodded and they stood in silence, watching the birds again for a moment until Kaylem gathered himself enough to speak.

"What if we go back to my home?"

A wave of images assailed her; of the well of sweet silver water in the courtyard, the massive cooking hearth in the heart of the household, and the surrounding desert wailing in the constant wind. The deep blue of the sky where eagles swooped and shrieked, and the movement of the stars in the velvety darkness of night. It was also the place where she had toiled for Kaylem's mother as little more than a slave for the entirety of her childhood. "What of it, Kaylem?" Her hands tightened on the wall until the knuckles were white and the skin of her fingertips hurt under the

CHAPTER 1

rough mud-brick.

"It's closer to Ur than anywhere else, and we won't have the deluge of refugees likely to swamp any of the local villages."

"Your mother sold me to a brothel, Kaylem, in case you forgot. Do you truly think that me going back there now and begging her for refuge would be such a grand idea?" Kaylem almost took a step back, but stood firm. She could see a war raging inside him. The determined set of his chin and sadness in his eyes hinted at his next words.

"My mother is far from the woman you knew, Shaji," he murmured. "The last time I visited... I wasn't sure I should leave in case it was the last I ever saw of her."

She wanted to tell Kaylem how glad she was to hear it, but instead Saoirse bit the inside of her cheek and nodded, swallowing down the burn that made its way up her throat every time she thought of Kaylem's mother. The mistress. She tried to make a sound of comfort, unable to form words even though she knew what it was like to have lost her own mother.

"It's unlikely she'll even recognize her own son let alone anyone else..." Kaylem's voice choked in his throat. "The people will wish for their new Oracle to be away from the dangers of Ur over the winter. The prospect of your safe return will give them hope."

"I should stay to help rebuild and tend to the sick and dying—"

"Shaji, have you ever built anything with those hands?" He took both her hands in his and turned them over, inspecting the skin of her palms, soft now that she had spent so long away from the drudgery of Kaylem's birth home. A thrill pierced deep inside of her as his thumb passed over the sensitive skin.

"I happen to be of very strong mind and can learn to do anything!" she shot back at him, attempting to bring her attention away from her core and back to her mind.

"And yet another mouth to feed on the stores of rations which may, or may not, be salvaged..." His voice rumbled deep in his chest, causing her body to reverberate with its echoes. She took a deep breath and turned back to the sky. For once she had no answer.

CHAPTER 2

For Saoirse, the worst part of the journey to the remote desert household was her dread of once again crossing its threshold. Staggering through the endless mud which sucked hungrily at her feet, her tears fell for the years of hardship the people of Ur would now have to face. Yet, behind her grief, her insides contorted with knots at the prospect of returning to the place of her childhood servitude. Not to mention the mistress, whose hate-filled voice she could still hear. Unfortunately, Kaylem was right. There was nowhere else to go that could offer the sanctuary they sought.

At least so far out in the desert, where there was not a shimmer of water as far as the eye could see, they would be safe from angry rivers and could take refuge while the city of Ur began its recovery. The isolated household would also be a haven from the Temple elite, who would lodge themselves like parasites in the few surviving dwellings, being so far from the river on the less privileged outskirts of Ur.

The elite would be deaf to the sufferings of the dwelling's true owners, evicted out into the mud. Saoirse was horrified when Kaylem told her of this injustice, his words convincing her once and for all to leave Ur for now. The prospect of associating with such monsters at all on their return to Ur, let alone to soon be living among them, was one she preferred not to think about as they slogged through the slime that strove to greedily suck the sandals from her feet and her spirit from within.

As they made their journey, weighted down by water bladders and food supplies pressed onto them by a simpering servant for

CHAPTER 2

the journey, Saoirse was sure her legs would collapse if she walked a single step more. But she pushed herself forward, most of it barely more than staggering. The striving to put one foot in front of the other consumed every other thought and fear she had been harboring. The setting sun turned the sky into a spectacular display of colors, and gradually took with it the stifling heat of the day.

Once they finally crossed the threshold of Kaylem's childhood home, it was under the faint light of the waning moon, not far before dawn. Saoirse was so numbed with exhaustion and shivering with cold, she was almost indifferent to the familiar gate. The gate was smaller and shabbier than she remembered. It stood shadowed under a burning torch, much as it had on her first arrival as a child. An aged servant bustled out to receive them, stopping for a moment to consider Saoirse. With a shock, Saoirse recognized the woman as the mistress's personal servant who lived within the dwelling and rarely went outside. Saoirse bowed her head in alarm, expecting to be turned away.

"Welcome," the servant murmured to Saoirse in a curious and wondering voice, as though she had expected Kaylem to be returning alone to the compound for the remainder of his days. Saoirse bobbed her head silently, hoping the servant would mistake her dismay for meekness.

They were escorted into the household and Saoirse looked around at the dim surroundings, which she had spent so many years imagining in her time there as a servant outside its walls. Never before had she entered it, aside from Kaylem's chamber on that fateful day of the sandstorm when everything changed. Now, she couldn't help but walk with a sense of unease. Kaylem's mother might at any time appear in front of her and shriek at her for her trespass.

The servant brought them to Kaylem's sleeping quarters. Saoirse hesitated. More memories assailed her, too strong now to keep up her timid act, and her chest became so tight she wondered if she was breathing at all. Black spots began to form in her vision and, to her relief, Kaylem took her arm as she began to crumple.

"It's been a long and dreadful journey," he told the servant. "My lady needs to rest." After lighting candles, the servant turned, leaving them alone in the chamber.

"I can't... not here..." Saoirse's throat closed, forbidding exit of the words she wanted to say. The howl of the wind from a ghost sandstorm, existing only in her memory, overwhelmed her. Marsi's lifeless face flashed before her vision, mouth and eyes craters of sand. An image of the only surviving servant, Bo, his eyes brimming with tears as he backed away from her for the last time, filled her with a clash of grief as well as a vain hope that he may still be outside in the servants' quarters.

In between the rush of memories, she dimly wondered where she'd be expected to sleep. Would it be beside Kaylem? Would she be expected to lie with him? The last thought was too much, and everything went black. She woke later, unsure of how much time had passed, to find herself on Kaylem's sleeping pallet, a single candle sputtering beside her. Kaylem's form loomed out of the shadows as she stirred, and she put herself into another panic at the thought of being in his intimate space.

"Shaji, you're awake. I've brought you some bread and cheese when you're feeling like you can sit up, and some dates from the cellar... Shaji?"

The mention of the cellar took her spiraling into darkness once again. Having been blamed for bringing the sandstorm which killed Marsi and Deni, the taste of dates had still been fresh on her tongue as the mistress had thrown Saoirse into the cellar to await her fate. A younger version of herself sobbed and shivered into the darkness in her memory. That had been only a thirteen-moon ago. Before the evils of the brothel in Erech, before the fateful dream and the flood. Back when her days had been filled with toil from dawn to dusk, under an endless sky.

Her heart suddenly jumped around in her chest, as though it had only been yesterday that she was taken from the household by the merchant, unsure whether she would live or die. Images of being tied to a cart, her headscarf flying in the dry desert wind as the merchant leered...

No! she told herself as she could sense madness hovering. She struggled to force her eyes open, but they stayed firmly shut. She could feel Kaylem holding her hand, hear him calling to her, and that gave her a sliver of comfort, even though her body was limp and refused to obey her command. The disturbing images calmed, leaving her for a moment in blissful peace.

Then a point of light flashed bright against the darkness of her closed eyelids. She tensed in anticipation of more traumatic

CHAPTER 2

memories, but was surprised when the light expanded and opened out onto a completely different scene than before.

It was Lania, one of the girls who had escaped the brothel of Erech with Saoirse, back when Saoirse was called Girl. But now Lania looked sicker, thinner, grayer. Lania lay dying in a sea of mud, while the innkeeper and the other girls stood around her, wringing their hands. Lania looked to be more at peace than she had even when she was well, despite the grief of her companions. As the breath left Lania's body, the others tore their hair and the girls' cries were shrill in the too-still air. Saoirse saw Lania's spirit drift from her body, and Saoirse's dream-self met Lania's somewhere above. They embraced in joy.

Lania was free of her body at last; free from the constant pain of her illness which had its roots in Salik's ill-treatment of her at the brothel. Her face in death was serene and Saoirse wished she could show the others what a joyful occasion this was.

The dread and sorrow of the still-living grew in a cloud above them, momentarily hiding Saoirse's view of Lania. Saoirse's dream-self contracted in panic as she searched and called out for her friend. Soon, Lania appeared again through the gloom, her face now filled with confusion. Saoirse took her hand and turned them both toward a direction where a soft light was growing. Lania tensed beside her, her eyes now grave with panic and fear.

Lania shook her head sadly at the light and turned in a different direction, toward a dark, descending tunnel reminding Saoirse of a cellar, smelling faintly of rotting things and mildew. Lania's eyes told Saoirse that this was where she expected to go after the evils of her life of prostitution.

"Lania, no! You were not deserving of this life." Saoirse waved away the entrance to the tunnel, as though she might make it disappear. "Even if you'd deserved to live the way you were forced to, you've now paid the price. Don't believe the teachings of the Temple. Look at yourself, you're already glowing. You can be free!" Saoirse held up one of Lania's arms so that both could see the pulsing light shining from her.

Hesitantly, gradually, Lania's face turned to Saoirse, her eyes looking longingly in the distance where the light still glowed.

"Hurry, Lania. Forget all of this. Move toward the light, it won't be there much longer..." Saoirse nudged Lania's form away from the darkness of the tunnel and toward the light which *she could see was pulsing gently as it faded. "Go now... There, now... Go, Lania... You're free! Finally, you're truly free!"*

The tension in Saoirse's chest eased. Tears flowed from her closed eyes as she saw Lania disappear; not into the stinking, dark tunnel created by the superstitions of the Temple, but toward something much more beautiful. For a terrible moment, Saoirse wanted so much to follow Lania to wherever she had disappeared to, and sobs shook her body as she brought herself reluctantly back to Kaylem, who held her hand so hard it hurt...

"Girl, please... I mean... Saoirse... Shaji, please, I don't know what you need."

"Kaylem..." Saoirse managed to croak, before attempting to loosen his grip on her hand, which was beginning to throb.

"Oh you're alive! I've been so afraid for you. You must eat, drink! Allow me to help you sit up..."

"Kaylem!" For a dreadful moment, Saoirse only wished to slap him across his cheek, as he gripped her hand so strongly, she could feel the bones grinding underneath her skin.

"Kaylem, my hand." As she spoke, she attempted once again to swipe Kaylem's hand away.

"Thank the gods for your recovery. Shaji, you weren't breathing!"

"Kaylem, let my hand go and fetch me water from the well." She spoke more sharply than intended and Kaylem jumped back as though stung. Her hand, finally free, throbbed in relief.

"But I don't want to leave you alone... You stopped breathing!"

Saoirse softened. "I was very much alive, Kaylem, thank you for your concern." He stood and turned reluctantly, calling for the servant whose footsteps Saoirse could now hear bustling outside in the direction of the well.

She pictured the silver disc of water, deep at the bottom of the shaft, reflecting the moon's shine as the servant woman broke the smoothness into a thousand ripples to fill the bucket. Something inside of her eased and she smiled, feeling that despite the horrors in her memory, she had returned to the only home that still existed for her in the known world.

CHAPTER 3

All of Saoirse's fears about sharing Kaylem's intimate space had been for nothing, she now saw as the sun streamed in through the wall vent and she found herself alone in Kaylem's quarters. She had slept for an entire day and night, she realized with a start. Unsure where he had slept, Saoirse stretched and sat up, a new dilemma at hand. It would be unseemly to use the servants' latrine and be seen in their area, but she had no clue where the household privy could be found and her immediate need for it was great.

Wrapping a shawl around herself for modesty, and in case there was a need to suddenly hide her face, Saoirse stood carefully, holding onto the wall until her dizziness faded. Her body felt as though it had withered like a plant sitting for too long in the sun. She slowly wandered the inside of the household for the first time. Smaller than she had imagined it to be, the outhouse was maddeningly impossible to find. In resignation she crept to the servants' area, knowing they would already be about and hoping she could sneak past them without being seen.

The great hearth in the main courtyard was glowing softly, and as always, there was a pot of lentils on to simmer. Bread cooled, as it always had, on the mud-brick surface beside the fire as though she had never been away, although Saoirse knew with a pang that it wouldn't be Marsi's bread and it would taste very different, even if it looked so similar.

The same tiny broom, that had held the evil widow spider which almost bit her, lay tidily in a corner. Her feet disturbed its long sweeping tracks in the yellow-brown dust, and she felt sorry for whoever had that job now. The hens cackled noisily in their enclosure just the same way as she remembered. Saoirse was assailed once again by a wall of memories so strong she wondered if she could continue along her way without bursting into floods of tears.

Just ahead lay the latrine, with not a soul around to disturb her and she rushed toward it urgently. She stood to the side in case anyone happened to be in there. As her hand rose to move the tattered curtain, it was heaved aside and Bo clattered out of the tiny cubicle, running his other hand through his hair which spiked upward at all angles. He was much taller, and his previously skinny arms were now roped with muscles, she noticed.

With a shock Saoirse froze, certain he would turn just slightly to the side and see her. She *wished* for him to see her, if truth be known; wished only to call to him and hold him to her as though she had never left. She checked herself before she opened her mouth to speak. It would be madness to make her herself known, especially as she stood outside the servants' latrine, no longer a servant. Bo noticed nothing but the angle of the sun, and his wide eyes told Saoirse that he would be in for a chastisement for being so late.

Saoirse watched in silence as he dashed away. Her mouth moved into a tiny smile as she made her way into the stinking mess of the latrine, heart suddenly full to bursting with the joy of knowing he was still here, still alive. She had hardly dared to think of him in the months since her eviction from the household and it eased something within her to know that he was healthy and strong.

After making her way back to the household, careful to dodge the other servants bustling about in the distance, Saoirse returned to Kaylem's quarters to dress.

"There you are, Shaji! I've been searching for you all over." Saoirse jumped as Kaylem appeared out of nowhere and both of them hesitated, each staring at the other wordlessly. Saoirse, unwilling to tell Kaylem of her morning so far, stood stiffly, mortified that Kaylem had now seen her in her sleep shift. The intensity of the moment grew between them, and Saoirse's body stiffened even more. Kaylem blinked at her and, awkwardly, shuffled his feet on the rug so vigorously that his foot hit hers

CHAPTER 3

repeatedly without him noticing. His long sheath of hair also stuck out at all angles and Saoirse smiled despite the pain of her toe.

"Er, Kaylem?'

"Yes, Shaji."

"Will you show me to the bathing quarters? Or, at the very least, remove your foot from mine?"

"Ah, a thousand apologies!" As Kaylem scrambled aside for Saoirse to collect her day garments, he stumbled a little and she could not resist a small, silent chuckle at his oafishness. She still felt the smile already tugging at the corners of her mouth again from seeing Bo.

As she passed Kaylem, his scent wafted past her again. The far stronger smell of his sleep essence still didn't completely erase the faint, but maddening, scent of oils she still could not quite place. It tugged and throbbed at a place deep inside her core and made her blush yet again.

After a hearty breakfast of eggs, dates, bread, and besan paste, which Saoirse noticed did not taste quite as delicious as when they had been made by Marsi and Deni, Kaylem led Saoirse to his mother's chambers.

"But Kaylem," Saoirse grumbled for what may have been the thousandth time, "Why must I see her? Can't you just tell her about me? What kind of horrors are you inflicting onto your dying mother, bringing in the one who, according to her, caused the downfall of her household?"

"Shaji, that is dramatic. The storm did not cause the downfall of the household. In fact—"

"I don't want to hear about that right now, Kaylem..." She followed him reluctantly up the narrow steps.

"It was my mother's final, dying wish to see me married. I know that even though we may not technically be married quite yet, I'm certain she won't be aware of that if we don't tell her. And, if you don't want to talk to her, just stay silent. Pull the shawl across your face if you must, but I promise you she won't even notice..."

Heart in her throat, Saoirse could already smell the musty, rotting stench of the dying. It reminded her of the tunnel she persuaded Lania's spirit to avoid in favor of the light, and she blinked in wonderment that it had only been yesterday that such a thing had even happened. She allowed Kaylem to usher her into the small chamber where his mother lay on a pallet. Saoirse smothered a gasp. The woman on the pallet was unrecognizable. Her once smooth, tanned skin was now withered and yellow-gray. A toothless, shrunken mouth worked and gnashed as she wracked on her pallet in obvious agony.

A shell of the vigorous and intense woman Saoirse remembered, the mistress seemed unaware of their presence, save for a fluttering of her eyes and a choked murmur of unintelligible sounds. Saoirse was uncharitably surprised that the mistress still possessed any measure of the breath of life, for it looked to her like the mistress's body should have long been at rest.

Kaylem knelt to cradle his mother's head and sprinkled some water into her mouth from a vessel beside the pallet.

"Mother. It's me, Kaylem! I've come to see you and bring my lady for you to meet. Her name is Shaji, and she is the love of my life. Here. Open your eyes and see her for yourself." Kaylem tried to prop up his mother to give her a better view of Saoirse. Instead, the mistress's head flopped to the side, her tongue lolling like a drunkard's. "Mother, I've found the one I wish to spend the remainder of my days with, and it is my desire that you meet her." A warm tingle filled Saoirse at Kaylem's words and for a moment they shared a smile despite the bleakness of the situation.

"Kaylem?" the mistress moaned indistinctly, and her eyes rolled in their sockets as they tried to focus on his face. Her hand clawed at Kaylem's chest, reminding Saoirse of a vulture's talon.

"I'm here for you, Mother. Can you see us? Here, I'll hold your hand and sit with you awhile." The tremble of his voice betrayed his distress at seeing his mother's suffering, and Saoirse could not help but wish to be elsewhere. Even the servants' latrine was more pleasant than the reek of this airless room, which rose around her until she was forced to move toward one of the wall vents, turning her face greedily toward the growing heat of the day outside.

Close to the wall vent, Saoirse found that she could see the whole of the servants' area, and she wondered if the mistress had previously spent much of her time watching the activities of her staff. That would certainly explain how she found so much fault in the workings of the servants.

She remembered the hours spent lining up in front of the

CHAPTER 3

mistress, listening to tirade after tirade in the baking sun of the courtyard below, which now seemed so small. Despite her resentment of the mistress, a part of her pitied the woman for having so little in her life but to secretly watch servants at their work.

"Shaji, why is she breathing like that?" The panic in Kaylem's voice was raw, and Saoirse turned to find the mistress clutching at her throat and bucking her body in an alarming way.

"Oh, Kaylem, she is passing. Hold her close. She must have waited for you to return so that she could leave in peace, knowing you were safe." Two deaths in two days, thought Saoirse in alarm as she watched the mistress's final moments. She wondered why the gods had chosen her to be present at the death of one she still held so much anger for.

The bucking became violent as the life-breath was sucked from the matriarch in a visible whoosh. Horribly fascinated, Saoirse blinked and shook her head as she saw the spirit rise from the gaunt and now completely lifeless flesh. Once clear of the body it turned toward Saoirse, seeing her truly for the first time. A menacing surge of red, spiky waves strained toward Saoirse and encompassed the mistress's spirit form.

You! she howled furiously. *You dare to return here with your black magic, luring my son into your sordid web and allowing him to believe you are the love of his life! Begone, filthy piece of dung, before I...*

Before the matriarch could curse her, Saoirse held out her hand toward the corpse and spirit hovering above. Unaware of what she would do next, her throat opened and sound made its way out of her. It began as a tune, one she remembered from the forbidden chanting group of Ur where she had first seen Kaylem again before their reunion.

Now the strange and powerful words of the chant came from deep inside her chest. They emanated from her flawlessly, despite her hearing it only the one time so many moons before. Kaylem's mother's spirit hesitated, and her eyes widened. Soon the jagged, red spikes surrounding her softened, the red gradually fading away.

Confused, the mistress turned to look at Kaylem and, filled with wonder, she moved slowly toward him. Kaylem stood from his crouch next to her body, peering in terrified awe at Saoirse.

Following Saoirse's line of sight, he turned to stare in the general direction of his mother's now glowing form. The mistress watched her son for a moment, raising a hesitant hand to stroke his cheek before wandering in the direction of the stinking tunnel of the afterworld.

There was no glow of light that would open from the heavens for the mistress, who had been so angry and bitter for so long. Kaylem put a trembling hand to his cheek where his mother had touched it. He kept it there, frozen.

The mistress took her first steps into the tunnel of the underworld and Saoirse kept up her singing in case the power in the chant could lessen the darkness for her, even a fraction. With a flash of sadness as she sang, Saoirse realized she did not even know the mistress's name.

Now, Saoirse noticed, the woman's life was playing before her very eyes on the walls of the tunnel itself. A childhood spent cringing away from an angry father and cheerless mother was replaced with the fleeting joy of pairing with Kaylem's father. Another moment of joy brightened the walls of the tunnel as Kaylem arrived into the world. It was a moment shared together with the new baby and his father, obviously replayed over and over like a well-thumbed prayer-tablet.

Trips away, dominated by laughter and sunshine flashed by too quickly and then faded, replaced with gray sorrow at her beloved husband's passing. The interminable hours after his death stretched into eternity, where a glimpse of Kaylem's face, so like his father's, was enough to send the mistress into fits of frenzied weeping each time her son came near.

Eyes streaming with her own tears, Saoirse's throat choked over as Kaylem's mother trod further into the tunnel, looking back only once at her and Kaylem. To Saoirse, the tunnel seemed less dark and forbidding than it was before. With a whispered final blessing, she watched the tunnel gradually disappear along with the mistress's spirit as she made her final journey into the underworld.

The room around them now felt empty, bereft, aside from Kaylem's weeping where he had fallen into his previous kneeling position beside the lifeless body. His hand was still fixed to his cheek as though keeping her ephemeral touch with him for a moment longer. Saoirse put her hand to his shoulder, rubbing in

CHAPTER 3

gentle circles for a moment before slowly descending the stairs to alert the servant woman of the mistress's death.

Later, they watched the sun set spectacularly over the desert sky as they sat together after a meal and ale in the coolest courtyard of the household. Kaylem finally spoke for the first time since the passing of his mother. "What did you see, Shaji? What happened?" His face was still pale and drawn, almost glowing in the twilight gloom. Saoirse tried not to shiver in the rapidly cooling air and sat quietly for a moment to watch the sky. She sent a silent plea to the gods to give her the wisest words possible for this. "Kaylem, I saw her. I saw your mother after she left her body."

"Yes, that I understood, and I'm sure I also saw a glimmer. But your face! It held such fear, and then when you began to sing, the fear changed to this radiance that filled you. And then you filled the chamber with such power and joy! I'd be hardly surprised if the tutor comes knocking on the gates to wonder what great and magical deeds have happened here."

"Hardly, Kaylem. Your mother... she saw who I was, and in her fury, she tried to curse me. I don't know where the chant came from inside me. It was the one I heard that made me leave the inn of Ur and find the tutor and the chanting group back before the flood. But this power, it didn't come from me. It moved itself through my body as though I was just the vessel."

"Truly, the power of the gods moves through you," Kaylem whispered in awe. His hand moved back to his cheek, as though his mother had left an imprint on the skin, and he heaved a shuddering breath. Saoirse took his other hand, which was warm, and they sat side by side. A pleasant buzz filled the air between and within them, as though it was alive with static.

As they sipped their ales and watched the dusk turn to darkness, the aging servant woman brought them blankets to fend off the growing cold. The first stars began to blink in the great sky spread before them and Saoirse, listening to Kaylem breathing beside her, could not remember a moment past when she had been filled with such peace.

CHAPTER 4

The next day marked the funeral of Kaylem's mother. Issa was her name, Saoirse discovered from Kaylem, who had spent the previous night beside his mother's body as was the custom. To know her true name further softened the memories Saoirse carried of the sad-angry mistress of her childhood. The grave of Kaylem's father now sat open and raw, after the manservant and Bo had spent much of the night and early morning digging until they hit the gold-encrusted cloth of his shroud.

The household was too remote for a coffin to be brought so far at such short notice, even though there was coin in the coffers enough to easily afford one. The searing heat and the sorry state of her body demanded that Issa be buried immediately, no matter the custom of waiting three days. By that time, Saoirse and Kaylem figured, there would be little left of her but stinking liquid. A shroud matching that of her husband was wrapped around Issa's body, a tiny, shrivelled thing lying on the mud-brick altar. To Saoirse it was more like that of a child than an adult.

The manservant and Kaylem worked together to lower Issa's body into the hole beside Kaylem's father's body so they could lie together for eternity. Saoirse watched as Issa's handservant approached with a platter of her favorite foods and trinkets. There were dates and a tiny bowl of some hastily, and miraculously, procured honey placed in the center of the platter. Pieces of freshly baked bread, liberally dipped in besan paste, were arranged around golden statuettes of the gods and goddesses. The sun brought its blaze to a golden, jeweled bracelet which Saoirse supposed was

CHAPTER 4

gifted to Issa by her husband.

The servant bent to gently place a large flagon of ale down next, Issa's favorite beverage. Squares of meat that looked to be desert hare lay scattered artfully among the other objects, and her stomach grumbled in anticipation of the meal to come. Animal flesh had been a rare feature in her diet, and she looked forward to it, even as her stomach turned with the smell of death filling the air.

"Please, will you farewell her," Kaylem begged her for what seemed the thousandth time.

"Kaylem, I've never even been to a proper funeral before and I don't know the Death Rite as they do it at the Temple. They're all waiting. I can feel their eyes on us. It must be you. I don't have any idea and I'm only going to offend them all with what comes out of my mouth."

"Just sing the same chant as yesterday, Shaji," Kaylem asked, his eyes like those of a lonely, stray dog.

Saoirse remembered Marsi's face from long ago as a younger Saoirse was caught laughing at the omens. The consequences of speaking out about her own deeper experiences of the gods had been disastrous back then. What little peace remained inside from the night before dried up. Anything she did in front of these people would always be seen as heresy, unsanctioned by the Temple.

"But wouldn't that be considered sacrilege?" Saoirse pulled her scarf over her face again, knowing Bo would be watching closely. A knot tightened further in her stomach.

"Please?" Kaylem whispered urgently.

"The blessing has already happened, Kaylem, and if I sing some unknown tune and blessing, the servants will be very upset. Think about how they would cope with a strange woman showing up and speaking so differently to what they expect."

It was suddenly too quiet. Kaylem's eyes began to gleam as his tears formed once again at the corners of his eyes. He gazed at her in quiet distress. She sighed with resignation and pulled her head shawl even further over her face despite the heat. Hoping Bo did not recognize her voice, she began a similar prayer to the one she had heard the high priestess intone at the eve of the new year atop the Temple.

To Nergal, the god of death and destruction, she implored him to convey Issa's spirit with gentleness to the underworld.

Her voice, shaky at first, rose into a tune that formed itself in her throat. Saoirse then voiced a prayer to Ziku, the god of prosperity and fortune, to bring abundance and contentment upon Issa's spirit on its journeys yet to come. She petitioned Anu and Inanna, the great father and mother, to allow for Issa's spirit to eventually be reborn with their blessings and wisdom.

Wondering how the prayer was being received so far, she cracked open an eye to a group blinking at her in stunned bewilderment. Kaylem stood slightly apart, listening peacefully with his eyes closed, a hand on the altar to steady himself. To her great relief, she could sense no outrage that she wasn't following the exact traditional rites.

She pushed away the memories of those terrible days where the servants' superstition had caused such hostility and led to her exile. Here and now, the people around her seemed touched by what she sang. The memory of the past, which caused a momentary tremor to her voice, loosened its fist around her, and she renewed her focus inward once again and continued.

To Tammuz, the god of the earth, she prayed that Issa's body would be returned to the great Mother Earth from whence it was made. To Enki, the god of water, she asked that the thirsts of Issa's spirit may always be slaked; and Ninlil, goddess of air, to bless Issa with peace and the breath of eternity.

To Erishkigal, goddess of fire, she implored that all of Issa's evils be burned and purified from her spirit to begin the next life cleansed and anew. And last of all, to Ashur, god of the aethers, to weave the other elements together for Issa's spirit substance, under the wisdom and guidance of Anu and Innana, to be created anew.

Bringing the prayer-chant to a close, Saoirse allowed the silence around the group to envelop them into its embrace. It caressed and comforted and allowed the grieving of the living to be eased into a state of peace. As she opened her eyes into the space still resonating with her prayer, she saw that not a cheek in the small group was without a silver trail of tears.

Kaylem's smile of gratitude shone from his face. She went to him. The others, now released from the prayer, began to wander aimlessly from the graveside. A couple of them, she noticed from the corners of her vision, turned to look at her in wide-eyed awe and she tightened the scarf over her face to protect herself from

CHAPTER 4

their stares.

The elderly handservant, who had lowered the food and drink onto Issa's body for her to find later as she hungered on her journey, dawdled absently into the household as the other servants also eventually wandered away. Yet to come was the meal to honor Issa's passing, although Saoirse suspected it would be a while until the food was ready.

Once the meal was served, the servants would be seated to eat their own food in their courtyard. Saoirse and Kaylem would eat together in the formal reception alcove at the front of the household, which struck Saoirse as somewhat dismal that they should be separated from the others out of custom. A part of her yearned to be able to draw comfort from the others and sit together as one group, just as it had been during the ceremony of mourning.

Bo, Saoirse noticed now, was watching her with narrowed eyes as though he recognized something about her but couldn't place exactly what it was. Making a note to herself to mention Bo to Kaylem later, she turned to make her way back inside and avoid further scrutiny. She left Kaylem bent beside the manservant as they refilled the hole from the pile of turned, yellow-brown earth nearby.

"*Mistress?*" Bo's timid voice stopped Saoirse short. He had used the formal, proper address for her as Oracle. Her chest locked. Surely he would laugh and then recognize her as Girl, the one who had been sent away. She wondered if he would be hostile to her, whether Issa had succeeded in poisoning him against her all those moons ago, and whether the servants would accept her as Oracle if they knew of her past.

Out of the corner of her eye, Saoirse noticed that Kaylem and all of the servants had stopped where they were and were listening closely. Saoirse turned to Bo and nodded, hiding her face even further behind the shawl, which suddenly seemed too flimsy a barrier between them. It was not the time to be reuniting with Bo, and she hoped against hope for him not to have recognized her, even though there was still a part of her that yearned to hold him close again.

"Our deepest gratitude for such a wondrous burial rite, *Mistress*." His voice, alternately squeaky and deep with the first crackings of adolescence, was filled with wonder and awe. Saoirse took a step back in confusion at the title. He had now, twice, used the formal word for *Mistress*, but surely it was too soon for him to have known. Nodding awkwardly at him, she resumed her steps to the household.

Soon, Kaylem found her alone in his sleeping chamber staring absently at the well from one of the wall vents. Saoirse turned to him.

"Kaylem, why did Bo call me *Mistress*?"

"Hmm?" Kaylem looked confused.

"What in all the worlds did Bo mean when he called me *Mistress*?"

"That's the correct term to address the Oracle, Shaji."

"They know?"

"It seems so... *Mistress*."

Saoirse nudged him with her elbow. "But... did you tell them?"

"No, I haven't."

Saoirse turned and looked at him with a frown of confusion.

"I promise you I haven't said a word. But there was a merchant from Ur here this morning. He left for Erech after a meal. He did talk to a couple of the servants, which may explain things."

"Ah..." Saoirse sat for a moment to digest his words.

"And Kaylem?"

"Yes, Shaji."

"How should I make myself known to Bo?"

"What do you mean?"

"When I was banished from the compound, Bo was devastated. I was like his older sister. I can't believe he didn't recognize me." She huffed out a breath, unsure whether to be relieved or disappointed. "Marsi was more like his mother, and we were the only family we had. I was so sure I'd never see him again." Saoirse's own eyes filled with tears, and she lowered her head, swallowing.

"It's... awkward..." Kaylem stared at the floor, his face set in a frown. "I know we shouldn't have mingled with the servants for the death ritual for my mother, especially with you as Oracle, but we didn't have enough people to satisfy the requirements of..."

Saoirse looked at him slyly. "Of course, Kaylem. But it's not like you were ever that strict with keeping away from the servants."

CHAPTER 4

Kaylem grimaced. "How could I forget? And look at the consequences."

Saoirse raised her eyebrows and folded her arms in front of her. "Were they all bad, then? Do you regret it?"

"I don't regret not staying away from you for one second. From the moment I saw you when you arrived it was like a magnet drawing me to you. But maybe this is different. Imagine how Bo might feel to find that Girl, the servant he knew from before, had suddenly, magically transformed into the great and powerful Oracle of Ur?"

"I don't know, maybe he'd be happy for me?"

"Don't forget, he's been nowhere aside from here. To suddenly find that his world is turned upside down…And unfortunately my mother did drill into him how terrible and evil you were." He looked down at his feet and she could feel waves of shame emanating from him.

Saoirse looked back out at the well and pondered for a moment. "I guess… I've been kicking myself for being dishonest to him, for hiding who I am from him."

"And then, imagine if all the servants found out that you were here previously as a servant. How would that be?"

Saoirse's shoulders dropped and she sighed. "I suppose you are correct, Kaylem."

"I am here to serve, *Mistress*." He intoned with a twinkle in his eyes.

"Oh, stop it." She batted him lightly in his chest and was struck by his closeness, his aliveness. Her skin burned and she knew it flushed traitorously scarlet. "I still wish I could let him know I'm safe, rather than hiding from him like this."

Kaylem nodded slowly and then shrugged. "For what it's worth, it truly was a wonderful Death Rite, just as Bo said," he murmured as he looked into her eyes, which made her flush deepen. This time the heat travelled down to her lower core which thrummed and throbbed delightfully in time to her heartbeat.

"Kaylem, the earth is not yet fully turned over your mother's grave…" she whispered, half wishing that he would move himself even closer to her. Silently, she chided herself for having such feelings at such a time.

Kaylem's face fell and he looked at the floor. "I suppose so," he said softly, wistfully. Saoirse wished he'd look at her again the way he had done a moment ago. She stood like stone, unable to move while he raised his face and their eyes joined. He smiled sadly.

"And yet…"

"And yet… what… Saoirse?" He pronounced her name perfectly, the syllables rolling from his tongue, falling from his lips with such precision, she felt the flush begin all over again. It was the first time he'd used her true name in a while and it was shockingly intimate in the quiet space between them. The place in her lower core writhed and glowed as though being simmered with gently burning coals.

"Yet…" Unable to quite recall what she had wanted to say, she noticed that the two of them were breathing in the same rhythm. The thin strip of air between them thickened as though her substance and his were straining to meet and entwine themselves together.

Even closer he leaned, slowly but surely shrinking the distance between them and her lips parted, her body becoming fluid. Kaylem's shoulder brushed hers which sent a thrilling jolt through her. Never in her wildest wonderings had she imagined such sensations. Kaylem's caress of her cheek somehow involved the whole of her body. Tendrils of silver and fire made their way downward, and then up again, only to burst, tingling, from the top of her head.

Saoirse moved her face so that her lips aligned with Kaylem's, which echoed a dream she remembered vividly from long ago. His beard was thicker. She anticipated its tickle on her cheek before it brushed lightly against her, sending more shivers and tendrils running through her.

Breathing in with a slight gasp as Kaylem's lips tentatively grazed her own, Saoirse's core became molten, like a wad of ore as she had once seen at the smelter's. Tendrils of fire flickered from the glowing heart of her, licking and flicking at Kaylem's solid earthiness. He did not flinch. Instead, he basked in the heat of her, moving himself even closer as he gently cupped her face in his warm hand—

"Ahem…" The voice originated from outside the chamber and Saoirse mourned as the pieces of the fractured spell fell around them. Then a hot flush of shame made its way up her cheeks.

CHAPTER 4

"Yes?" Kaylem's voice was perturbed, with a hint of resignation, as both of them realized it must be time for the meal.

"Master Kaylem, we have a visitor, and I wonder if you would prefer for him to dine with yourself and the *Mistress*?"

"A… visitor?" Kaylem's forehead creased in puzzlement.

"He is the tutor returned to us, master."

"Oh, master Hos! Yes, please lay another setting for him." Kaylem turned to stare at her with wide eyes.

"The tutor," she whispered, her own eyes just as wide.

"See, he's come to meet the one who has been performing such amazing wonders on the inner worlds."

"Nonsense! But it will be good to see him." Saoirse spoke with a joyous smile on her face, remembering the way the old man had glowed during the illicit chanting she had attended before the flood of Ur had changed her entire life's path.

He was also the man who had been Kaylem's tutor in his childhood, and Saoirse had attracted endless punishments for being caught secretly listening to him rather than doing her work. They hurried out to greet the man who stood awaiting them in the reception alcove, strangely as fresh as the day she had seen him in Ur. He looked as though he had not traveled even a footstep on the dusty road.

"Master, it is a great pleasure to receive you." Kaylem embraced the man, who then turned to Saoirse.

"*Mistress*." He dipped his head with a glint in his eye that Saoirse could almost call cheeky. She blinked.

"Master," she managed to choke out. To see him so close was suddenly unnerving. He literally thrummed with power. It emanated from him so strongly, her hands began to throb, and her chest felt as though it might crack open.

"Call me Hos," he told Saoirse. "It's a word derived from an ancient and far-flung dialect meaning aether, similar to the language your own names originated from, by the way."

Nodding again, Saoirse could not help but wonder at how well the name fit, and she smiled.

"Please, join us for our meal, master Hos. I'm comforted that you could be with us for our Feast of Mourning." As Kaylem spoke the traditional words, he indicated the low-lying bench surrounded by colorful and ornately embroidered cushions. Hos nodded and they sat to begin their meal.

31

"Master Hos?"

"Yes, master Kaylem." Hos began to help himself to a plate piled high with fragrantly spiced meat, roasted eggplant, okra, and lentils, a delicacy especially prepared by the handservant herself for the occasion. Saoirse wondered if she was taking too much of the meat, but her stomach was growling like a rabid dog in response to its delicious smell.

"I can't help but notice how… refreshed you seem. The merchant who visited earlier looked very dishevelled after his travels in comparison." Saoirse raised her eyebrows at Kaylem's impertinence.

"Ah, ever the observant one here, are we not?" Hos winked at Kaylem in a fatherly way and Kaylem beamed back at the man in adoration. "Well, since you've pointed out my freshness, permit me to explain my arrival to your threshold." Hos dabbed delicately with his cloth at a spot of grease beside his mouth, wrapped a piece of bread around another mouthful and ponderously chewed as though it were fare of the gods. He then washed it down with a large sip of his ale.

Saoirse had crammed so much of the meat into her mouth she could hardly chew it. It was the most glorious thing she had ever tasted in her life, and she moved it around as best she could on her tongue to savor the taste fully.

"It's true, that I've traveled far…" His eyes took on a dreamy sheen. The meat suddenly turned to grit in Saoirse's mouth. Her stomach clenched in a strange sort of dread as though it knew what the master would say next. She wanted to interrupt him, throw her bowl at him and storm away. Shocked at the intensity of her feeling, she forced herself instead to sit still and work her way through the mouthful as best as she could.

"How did you travel, master Hos?" The words forced their way from her suddenly as though they did not belong to her. Her voice sounded faint and far away to her ears.

"Ah, yes… I suspect the answer will not please you, Saoirse."

Saoirse drew back from him and gulped down a mouthful of ale to rid her mouth of the now unpleasant remnants of food. She took another sip to bolster herself against his next words, her eyes locked to his.

"It seems that the Anzu have been busy in their latest bout of prying into the affairs of human-kind," he began in a mild

CHAPTER 4

voice. Saoirse took a tight breath, frowning at the image of the large bird-like being held vividly in her mind, still fresh from her prophetic dream.

"It seems so, master Hos, as the city of Ur and its people have been laid to waste by their so called… prying," she answered with more venom than she expected in her voice. "Why are they even here? They should all get in their craft and go back to wherever they came from." Saoirse's voice was cold as she remembered the dream, in which the Anzu had told her of the coming flood and implied that their kind had caused it in some way.

This was, the Anzu had briefly explained in her dream, because of the great evils wrought by the Temple priestcraft, performed in the name of the gods, who in truth, would never condone such horrors. The Anzu were said to be agents of those gods, acting in the known world to carry out the gods' will.

"And what exactly is your involvement with the Anzu, master Hos?" Saoirse asked.

Kaylem looked at each of them in alarm.

"Not as you would assume, *Mistress*," he answered, his eyes never wavering for a second from hers.

"Is that so, master?" Saoirse glared at him, her eyes narrowed to slits.

"What is true, *Mistress*, is that the Anzu and I have been… partaking in negotiations in order to… minimize their impact on the people…" Hos said softly.

"Please, master Hos, do not address me as *Mistress*. You may call me Saoirse, or anything else you wish to as far as I care… Yet, am I truly to believe that you did not conspire with these… creatures… in order to gain favor? The same favor the Temple elite seem also to seek so keenly from the Anzu? After all, they caused the flood, master Hos." Her jaw was clenched so tightly she could hear her teeth grinding against each other.

"The Temple elite, Saoirse, do not see the Anzu for who they truly are, and it would completely destroy even the most powerful of them if they did." Master Hos held out a hand to quiet Saoirse as he sensed that she was about to interrupt. "Neither, it seems, do you, dear Saoirse, despite your gifts. It is of great importance that you should better know their nature before you come across them for yourself." The tutor's voice remained gentle despite the authority and warning his words implied. Kaylem sat stiffly and silently, eyes wide, his mug of ale held frozen halfway to his lips.

"I don't want to hear a word of it from one so ensconced within the favor of these savage and destructive beings who have brought about the total destruction of Ur. Not to mention how many deaths will follow with winter and no food on the way," Saoirse muttered furiously. Without quite being aware of what she did, she raised herself from her cushion, turned on her heel, and stalked from the alcove.

Wondering vaguely why she did not stop at the threshold, Saoirse marched into the yawning emptiness of the desert, the sun well on its way to the horizon. She strode in a straight and stubborn line away from all that she knew, pulled as she was by a force that she had somehow awoken and called upon from the unknown depths of herself.

Even Kaylem's desperate cries for her to turn back did not stop her and her senses became acute as she became a predator hunting for her prey.

CHAPTER 5

The walking gradually helped Saoirse come back to herself. It was just past sunset, and the sky was beginning to dim. Wishing she had brought, at the least, a bladder of water or ale, Saoirse swallowed with a dry click and stayed on her course, the mysterious force drawing her forward in a direct line. On and on she walked, through the increasingly darkening night, on legs still tired and shaky after her recent journey from Ur. The heat, so strong in the day despite the proximity of winter, leached quickly from the air around her, the earth beneath her, and from her now shivering body.

By the time she slowed, Saoirse could see nothing aside from the winking stars, spreading in a majestic panorama above her. This was the place the pull had originated from, and she sat on the stony, now-freezing ground to wait. The walk had calmed her somewhat, and her head was cool as she contemplated what it was that she awaited. She wondered at her certainty that they would come, for if she was mistaken it would mean death, if not from thirst, then from the increasingly freezing air around her.

Feeling faint, she allowed herself to go into a trance to prepare herself for this meeting and escape the uncomfortable sensations of her body. Even in the total darkness, now that her inner world was still and in harmony with the silence around her, Saoirse could see a medley of colors and shapes. Each of the objects around her contained an inner glow of their own which continued irrespective of the sun's position in the sky.

Sitting as still as she could with her eyes half open, Saoirse merely observed, caught up in the beauty and wonder of the worlds both within and without as the two merged and fused, becoming one. Reaching out with her awareness, she sensed a silver ribbon snaking its way to Kaylem, and she sent a pulse of reassurance back to him, knowing he would be frantic at her abrupt departure. She also sensed Hos, instructing Kaylem to wait for her rather than following her out into the dangers of the desert night.

Opening even further, Saoirse sensed another presence. An instant later, a burst of blinding light appeared from the patch of sky directly above, glowing so brightly that she shut her eyes against it. Even with her eyes closed, light branded itself onto the backs of her eyes. There was the strange sensation of seeing the light fade and a figure appear, even though her eyelids were still firmly closed.

Eventually she did open them in order to better see the being before her. In mild surprise, Saoirse saw that the Anzu was female, made obvious by the swell of breasts under the tight leathers worn by the creature. The being was familiar, and Saoirse was immediately reminded of a dream from back when she had first arrived at the household as a child. The very same being had taken her far away in a craft and shown a much younger Saoirse the well in the courtyard. It dimly crossed her mind that to send the female was an attempt at a more gentle introduction to their kind, and Saoirse couldn't choose whether to feel insulted or grateful for such thoughtfulness.

The female's wingspan, and in fact the whole personage of the bird-woman before her, was more remarkable than anything she could ever have imagined, even if she had already met her in a dream. Folded neatly behind the female, her wings towered far above her head, which was set at a regal angle and covered in a fine down of feathers over bluish skin. The Anzu towered far above Saoirse, and her neck ached as it craned to meet the female's dark gaze.

Both stood silently, each appraising the other until Saoirse noticed that a hole in her awareness had begun to form. It was not a forcefully created hole, but one through which another's awareness may enter her own, like a wall vent or doorway. An un-worded question formed in Saoirse's mind as both sets of eyes locked upon each other. It was a request for permission of sorts, to which Saoirse gave a sharp nod of affirmation. Too soon, the

CHAPTER 5

Anzu's substance had entirely pervaded her own. Saoirse stiffened in mild panic as she found herself discarding any prior notions she may have had about communicating with the being.

As though facing a mirror which reflected every one of her own thoughts, feelings, and impressions, Saoirse was suddenly bombarded by a tidal wave of her own being. She was aware of the creature absorbing the whole of her knowledge, the whole of her spirit, in a way that allowed Saoirse herself to see so far within herself she somehow did not know herself any longer.

Darkness and light warred with each other in an endless dance that reached to her very core. Completely unprepared for such a deluge, Saoirse fell shivering to the ground. She whimpered as the enormity of her inner being opened.

A crease in her chest appeared, which expanded and opened. Saoirse felt a glimmer of panic until another different body appeared underneath. This also peeled away to reveal yet another, and she understood that these were different skins, different bodies she had worn throughout the ages. Sometimes she was a man, Saoirse saw in astonishment. In others, she was a woman. Strange and different outfits appeared and melted away, along with the flesh, and soon the impressions passed by too quickly for her to register.

The visions slowed and focused on a woman with impossibly long hair tied into many elaborate plaits, who slashed two swords around herself in movements akin to a dance, against a spectacular rainbow sky. This Saoirse recognized from a previous vision, and she gasped in wonder at the realization that this woman had been herself in a different skin, a different time. This was the woman who had saved her miserable life at the brothel, who had given her the fortitude to kill the brothel owner and lead her friends to safety...

Blackness followed and Saoirse breathed a sigh of relief that it was all over. Then, the blackness parted, and Saoirse blinked and looked down, hoping to see her own body restored to her once again. Instead, she was impossibly tall, wearing leathers reminding her of the Anzu who was still standing before her. In her peripheral vision a pair of wings stretched behind her own Anzu body.

Before she could blink, the scene opened out and she saw a dying planet where many Anzu lay floating, their wings spread lifeless and black on a sea of water that glowed a toxic green. She understood that the Ushum, their mortal enemy, had caused the destruction she saw all around her. Other dead sea creatures, bloated and rancid, surrounded her along with the bodies and she wondered what the Ushum could possibly have done to cause this. Looking downward again, she noticed her own lightly feathered, bluish skin turning black, as whatever had killed the others came for her.

A strange sense of relief and resignation filled her as she lay waiting for death to claim her, too. As she allowed the life-force to ebb from her body, the flash of a craft appeared with none other than Kaylem, also in Anzu form, standing at an opening in its side. He was wildly gesticulating and yelling something at her.

It was too late, and triumph filled her because she would die here on this planet and her spirit would be trapped here among her fellow beings. The thought was followed by an instant of regret before slipping mercifully into blackness. Before the blackness could completely consume her, something grabbed at her consciousness like a hook, tugging her back from the void. Again, it rudely pulled at her until her spirit hovered, bodiless, before Anzu-Kaylem. Her essence hovered inside the ship now, and Kaylem took a giant breath in, somehow pulling her spirit inside his body.

Outraged, she struggled and attempted to escape back to the dying planet. It was not supposed to be this way. He had no right to force her away from this world in which she wished to die. If only he'd left her to die back there, her spirit would be free of him, free of the great burden he had so violently forced upon her so many aeons ago...

To go with him would mean enslavement to another planet, one she wished never to see again...

After another period of blessed blackness, there were more images. She was flying over the Earth. A great ocean stretched as far as the eye could see, broken only by a small islet of land. One of the Anzu's craft landed in a flash of light onto the small shore. A female Anzu stood at the craft's opening, carrying a human babe. Saoirse cried out as she saw the now sobbing Anzu hand the babe to a cowering human woman standing below. The human woman was clad in tattered woven grass and hid her eyes as the craft disappeared in a blinding flash of light.

CHAPTER 5

More humans wearing similar garments approached and crowded around the babe, who Saoirse noticed was a girl-child; an orphan without a family, just as she herself was. The ragged group stood beside a stream of silver water in their midst, which glittered as it flowed down the sloped sand toward the ocean brine. A small boy reached his hand reverently, tenderly toward the babe. Saoirse could clearly see that already he was unusually tall compared to the others; so tall that he would grow to tower over the others around him, just as the new babe would as well.

Her last glimpse of the scene was of the stream of silver water, which her spirit-self plunged into. The water was cool and cleansing, a blessing to the early humans from the Anzu. Saoirse found herself suddenly immersed in the silver spring, swimming upward toward a bright light. As she broke the surface, she discovered that she was at the bottom of the well in the household, watching the water lap against the ancient stone.

Saoirse gasped and drew her breath in with a whoop, as though emerging from under water.

"No!" screamed Saoirse and she sensed the Anzu female withdrawing her consciousness, soothing the screaming layers of distress until Saoirse returned to her own body, gaping and panting and writhing on the thistle-pocked ground.

A part of her wondered why she had tried to escape from Kaylem in that vision, but the rest of her threatened to pass out from overwhelm and she blocked off the possibility of anything else coming into her consciousness. After a time, the coldness of air and earth soothed her distress, and then there was nothing but the terrible knowledge she had absorbed. The Knowing settled over her like the heaviest of burdens and she sobbed and sobbed until her throat could no longer make any sounds but a harsh croak.

Only a heartbeat after she had recovered somewhat, another tidal wave overwhelmed her; that of the bird-woman's entire being as she felt herself being drawn into the bird-woman's essence.

Once again, she saw their dying planet, and this time she was only bodiless awareness, observing as they moved rapidly away in a different craft packed with Anzu of all shapes and sizes. Thousands of other craft flew around them, and all watched their planet shrink into the distance as they readied to travel the reaches of space to another home far away. The inner space of the craft was full of keening of grief and remorse, for the damage done to themselves and their Mother-planet. For now, the Anzu would struggle to survive on a hostile planet, carrying the burden of this war with their enemy, the Ushum, forever.

After much travel, the new planet loomed, enormous and red-hued, its air too thin to breathe and crawling with foreign and threatening life forms. They made the new planet their home to the best of their abilities. Many died. Craft were sent to explore the region and returned with the discovery that another, smaller planet in their system held a valuable and sacred element blessed to it by the gods, which would enable their lives to continue.

Two primitive beings from the small planet had been brought back with the explorers. Clad in tattered woven grass garments, the two humans, a man and a woman, huddled together as far away as possible from the Anzu, tears flowing freely down their faces.

The human's planet held little but endless ocean, broken only by the occasional tiny isle on which the humans had eked out their existence for millennia. Yet the Anzu knew that the oceans would soon recede, revealing lands rich in the metal that glowed like the sun and could be turned into a mist that would render the new planet's air heavier and more friendly to their bodies.

The more perceptive of the Anzu received visions from the gods who instructed them to bring the primitive humans of Earth out of their dark age; to show them, with kindness, the way forward, and to interbreed with them in order to give the human race a brighter future. The less perceptive ruffled their wings in greed at the prospect of ripping the sacred sun-metal from the earth for their reward, using the humans as their slaves to dig for the precious stuff.

Debates turned to arguments as those who could hear the whispers of the gods begged for mercy toward the humans. The others argued that all would die unless Earth was stripped bare, the humans reduced to less than the animals they lived beside...

Saoirse shrieked as she felt her own essence pulled from the bird-woman and deposited back into her body, which shivered and ached as though wracked with fever. A distant part of her awareness screamed at the unfinished stories still yet to unfold, the process of the Knowing continuing behind a thin veil. Saoirse turned away from that veil and toward the hard earth, which

CHAPTER 5

prickled and froze her skin, until she returned to the dull vessel of flesh that she reclaimed as hers.

Shuddering and weak, Saoirse was only dimly aware that the Anzu was picking her up and gently carrying her prone body into the still-glowing craft nearby. Saoirse vaguely registered that there was another of the beings waiting inside the craft; a male this time, although he compassionately kept his essence entirely closed to her.

The craft flashed once again through her closed eyes, then moved so rapidly that Saoirse felt violently ill despite the dimness of her consciousness and empty belly. Within seconds, the craft stopped, and she found herself puddled at the open gate of the compound, half aware of Kaylem reaching frantically to carry her back inside.

CHAPTER 6

Saoirse slept and slept while night turned to day, and day to night. Unsure and uncaring just how many times the sun watched the earth make its turn around the heavens, she didn't want to open her eyes ever again. Things would never be as they were before and waking up would mean facing the reality of the terrible wellspring of knowledge released by the Anzu. It would also mean facing Hos, whose words and actions, she now saw with great shame, had been meant in kindness in order to protect her.

Eventually, nature's requirements for her body dictated that she force open her unwilling eyes, bright sunlight blinding them as she hoisted her aching, withered body upright. Kaylem was beside her in an instant, and she struggled with a moment of such violent anger toward him she was glad she could hardly lift her arm. She reminded herself that the man standing before her was not the one who had somehow captured her spirit against her will and forced her back to Earth from the dying planet of the Anzu.

Even though his innermost essence was one and the same, she told herself that this man in front of her was someone entirely different, and much time had passed since. Kaylem assisted her to the bathing chamber, then led her back to bed and insisted on spoon-feeding her some kind of broth, the only food her protesting belly would receive.

For days, until she was steady on her feet and able to join Kaylem and Hos for their meals, Saoirse did little but rest and contemplate, allowing Kaylem near her only when she was unable

CHAPTER 6

to tend to her own needs. Hos, in his wisdom, remained silent on her encounter with the Anzu and, she figured, must have advised Kaylem to do the same. By the next ripened moon, Saoirse understood that the terrible knowledge would change nothing about the particulars of her every-day life at the compound. She allowed the images to gradually fade into the back of her consciousness, not quite sure what else to do with them.

As Saoirse made small incursions around the courtyards, Hos occasionally nodded to her in acknowledgement as she passed him by. She found herself unable to look into the well and would hastily pull up the occasional bucket of water only to slake her strongest thirst. She refused to see the water's silver sparkle, reminding her so much of her visions of a much younger Earth.

The days blurred into a long stream of idleness and eventually Saoirse found herself becoming restless. Her dreams became filled with stinking yellow-brown mud, which found its bitter way into her mouth and ears, as she watched the people of Ur sicken and die. Those who survived fought and killed each other for what little supplies remained. Others worked to their deaths rebuilding for the elite in return for barely enough food to keep a rat alive.

Not one to tolerate inactivity for long at the best of times, Saoirse became increasingly irritable with Kaylem's fussing and insistence that she rest.

"Enough, Kaylem. I'm not a delicate waif and I'm feeling much better."

Kaylem sighed and watched her warily, as though scared she would slap him. "Shaji, why does your voice suddenly hold so much anger when you look at me?"

Saoirse drew in a breath and let it out in a whoosh, wishing she could somehow erase the images of her visions shared with the Anzu that now sat within her like small drops of poison.

"It's just impatience to take some action, Kaylem. Too much time has passed, and I see too much of the horrors that are unfolding in Ur in my dreams. We must ask master Hos for some lessons to help prepare us for our return."

"We could always just stay here..." He stroked her arm idly and she suppressed the urge to fling it away. "Now that I'm master of the household, this is truly ours. It's far away from the evils of the elite, but close enough to Ur that we could visit now and then." Kaylem stared into the distance, his voice wistful.

"Kaylem, the people of Ur are suffering. I feel their pain as a constant shriek at the back of my awareness."

"We could find a way. The people will continue to murder each other without thought of the gods, whether your guidance is with them or not"

"Maybe. Whether my presence is desired or not by the elite, the people of Ur must be protected from those very evils you speak of. Who else will dare speak for the people?"

Kaylem toyed with the hem on his robe and scrunched up his face. For a second, Saoirse wanted to reach out and run a finger softly down his cheek to feel the tangle of his beard. She stopped herself and rearranged her face into an expression of severity.

"I know we have to go back," he murmured. "I wish I could tell you how you're going to live a life of ease and contentment once we're there. But my biggest fear is that they might find their way to killing us both. I don't care about me, but if they laid a hand on you... I couldn't bear for that to happen. After seeing what the Anzu did to you..." Kaylem looked away, his throat bobbing.

"Kaylem, don't be afraid. My flesh... our flesh is only the bark of the tree. For one or the other to lose that skin is just an inconvenience, don't you see? We have endless chances, unfortunately. We're trapped here, coming back in different bodies until..." She blinked and pinched at her arm in frustration. She didn't actually know if there was an end to it. Kaylem watched her patiently, waiting for her to continue. "There's no stopping the process, Kaylem. We just come right back. I've seen it! If the price I have to pay for fulfilling the task of the gods is my flesh, my body, then I'll gladly pay it. Maybe then we'll truly be free..."

"Free? Like the gods themselves?"

"The true gods, yes. But the true gods are not the Anzu and the Ushum. They are only agents of the gods. Imagine being free of this..." Saoirse punched herself in the arm.

Kaylem's eyes widened and then blinked rapidly. "No, Shaji, please don't talk like that. Our flesh is sacred, given to us by the gods. It may be of no consequence to you if you lose your life, but what about me? I couldn't live if you weren't here beside me."

"But to lose the body is not to lose your life. Surely you know that, Kaylem."

"Of course I do, but surely you wouldn't want to just die

CHAPTER 6

when there's so much life to be lived... when we've only just found each other again."

Saoirse, taking a long draught of small-ale from a mug which stood beside her, and breathing a long breath before she continued. "After the Anzu communed with me, something opened inside of me, and the visions have increased. I've seen two paths, Kaylem."

Saoirse fought her way past the constriction in her throat. She had yet to allow herself to accept the reality of what she was about to say. Still, the words were there needing to be said. "One was the path planned by the gods, and the bright future that lies before us if we follow their guidance. This path requires great faith and courage, from both of us together, and there is such a small chance of it happening." Saoirse took his hand and glared at him. "Believe in me always, Kaylem, even though your faith in me might fade, and then we may have that chance."

Kaylem shifted and fidgeted for a moment, blinking rapidly. She softened her expression, and he squeezed her hand. "I'll never stop believing in you, Shaji, you should know that."

"I know you were the only one to believe me before the flood. But Kaylem, there's another path. The will of the gods is not fulfilled. An action taken in fear means a victory for the darkness. Then, everything we've worked for will be lost, and we'll be doomed to live in darkness for the remainder of our days until our bodies die. Then, we'll have to wait until another time far in the future, when circumstances are once again favorable to bring about the plan."

"Surely it won't rely only on us," Kaylem replied, his eyes wide and his skin pale. "Us against the entire Temple elite?"

"It won't. I think that's also the difficult part, Kaylem. This relies on a whole lot of people working together to bring it about. You and I are central to it succeeding, but we also have to trust others to do what they must, as well. And, this plan will unfold over the next few years when we'll have to face our darkest fears."

She sighed and reached for his hand. "We must both remember, Kaylem, when we face our trials, that the gods and their messages are not always spoken through the ones you would trust or expect. And sometimes the ones we trust the most will speak from the darkness within, instead of the heart."

Kaylem took up her hand and squeezed gently, his face creased with worry. "Such grave words, Shaji."

"Darkness has won too many times, Kaylem, and it's through fear that darkness gains power." Saoirse allowed him to keep hold of her hand this time.

"Then, love of my heart, allow me to speak despite the fact that my body is right now trembling in terror." Kaylem, still holding her hand, knelt at her feet, a wry yet vulnerable expression on his face. Her throat spasmed as she realized what he was doing. "I give of you my body, my spirit, and my undying love."

Saoirse could not speak, but watched as he spoke the traditional words of the marriage proposal usually spoken in front of both the bride and groom's families just before the wedding.

"Be the woman to live as one with me, Saoirse. Be the one to share my body, my spirit, and my life. You are already the one my heart beats for. Let us be man and wife here and now, today, so you can see how much I believe in you." His voice trembled in its passion. "I'm sure master Hos will be happy to perform the ceremony to unite us. Say you will. Please, Shaji? This time, say you will."

Saoirse looked deeply into Kaylem's eyes. For all their darkness, they shone with his love for her. After a hesitation, Saoirse breathed out the heaviness that lay on her and shrugged the fears from her heart. She could hardly lecture Kaylem about his fear if she was filled with it herself, and what happened in the past was past. They had another chance now.

A hesitant smile formed itself on her face, which Kaylem caught with his eyes, and they crinkled back at her with joy. Her own smile grew, which she saw reflected in Kaylem's eyes until tears streamed down both of their faces. She laughed as her teenage dreams flashed into her mind.

"Kaylem, I'd be honored to live as one with you; honored and filled with joy that the gods have found a way for us to be together." Kaylem arose and, spinning her around in the small chamber, they danced a Dance of Celebration, all of the darkness forgotten.

CHAPTER 7

Later, the handservant was sent muttering to the cellar in search of any delicacies left since Issa's funeral and the manservant sent to hunt whatever unfortunate animal he could find. Master Hos stood with them together under the palm-shade, ready to perform the Joining Ceremony. There was no need for crowds of people or fancy robes. The glory of the moment lay in the glow of their hearts, which grew to encompass the entirety of the vast desert as Hos intoned a lively chant of celebration and union.

Saoirse found it difficult to focus on anything but Hos's reedy voice rising and wavering through the different notes as he blessed the couple in the name of the gods. She was tempted to close her eyes and float away as the chant made her feel like she was flying through the heavens as easily as a desert eagle, soaring through galaxies and solar systems far from where they stood.

Then the tone changed, and she found herself deposited back in her body, her hands warm where Kaylem held them gently in his. Kaylem was watching her, and she could see the relief on his face that they were finally able to have this happiness to share. Looking deep into his eyes, she sensed a weaving together of their spirits, hands, and hearts as the tutor wove the sound around them.

As master Hos's voice fell silent, the newlyweds turned to him and bowed. Then they moved to the dining alcove where two settings lay, side by side. Hos took his meal elsewhere, insisting that he would feel like a fifth leg on a lizard if he stayed. They fed each other small morsels of tender meat, along with bread dipped in the fragrant juice of the stew. In between mouthfuls were sips of ale and even a small vessel of wine for a toast at the end of their meal. Then they sat for a while in silence, bellies filled to bursting as they contemplated the ceremony, the meal, and what was still to come.

As her thoughts turned to the evening ahead, nervousness began to creep in. Hardly detectable at first over the contented buzz of her body, it wormed its way into her, turning the food in her stomach to coarse desert sand. Soon, she would be sharing Kaylem's bed with him. No amount of telling herself she shouldn't worry made any difference.

Too soon, he looked at her and his desire was plain on his face. "Come, my radiant bride. It's time to join our bodies together."

Saoirse sat watching the congealing remains of the meal and Kaylem's smile dried up. "What is it, Shaji?"

"Kaylem, I'm not the pure, untouched bride you deserve."

Kaylem made to interrupt but she held up her hand. "There's a darkness in me. I'm afraid..." Unable to go on for a moment, Saoirse breathed in deeply and forced her voice to continue.

"I'd gladly die before losing your regard, Kaylem. You know my history. You know what I've done, what I've been through. You know I can never pretend to be anyone other than myself, and..." Saoirse cleared her throat and shuffled. "I'm damaged, Kaylem. I might seem well enough most days, but you haven't seen the dark times that..." She sighed and her shoulders slumped.

"I know enough about that time, and I'm here for you, Shaji." Kaylem moved closer and Saoirse wasn't sure whether to push him away or welcome him.

"But I'm not a virgin, Kaylem. I know with the Temple elite and the rich... it's so important for the families to accept a virgin bride..."

Kaylem's mouth twitched.

"Are you... laughing at me?" She sent him daggers with her eyes.

"It's just that... well... I don't know how to put this delicately. The Temple practices involving the juniors are..." He shrugged and gave a rueful huff. "I'm not a virgin either."

"Oh," she said after a lengthy pause.

"Do you care?"

It was her turn for her lip to twitch. "That would be a little..."

CHAPTER 7

"Yes, well I was hoping you'd—"

"But, Kaylem, what exactly—"

"I don't know why prostitution is so frowned upon. Truly, what they do in the Temple is…" Kaylem averted his gaze for a moment and pursed his lips. "The girls given to the Temple do their training knowing full well what's involved once they become priestesses. I can't imagine it's terribly different really, aside from the rites and rituals around it in the Temple."

"And I doubt they'd allow the priestesses to be treated with violence," she said darkly. "Yes, there is that." They both stopped for a moment to listen as the night insects outside the wall vents began to take up their chorus.

"Would you like to sit outside for a while and watch the rest of the sunset?" Saoirse asked suddenly, feeling the walls close in on her. They moved outside and sat under blankets while the sky slowly darkened above.

"Shaji, I know you've endured things beyond what anyone should ever go through. I know you'll need time to heal. We don't have to lay together tonight if you don't want to. I can return to my mother's chamber like I always do. We have all our lives to move toward this." Kaylem took her hand and Saoirse could see his eyes gleaming in the half-light. "The last thing I want is to push or force you in any way. We can go at your pace, whenever you're ready."

Saoirse felt the tension leave her body in a rush. "Thank you, Kaylem. I needed to hear that. It's never been at my pace or at my choice." A sob tore through the last of her words and she buried her head in her hands as Kaylem scooped her up and brought her close. He smoothed the hair from her face and rubbed her back as wave after wave passed through her. Eventually the storm settled enough for them to both sit quietly, and Saoirse listened to Kaylem's steady breaths, feeling his chest rise and fall in a reassuring rhythm.

"There's a ritual…" Kaylem's voice rumbled into the darkness, and she felt its resonance throughout her body. "It's to welcome a new priestess into the full rites of the Temple once they come of age. The priestesses are young virgins when they're accepted into training and then some of their learning is directed toward what is called their *Temple duties*." Saoirse could hear

Kaylem's smirk in his voice.

"All the Temple men talk affectionately about the priestess's *Temple duties*. There are many other duties the priestesses must learn and carry out, but the most sacred of all are these. It is said that when *Temple duties* are carried out correctly, both the priestess and her partner may become one with the gods."

"Really? Then it must have been very different to the kinds of duties I had to carry out" Saoirse spat with a frown.

"And it must be done with consent from both partners, according to Temple law. Sometimes this didn't happen and there were many whispers about Milar and other Temple men who thought they were above the law. I'd imagine that was why they frequented the inn so often, since they could do what they wanted with far less scrutiny."

Kaylem traced a hand gently over her cheek and throat, where a fine network of scars still lay to mark where Milar had tried to kill Saoirse when she had been working as a prostitute at the inn of Ur. Milar was one of the most senior Temple leaders. He had threatened Asher, the innkeeper, with death of all working at the inn so he could gain unfettered access to Saoirse and the other girls. All were terrified of Milar as he was well known for his brutality. Even though it was considered an abomination for a Temple man to visit a prostitute, Milar and his colleagues had been regular visitors to the inn.

The night that Milar tried to kill Saoirse, she had defended herself with a knife and unintentionally killed him. Anan, the highest leader of the Temple, had seen Milar's death as an opportunity to rid himself of one who was beginning to tread a little too heavily on his toes. His death would also allow Anan access to the large stash of opium poppy Milar had seized from a merchant dealer. Saoirse had resigned herself to the prospect of her impending death in the stoning pits, but Anan decided it would be best to cover up the entire incident. Milar's death was announced as being caused by a gripe and he was given an honorable funeral with the finest of professional mourners.

Saoirse shuddered at the memory and forced herself to breathe deeply to allow the hard, cold knot at the center of her stomach to loosen a little. "I can't imagine being a priestess and having to allow those... animals... whenever they wanted..." She made herself unclench her jaw, which had started aching. "At least we

CHAPTER 7

were far enough away that they could only come occasionally. Never would still have been too often, though."

Saoirse thought of the knife she had used to kill Milar, and before that, Salik, the owner of the brothel Kaylem's mother had sold her to. It was this act of self-defense which had liberated the girls from the brothel and brought them to the inn of Ur. When Kaylem and Saoirse arrived at the household after the flood, Saoirse had scratched away a small niche low down in a corner of Kaylem's chamber and hidden the knife there. She wasn't quite sure why she had even kept it. It was rusty and covered in dried blood that she couldn't completely clean off. Except, the knife had saved her life twice now, and its presence helped her feel safer somehow.

"I felt for the priestesses. During their training, they're told of the wonders of serving... of doing their *Temple duty*. It's built up to be this journey to ecstasy and union with the gods."

"And then they have to lie with those sweating savages who know nothing of the true ways of the gods, and they just take what they want." Saoirse massaged her cheek where her jaw muscles twitched and cramped from their violent clench.

"Those men are also trained in the arts of *Temple duty*. They know what they should be doing. They just choose to do otherwise because they don't understand."

"What's there to understand? It's all about the man and his cock... pleasure for him and the spilling of his seed—" Saoirse made a jerking motion with her hand, a bitter look in her eyes.

"Their preference is for that, it's true. But in the rites, it shouldn't be like that at all. There are preparations, and the man isn't actually supposed to spill his seed. He breathes in a particular way that inhales creative energy inward instead."

Kaylem sucked in a great breath. "The energy travels up the spine and joins with the greater cosmic creative energy. If they do it right, it brings both of them closer to the gods and the highest experience of ecstasy. Of course, the priestess in training has her own breathing and inner work to do, too."

Saoirse nodded, interested despite herself.

"Both the priestess and her partner must bathe separately beforehand," Kaylem continued. "They must both fast for the day before and observe a number of hours in one of the chambers at the top of the Temple steps. That's what the chamber was for that we were in after you were pronounced Oracle."

"The one with the fire god and the reptile god. That alone would make me want to run screaming from the place. Its eyes..." She shuddered again.

"What about them?"

"The reptile god..."

"Kusu? Gibil's consort?"

"It looks like an Ushum."

Kaylem made a sound of amusement. "An Ushum? Like those myths we were told as children?"

"Yes, Kaylem, the ones that suck the life force from a person like the juice from a citrus fruit. You might think they're mythical, but you might also have thought the Anzu were mythical had you not..." Saoirse broke off, aware that she was breathing heavily.

"The Ushum exist?"

"We spoke about this the night of the flood, Kaylem. Weren't you taking me seriously?" Kaylem shuffled on his part of the mat and cleared his throat.

"Shaji, I—"

"They don't appear before us in their craft like the Anzu do with us. They invade people and live inside them like parasites, Kaylem. One of them lived in Milar. I saw his eyes change. I don't know how else to describe what I saw. It was as though they flickered and then his human eyes became slitted like a lizard's. Salik was the same, the brothel owner."

"Oh," he said quietly.

Saoirse felt her teeth begin to chatter. "I don't want to talk about this any more. Can we talk about something else?"

Kaylem was quiet for a moment, and she could hear his breathing. "Do you want to hear about the rest of the *Temple duty* rite? It's quite beautiful."

"Only if it doesn't involve lizard gods or any practices that are violent."

"It doesn't. The true name for this rite is the Rite of Joining. So, after quiet contemplation, both the priestess and her partner sit in a special dedicated chamber in the priestess's quarters. It has images of the gods in erotic poses carved on its walls in order to bring the couple to a more... amenable mood."

"Yes, I see." Saoirse tried to imagine gods in erotic poses but instead kept thinking of the lizard god, so she looked up at the

CHAPTER 7

stars which now spread silently across the night sky.

"Once the couple is adequately... er... acquainted, they disrobe and sit cross legged with their knees touching. Both inhale a smoke of sacred herbs which bring the couple into a trance. Once the trance deepens, they are able to receive the gods into their bodies. The priestess actually becomes Inanna, and her partner becomes Dumuzid. What happens after that is only part ritual."

Saoirse allowed Kaylem's voice to fall like a balm on her frazzled nerves as she looked at the stars, nodding at his murmured voice.

"There are laws around what may and may not happen, but the outcome is to reenact the act of creation between Inanna and Dumuzid. If it results in a babe, then it's a strange mix between celebration and failure in a way, since the man's seed is supposed to be withheld, not spilled into her womb. But most of the priestesses are on herbs to prevent it happening anyway, so it's impossible to really know if it happens the right way or not."

"I would never wish to conceive with one of those... abominations." Saoirse grimaced. "I'd hate to be looking in the face of a small version of Milar, or Anan, while it suckles at my breast. Ugh." She shook violently as though to clear herself of the image.

"I'd say that's why they take the herbs as well."

"It really does sound just like a glorified version of what I had to do," she said with a note of wondering in her voice. "All this time, I believed I was somehow impure, or evil, after my body was used in that way. I didn't know anything about *Temple duty*," she said with a snort of humor.

"Neither did I until I was initiated into the Temple," Kaylem said with his own snort.

"What was it like?"

He went silent again for while, and Saoirse continued watching the stars while he readied himself to speak. "I got an older woman. She was... well... it was..." Saoirse could feel heat radiating from him. "She wasn't very patient with someone as... new to the whole experience... as I was..." He cleared his throat. "It's the only time I... the men were nudging me and calling out at me when I returned..."

"And did your seed make it to the gods?"

Kaylem snorted. "I didn't even get the chance to start the special breathing I was taught to do. The woman I was with... it was very embarrassing. She rolled her eyes and just walked away, leaving me in a puddle of my seed."

Saoirse found to her surprise, as they talked long into the night and watched the sliver of the waning moon make its way across the sky, that she relaxed enough to feel as though her insides had turned to honey. As the sky was beginning to lighten, and Kaylem suppressed a yawn, Saoirse took his hand and caressed it.

"Show me the ritual,' she said to him, and she was gratified to sense him stiffen. He cleared his throat and turned to her.

"Are you sure?" He asked in a high, tight voice.

Her only answer was a nod.

CHAPTER 8

Holding hands, they made their way to his chamber. The handservant had freshened the cushions and furs for the occasion, leaving behind a small bowl of a delicately scented oil which Saoirse picked up and held to her face in wonder.

"What is this?" She sniffed less than delicately, and Kaylem laughed. "Don't tell me..." She sniffed again. "Ohhh... it's rose! Gods, this is expensive, Kaylem. Don't waste it on—"

"Don't say that please, Shaji. This occasion is exactly what we should be using such a special oil for." He took it from her and dipped his fingers lightly into it. Then he transferred some onto his other hand and ran both sets of fingers lightly down the sides of her neck. She could feel the slight puff of his breath on her cheek as he finished by brushing his hands along her jaw, meeting in the middle. By the time he paused, Saoirse could hardly stand straight, as her knees were somehow unable to lock in place.

"Now, we don't have any of those special herbs, nor images of gods in erotic poses on the wall, but I could stand like this if you'd like." Kaylem affected a ridiculous posture, with his lips pushed into a pout and his eyebrows low over his eyes. Saoirse cackled and pushed him over so that he landed gracelessly into the tumble of cushions in the corner.

"Come, my sweet, savage beauty," Kaylem announced after righting himself into a kneeling position with his arm held aloft in front of him in a beckoning gesture, his hair in a ridiculous tangle. The sight of it made Saoirse smile. "Come join me in a sacred dance so that we too may become one with the gods." He sank down onto his rear and sat cross-legged, looking up at Saoirse with a glint in his eye.

"I thought you needed to disrobe for this part."

"It's true, but not just for me," he answered cheekily.

Saoirse nodded, her stomach uncomfortably tight. "Together, then?"

"Together,' he agreed, and the room filled with the rustle of fabric as they busied themselves with their task. Unable to look Kaylem in the eye, or anywhere else on his body, Saoirse stared at a small prayer-tablet lying scattered on the floor beside them. It was too dim to see what was on it, but its solidity kept her from rising off into her thoughts and away from the chamber where they now sat face to face.

She didn't know where to put her hands, which wanted to hug themselves around her exposed body. Kaylem seemed similarly tense as he shuffled and cleared his throat, settling for leaning forward slightly and dangling his arms at his side. It was chilly too, and she could see the evidence of it on their skin.

Saoirse's awareness narrowed down to the slight tickle of Kaylem's leg hair brushing against the smoother skin of her knee. A hint of the rose oil laced the air, mixed with the tarry smell of the candle. His skin radiated warmth which she could feel reflected on her own skin, and that maddening scent of his returned to taunt her. It was woody and spicy, deeply familiar, and yet she couldn't quite place it.

"Do you wear an oil?" she asked, knowing that if she didn't, it would plague her while she was hoping to have her mind on other things.

He smiled. "Bergamot and cinnamon in an olive oil base. There may be something else, too, but the merchant wouldn't say." His face clouded. "Do you like it? I can wash it off—"

"I like it," she told him and dipped her own fingers into the bowl rose oil. "Speaking of oil… what do we do with this exactly? Is there a set of rites for it?"

"That's for later, but you may begin anointing me now if you wish." Kaylem winked at her, and she dabbed it onto his nose. He grabbed her arm and licked it all the way down to her hand. Saoirse blinked, wide eyed for a moment, then squealed and they fell into a riot of wrestling.

"This doesn't exactly feel sacred, Kaylem," she said as

CHAPTER 8

he allowed her to pin him down, half buried in the mound of cushions. Both were panting heavily from their exertions. She brushed away the mess of hair sticking into his eyes and pulled her own tangled tresses over her other shoulder, so they didn't dangle into his face.

"It's all sacred," he answered. "The gods live already within us, within our bodies. We can't help but be sacred."

"But—"

The rest of her query was answered by a kiss which deepened as their bodies drew close. His bare skin was warm, so warm, and surprisingly soft against hers. She tried not to look down to where she could feel his maleness pushing against her thigh and inwardly shouted at herself for her timidity, unable even to hold his gaze. This was something she should know all about, given her history.

Kaylem stroked her arms, her back, and her face. The air around her thrummed and something in her head hummed. Where they touched, there seemed to be no boundary between her flesh and his. She took a deep breath into the slight curve of her belly, which was now loose and tight all at once. It sounded like a sigh, or even a moan of pleasure, which surprised her as she had heard others making similar sounds, but nothing like that had ever come from her own throat.

Kaylem responded by making a similar sound as he nuzzled into her. The place of contact with his lips on her throat sent a cascade of chills alternating with heat spreading throughout the entirety of her body. Her skin had come alive, every touch of his making her want to somehow get closer to him, if only they could climb inside each other entirely.

Hungry now, she hunted his mouth and nibbled and tugged at his lower lip. He breathed in with a hiss and sent his tongue smoothing itself over her lower lip, gently seeking its way in through the seam of her lips. Their tongues wrestled, tangled, and tasted. His breathing matched hers, urgent and sharp. So far, he had only touched her face, her back, her arms, her lips. Safe places, as though he was hesitant to take it further quite yet. A part of her was relieved, another part impatient.

Did she want him anywhere else on her body, she wondered, as he tangled his hands in her hair at the back of her head and guided her face back down toward his. How would she feel if he was above her, she asked herself, as their teeth brushed and clicked against each other, mouths working in a soft dance.

The candle flickered and made shadows on the walls, and their shadow-bodies loomed and danced along with the tiny breeze which carried the chirr of the night crickets through the wall vents. Saoirse pictured the night sky outside, the silent desert spreading into nothingness around them. She pictured the moon, its waning crescent fading now as the sky took on hues of purple and orange. The servants would be awakening about now and bracing for another day. She wondered how Bo coped with the knowledge that he would likely spend his entire life here within these walls, every day filled with the same drudgery as she had once, from dawn till dusk...

"Shaji?" Kaylem's face hung in front of her. "Are you well?"

"Of course, Kaylem." She framed his face with her hands and brought him closer, deepening the kiss. She trailed her hands down the firm curves of his shoulders, his chest, and the flatness of his belly. A trail of dark hair led her lower and she looked over his shoulder at the wall as she reached for his maleness, stroking and caressing and bringing it to a firmness that gave her a small shiver of satisfaction at her skill...

"Shaji." Kaylem drew back, his face creased in concern. "I can't feel you anymore. You're not there. You're empty."

Saoirse blinked in confusion. "Weren't you enjoying..."

"Yes, it was very..." Kaylem looked down at his feet and then back at her. "It's not just about enjoyment for me. It's about whether we can both together..."

Saoirse couldn't help the flush that made its way from her chest, which crept up her neck, and colored her cheeks. She wasn't enough. Of course, this parody of intimacy wasn't how it should be. They should never have committed themselves the way they did when all she had to offer was what she had been forced to learn in the most unholy places of the known world...

"Shaji," repeated Kaylem softly. He stroked her cheek, and she couldn't meet his eye.

"It's all wrong, Kaylem." Her limbs felt like they were made of mud-brick. Numbness coursed its way through her, leaving nothing in its wake. "I don't know what I was thinking, to let this happen. I don't think I'll ever be able to do this..."

"No, Shaji. This is only the beginning."

CHAPTER 8

"But it's over before it even…"

"Did you not feel it when we started?"

"Yes, but then I ruined it…"

"You didn't ruin anything."

"I did! It just left… all the feeling just left me, and I was looking at the sky, and thinking about the stars, and I floated away when I should have been…"

Kaylem took her hand and looked at her intently. "Promise me you won't be angry if I tell you something?"

"Why would I be angry? I'm the one who…" Saoirse looked back down at the floor. The rug poking from under the pallet was threadbare, she noticed, where on countless mornings Kaylem, or herself more recently, must have stood after rising from sleep.

"Master Hos had a long talk with me before we were married," Kaylem blurted. Saoirse brought her attention back to him.

"About what?"

"About exactly this… about how you might be at first, or even later too… after… after…" He shrugged helplessly.

"How would Hos know?"

"I don't know. He just told me I'd have to be patient, that I'd have to stop when I couldn't sense you there anymore, because that was when it became too much for you… and… and… that it was natural for you to do that after what you've been through."

Saoirse flinched.

"He also said it would take a long time, but it would be worth every minute we'd waited." Kaylem watched her warily. Saoirse didn't know what to say, so she blinked at him, her mind blank. Kaylem shuffled and winced some more, fiddling with one of the cushions that had somehow ended up in his lap. He looked at her, his eyes sad.

"Let's sleep now. I'm so tired, and you must be, too. Can I stay here with you?" He half reached out and then withdrew his hand back to his lap, still watching her with unnaturally wide eyes. "I can go back to my mother's chamber if…" He cleared his throat, and they sat in silence for a moment until his body tensed to stand.

"No, stay with me," she said in a small voice.

"This will be different after we have some sleep," he murmured into her hair. She felt him settle beside her, stroking her unresponsive skin as she stared at the morning sun making its way across the wall through the wall vent, unable to unclench her fists.

She didn't know whether to be grateful for his comfort, or feel guilty for waking him when she bolted upright with a scream not long after finally falling asleep.

CHAPTER 9

Saoirse tried to chew without the sound filling the silence between them. Hard boiled eggs dipped in besan paste were a favorite of hers to break the morning fast. She would usually be happy to lose herself in the tastes and textures as she rolled them around in her mouth, washing it down with a hearty sip of small-ale.

The preceding days since their joining should have been joyful and intimate. Instead, the time had been filled with heaviness. Increasingly, whenever they came across a moment which led to them becoming lost in each other, the moment would invariably collapse, leaving them both awkward and fumbling and lost.

"I wonder…"

"Shaji…"

Both of them broke off, as they politely waited for the other to say something, anything, even if it was only to remark on the smoothness of the besan paste, or the increasingly cold mornings. Kaylem gave her a sad smile which she was certain was reflected back on her own face. What more might there be to say?

"The best of mornings to the newlyweds," came Hos's voice all of a sudden, which made them both jump. Hos checked himself, standing and observing for a moment. "A thousand apologies, I do not wish to disturb you if you were—"

"Please join us, master Hos," Kaylem answered quickly.

"You're not disturbing us, master," Soiarse said at the same time.

"A lovely welcome, I thank you," Hos answered, his sharp

gaze making Saoirse shift uncomfortably on her seat as she sensed him observing far more than just their breakfast. They made room for him at the low table. Saoirse made a show of offering him the tray with the remaining egg and besan paste that she had just been eyeing up for herself. Hos ate with quiet gravity, sipping slowly on his small-ale that had been brought by the handservant when the master appeared. Once he had finished, he sat back with a sigh and eyed Saoirse and Kaylem for a moment, causing them both to fidget once again.

"It seems that, while your honeymoon is all important, circumstances have a way of intruding," he finally said. Saoirse wondered just how much Kaylem had been telling him about their situation, and she felt her irritation swell.

"Master?" Kaylem asked, looking haunted.

"The situation in Ur is becoming dire."

Saoirse had wondered about this, and the dreams that still plagued her sleep confirmed his statement. She suppressed a slight sigh of relief that he hadn't mentioned their personal situation.

"What can be done about Ur? Should we return?" Saoirse asked, hoping the edge of eagerness couldn't be heard by anyone else at the table. Lately, she thought she would rather face a quagmire of freezing mud filled with evil elite and diseased, dying people over even one more night of frozen awkwardness with Kaylem.

At least she would be useful in Ur, of service, where she could maybe try to keep the selfish Temple elite in line, nurse the sick, perform Death Rites, and help with rebuilding no matter how soft her hands had become. Here, nothing she could do would change what happened the moment she and Kaylem faced each other in the charged silences of their chamber.

"Absolutely not, Saoirse. Although I appreciate your offer to sacrifice your comforts and peace here, as well as special time with your new husband."

Saoirse tried her best not to narrow her eyes at Hos as his tone seemed very knowing.

"I merely thought it best to resume our lessons, given that you will need to return to Ur after the city is stabilized. Then your talents will be much needed... And no, Saoirse, you would not be more useful there than here right now."

Saoirse closed her mouth and lapsed into silence.

CHAPTER 9

"For those in Ur, I feel for them. Even for the elite, who have, of course, appropriated the only standing abodes far from the river, conditions there are beyond disastrous. Crime and violence are rife, and many of the people are dying from starvation and cold."

"But why must this be? Why does there need to be such suffering?" The outrage rose into her throat like bile. "It was the Temple elite who angered the gods, who murdered so many in the name of those gods, making so many of the people live in fear and suffering."

For a moment, her anger swept away the awful, deathly stillness inside of her and she relished the sensation. "The elite are the ones with the power to commit these crimes, and they still do. Now they're living in relative comfort while the people of Ur are once again worse off than before. Surely the gods could have asked the Anzu to come up with a disaster that would have affected the ones who actually perpetuated these evils, instead of the people who are mostly innocent."

Hos nodded vigorously and gave her a tender look that made her want to scream at him. "Let us move this discussion to the palm-shade. The heat is growing, and yet there is where my mind works best, especially when I'm sipping on a cool ale and looking out at the well," he said as his gaze never wavered from her eyes.

As the master creaked his way down onto a cushion under the palm-shade, Saoirse almost burst into tears. The last time she remembered being present for a lesson with Kaylem and the teacher she had been crouching in the blazing sun behind the structure. While sweat made rivers down her body, she had been constantly on the lookout for Deni or Marsi to make sure they didn't catch her idle. Not to mention the mistress, Kaylem's mother, who would likely have sold Saoirse to the brothel far earlier had she known.

Looking behind her at the spot she used to think she was hidden in, Saoirse realized that anyone sitting where they were now would have seen the silhouette of someone standing there in a heartbeat. The master's eyes glinted at her as he noticed Saoirse looking for the shadow of her former self, and he winked. Now, she was reclining in the shade on cushions as an equal, sipping on ale alongside Kaylem and the tutor, instead of fearing she might faint from thirst and heatstroke.

Despite her heat and thirst at the time, the master's teachings had been balm to her spirit and had helped her accept her circumstances, no matter how grim. Perhaps she had even valued his words all the more for how forbidden they had been to her. All at once she realized that the master had targeted some of his words especially toward her, and he nodded as though in acknowledgement.

"Why must we suffer? Why would the gods allow such suffering and injustice? I believe that was the question," the master prompted.

Saoirse nodded, suddenly deflated. The echoes of her previous outrage were still bouncing around inside of her, although she wondered at how clever the master was to give her time to calm down by suggesting they move here.

"Saoirse, you have had perhaps more than your fair share of suffering already. Losing your parents at such a young age, being sold into slavery by your uncle. Forced to labor as a servant for the bulk of your childhood, and then the horrors you have endured in the past year."

She nodded, wanting to eagerly agree with the tutor. But she knew from hearing him maneuver Kaylem so many times into uncomfortable conversations, that it was likely her turn now. She steeled herself for a challenge.

"What would you have to say about suffering, Saoirse, after what you have been through?"

"Master?"

"I figured you'd have some insight into suffering, since you've experienced so much. What would you say if someone asked you what was the point of it all?"

Saoirse took a long sip of her ale and drew a despair-filled breath to rant about spiteful gods meddling with the fortunes of poor, helpless people in order to amuse themselves in their boredom. She didn't truly believe that, but it would have been satisfying to say anyway.

Before she could form the words, she noticed something dark moving in her peripheral vision and she watched as an ant climbed its clumsy way up onto the threadbare rug near her toe. Its body was shiny and blue-black as it wandered ever more frantically over the foreign landscape.

She thought she knew how it might feel as she brushed it

gently back to the sand. Its limbs wheeled frantically for a moment until it finally righted itself and made its way out into the endless expanse of the courtyard. Why was it that people had to suffer? Or ants, for that matter. The ant was moving in the direction of the well, which was a mere few footsteps away for Saoirse, but may take an eternity for an ant. It would be a perilous journey at that, with the various desert birds and other creatures on the lookout for a tasty morsel.

Maybe there was still a tiny puddle of water next to the well that hadn't yet dried after she had spilled some on the ground earlier, and yet again maybe there wasn't. But, the ant seemed determined now to get to the well and she wondered how it knew there might be water still there that it could reach. Could it smell the water? What if there was none left by the time the ant reached it? Should she carry the ant to the water? But it might bite her, and maybe it wasn't interested in the water at all.

Kaylem cleared his throat, pulling her out of her reverie. She felt no more prepared to comment on her suffering than she was before, so when she opened her mouth, she didn't expect anything useful to come out.

"The ant must learn to find water. If the ant is always given water without having to suffer thirst, then it will not understand that it needs to learn how to seek out water for itself. Nor will it value the water as the water has come so easily. If it then must rely on others to bring it water, it becomes not only dependent on others, it's also likely to become tyrannical in order to continue to secure its needs, so the ant has then created its own loop of suffering that also causes others to suffer…"

Surprised, she looked over at where she remembered the ant had been. There was a tiny black speck a whole lot closer to the well than she ever imagined it might have reached by now.

"Not only that," she continued without being entirely certain what was going to come out next, "the ant becomes vulnerable and powerless if it can't find its own water. Its life now rests in the hands of others for something it really should have learned to do for itself. Then the ant lives in fear, in case the others supplying its needs come to understand that they are the ones who truly hold the power…"

"So, then the ant must lie and manipulate, and hold others in its thrall, which is really only a different kind of suffering. Maybe that kind of suffering, that kind of thirst, is even worse than the original suffering it would have had if it had sought out water for its own to begin with…"

She blinked and looked up at Kaylem and the tutor. Kaylem was looking at her, open-mouthed. The tutor was smiling and nodding beatifically.

"Tell us more, dear Saoirse." The tutor took a quick sip of his ale, as though not wanting to miss an instant of the action unfolding in front of him.

"I… I don't…" She looked at the tutor, blank.

"Who does the ant remind you of, Saoirse?"

"Well, the Temple elite of course. Anan especially, with his demands for me to find Milar's opium and willing to murder anyone who gets in his way… Well, all of them, actually, for basically living as parasites and feeding off the people… and yet…" She looked down at her feet.

It would be selfish to ask the master about the suffering her and Kaylem were going through, which had nothing to do with the situation affecting the elite. She was a little disappointed the analogy had only been about ants and water. It was entirely too simplistic to apply to her own issues, which seemed to have no answers.

"Might the water you speak of represent something in all of us, then?" the master asked casually into the stillness. He leaned back on his cushion as though reclining at a fancy inn, looking in the direction of the well; the same well that held water so clear and sweet that it felt like liquid silver as it made its way down one's throat.

It was also the same well that Saoirse still swore, as she peered down into it, that she could see the reflections of shining silhouettes standing beside her own in that gleaming disc of water so far down. The thought of what those silhouettes might represent made the old yearning return, as though there was something she truly thirsted for more than all the waters of the world could provide…

The thought slid from her mind as it did every time she tried to hold it, since there was nothing she could do about that yearning. She didn't even know what it was she was yearning for. It was just a bunch of watery reflections, and she had no control over whether they appeared or not, just as she had no control over her current situation. No matter how much she fought against floating away when lying with Kaylem, it would always happen. There was no use even thirsting for what her and Kaylem might have if not for her ruining it all the time, let alone…

"What would you sacrifice… what kind of suffering would you accept in order to be able to drink that water?"

Saoirse drew her breath in sharply and stared at master Hos.

"What choice is there, though? There's no changing some things…"

The tutor shrugged. "Maybe not."

Saoirse asked herself what kind of sacrifice she might make in order to fix the problem between her and Kaylem, even though another part of her was wanting to scoff and curse at the question. There was no answer, she reminded herself. She suppressed an urge to smash her fist onto the ground, throw her mug of ale, and yell obscenities at the tutor, who, she knew, was only asking general questions. Although, she noted as she couldn't help but glare at him, his gaze did seem very knowing.

All she had done was agonize over how their problem could be fixed. If only Kaylem's mother hadn't sold her to the brothel. If only the sandstorm hadn't happened when it did. If only the merchant hadn't sold her to the most evil brothel owner in the known world. She had been so innocent, little more than a child when she was forced into the brutal world of prostitution. How could it ever be possible now to find any kind of pleasure with a man after what she had been through? Was she cursed to forever shrink away from Kaylem's touch, no matter how much love she knew they shared?

"If I could sacrifice my memories of what happened and be back to my old self, I'd do so in a heartbeat." The crickets chirred around them, and Saoirse started as she realized she had spoken out loud. The tutor grunted neutrally, as though to acknowledge her words without inferring any of his opinion.

"But then…"

"But then?" he prompted into the long silence.

"Maybe I'd still be slaving away my life in that courtyard if it had never happened, or maybe… I don't know…"

The master nodded casually.

"I remember a dream I once had. It was when I first arrived at the brothel in Erech and I felt filled with terror for what lay ahead.

This dream... It was as though I'd found myself in the home of the gods..."

"*D'ingir*," she heard Kaylem whisper as she remembered the darkness of her thoughts back then, the desperation as Salik had roughly thrown her into the small chamber with the wall vent so narrow that she hadn't been able to see the sky.

That night, after finally falling asleep from sheer exhaustion, she had plummeted into a place of endless golden light, pulsing with joy. Countless other beings were infused into the space alongside her, within her, among her, as if she was the center of all, and yet so were they all. None of the beings had any form that she could have made out, but they were all existing simultaneously in the same space.

The dream had been a sliver of light reaching for her all the way to the netherworlds of the brothel, where she had afterward endured the worst of humanity for an entire thirteen moons.

"Being invited into the home of the gods, Saoirse. A true blessing indeed."

Saoirse could not stop the sob that arose from the depths of her being. "But why do the gods live in such beauty and harmony when it's so different here? Why can't we live as the gods do? I'm certain I've learned all kinds of things in my time as a prostitute, such as how to pleasure men in all the ways one could possibly imagine, but do you think my beloved husband and I can lie happily together?" She broke off, her breathing ragged, and rammed her fist into the carpet.

"I've managed to avoid slaving my life away in drudgery, and now I may be together with the man I've always loved. And yet do you imagine I can enjoy my freedom? I am not free in here." Saoirse slapped herself in the chest. "These blessings which came at such cost are ones I cannot claim as mine..." The desert spread its silence around them as the three of them sat motionless, aside from the violent sobs making their way from Saoirse.

"It is true, Saoirse."

Saoirse jerked her head up and glared at the master, wiping her nose on the sleeve of her robe. There would always be something he would add. She knew this from previous times. They sat for some time, the master serenely staring at an eagle swooping and dipping its way through the sky.

The eagle was free, with no need for anything but hunting

for food and riding on the winds. It would not be weighed down by terrible memories, nightmares, and attacks of terror and rage that came out of nowhere. It was not expected to behave within a restrictive set of social expectations. It was an eagle and would act exactly as an eagle does no matter where it was.

"The eagle has no understanding of itself as an eagle. This is only what we define it as. The eagle just is," the tutor mused. Saoirse wondered angrily to herself what that had to do with suffering. "It behaves according to its destiny, which is preordained." The eagle dipped and they lost sight of it for a moment. Everyone watched the empty sky until it soared back into their line of vision with something small and dark hanging limply from its talons.

"We humans are a little different to the eagle, in that we have our own will rather than the Will of the gods."

"So, why are we not floating around in a paradise of our own making like the gods, then?" Saoirse couldn't help but ask. "And why have the gods not helped us from where they are? Do they even care?" She felt Kaylem's warm, sweaty hand cover her own and wanted to push it away since she supposed he was likely only trying to silence her.

"In your dream, Saoirse, were you able to see the gods?" asked the tutor.

"I was not. They were there all around me, and yet…"

"They had no bodies?"

"They had no bodies. It was as though they were nothing but essence, but that essence was like nothing I've ever imagined and wouldn't be able to ever again."

"Nothing… No… thing," said the master and he fell silent again. The eagle was long gone, and the crickets were deafening all of a sudden.

"Is that why they are filled with so much joy? Because they don't have to live in bodies?" asked Kaylem.

"Why must we live in bodies then? Can we not be like the gods and shuck off our skin forever?" asked Saoirse. "How would one do this? It's not as easy as finding a way for this flesh to die, as it will only regrow around us all over again in a new body." She pinched her arm in disgust.

"Maybe the gods have had far more time to find the way to *D'ingir*," master Hos said musingly, still looking up at the empty sky. "Or maybe they chose not to be clothed in flesh, preferring never to experience life here in the known world as we do. Either way, Saoirse, I would say that the answer to your suffering lies within you. And while the gods may not meddle directly in human affairs, they may whisper guidance into willing ears, especially if the right question is asked."

"The gods within fell silent after I was sent away… after…" New sobs began to make their way out of her.

"Did they truly, Saoirse?"

She wanted to yell and scream at him. All the suffering had done nothing but harm her and ruin her for anything beautiful or good. The gods hadn't whispered to her since her childhood; since her innocence had been destroyed. The dreams and visions were different to the whisperings of the gods from the place of the Knowing. She could no longer go into the place of the Knowing at will and reach the place of utter peace.

And lately the dreams and visions had been rare, never giving insight into her own sufferings. Instead, they gave random flashes of useless and unrelated images. Or there were nightmares so horrific she woke from them screaming. Resentment crawled its way into her gut, and she reached into the nearby sand, taking a handful and squeezing it as hard as she was able.

Later, as she and Kaylem lay down to sleep after an evening of yet more awkward silences, she faced the wall and stared into the darkness until the gray light of predawn infused into the space around them.

CHAPTER 10

Saoirse woke up alone, the sun pouring directly over her through the wall vent. In her dream, she had been having a discussion with master Hos, although she couldn't remember exactly what they had talked about. She pictured Hos under the palm-shade with a mug of ale in his hand, hoping it would help bring some of the dream-conversation back. Something within her had eased just a little after yesterday, and it could only have happened while she was asleep.

Ask the right question... ask the right question... ask the right question ran through her mind while she dressed and made her way to the household bathing room, cleverly hidden under the steps that made their way up to Issa's old room.

Ask the right question... the words hounded her as she refreshed herself and made her way to the courtyard where she could hear conversation. There was no question she could think of asking, and besides, who would she ask it to?

"...and I'm so glad you're here, master..." she heard Kaylem say, and then his voice faded into a murmur. Were they talking about her? Is that why the master knew so much? Saoirse wondered how she felt about being the object of such discussion.

She decided she couldn't bear to face Kaylem's sympathy, or the sharp eyes of the master this morning. Her feet took her to the main gate, outside which the stifling heat and endless space of the desert could be found. The last time she had been wandering around the outside of the compound in such a way was as a child. Her main duty had been to collect the meager firewood that could be found among the prickly desert vegetation clinging to life outside the wall.

As she made her way out of the gate, Saoirse felt a weight lift from her chest. She breathed in a lungful of scorching air as though it was cool and fresh from the great river itself. Tracing the perimeter of the wall, she found a small shady spot and curled herself within it, as she used to do when she was a child. Back then, her fears were of Deni giving her a sharp word or retort for being found idle; or going to bed still feeling hungry after the evening meal.

Marsi would reproach her for her stomach being a bottomless pit and liked to joke that the mistress would cast them all out into the desert for chewing through all the food stores like rats. Now, there was food to be had whenever she wished. She was Kaylem's wife. She could ask for anything that she could ever desire, aside from the one thing she wanted the most.

Saoirse wondered some more about exactly what it was she desired. Was it merely to be able to lie with Kaylem and have pleasure? Men seemed able to have that pleasure with such ease. Was there more to her desire than that? Why was her desire the one thing she couldn't have?

There were so many questions and she wondered which might be the right one or whether she could have more than one. Was it too many if there were more than one? Did the master mean that she had to narrow down her questions until she came to just the one? How would she do that when there were even more fighting their way into her mind?

Saoirse remembered the time they'd sheltered during the sandstorm, after Kaylem had risked himself to help her haul the covering back over the well. That was the last moment they had spent alone together before she had been sent away. There had been no touch, only looking into each other's eyes and sharing in a stolen moment of peace.

The memory was filled with sweetness even if it was tainted with the pain of the mistress's fury afterward, of Marsi and Deni dying so brutally in the sandstorm, of being sent away from the only home she had. What, she wondered now, had been so special about their short moment together which had made that memory into one that she held so close to her heart? And, was this different to what she wished for now?

CHAPTER 10

As she watched an eagle soar above, maybe even the same one as the day before, she sensed a rare calmness within her as the noise of her mind fell away. Even the eagle in its movement somehow radiated stillness, the constant buzz of insects also part of the silence as she sat and watched. For a short moment, she was whole and desired nothing but to be exactly where she was, no matter the prickles poking into her buttocks through her robe where she sat.

The prickles became part of her senses, the same as the eagle's cry and the whirr of the wind. In that moment, something moved within her; a piece of understanding falling into place, and she nodded at her shadow with a small smile. After her tears were whisked away by the heat of the ground, she made her way back to the compound, and back to Kaylem, in peace.

"There you are, Shaji, I've been looking for you." Kaylem reached out to her and then checked himself. Lately she had shied from his touch. She reached for him and held his large hand, compelling herself to stand firm as the sensation of his maleness threatened to overwhelm her. Kaylem's eyes widened, and he stood still, watching her warily.

"Have you eaten?"

"I haven't yet. Is there anything easy on hand?" As she said the word hand, Kaylem lifted their joined hands and looked at them in wonder, his gaze flicking back to hers.

"Let's have a look." He smiled and led her to the smaller inside hearth, where some small loaves of bread sat neatly wrapped in palm leaves. A boiled egg waited in a dish alongside a generous dollop of besan paste, also keeping fresh under a piece of palm leaf. Saoirse smiled as she cracked the eggshell and peeled it, sprinkling the pieces into the still-glowing coals.

After satisfying her hunger, she led Kaylem to their shared chamber, and they sat side by side on the sleeping mat.

"I don't think I have the entire answer," she told him as he traced his finger down her cheek.

"I don't think anyone ever does," he answered as they joined hands again, leaning into each other for a kiss. It was intoxicating. Her breathing deepened and she smiled at him. He moved closer, shifting his body in a way that sent her thoughts skittering up to the ceiling as they always did.

"It's happening already," she whispered ruefully as she held his hands still for a moment. Instead of fighting against it, she sat and watched as it came over her like a heavy mist. Kaylem held her close, slowly stroking her hair.

"How long is this going to last?" she asked him after a while, not expecting him to know. Kaylem didn't reply but kept up his stroking. She continued to sit, blank now, filled with the same old horrible stillness that felt like death. It wasn't full of life and movement like the emptiness of the desert. It was a gray emptiness which, she feared, would yawn inside her forever and eventually swallow her up.

She had exhausted herself previously, fighting it away in case she became lost in its cold embrace. It had hunted her in nightmare after nightmare and each time she had run away. But there was no escape, and with Kaylem beside her, it didn't seem quite so terrifying.

Unsure how long they had been sitting for, Saoirse looked up at Kaylem, whose presence and warmth was the only thing keeping her tethered to herself. He met her eyes, his gaze soft and gentle, his own eyes reflecting her silhouette in their gleam. She had nothing to give. She was blank, but she allowed the void inside to swallow her up, because there was nothing else to do, and because Kaylem was there next to her, solid and alive.

He could be alive for her while this cloud of death sat over her. His hands softly swallowed hers and she allowed them to sit limply within his grasp, the skin of his palms soft against her fingers. It was a sensation she felt no connection to, as though her hands did not belong to her. She wondered vaguely if she really were dead, and yet Kaylem still sat patiently, watching her without expectation. The sound of his breathing reminded her that he was alive, and therefore so must she be, too.

Occasionally his eyes broke with hers as they traced the flight of a blowfly frantically bashing itself against the ceiling where an angled ray of sun from the wall vent split the relative gloom. Another time it was to track the shift of her body as she made herself more comfortable. He joined her in reclining.

Together, they watched the sun ray move interminably across the wall. It eventually disappeared altogether, although outside the bright chirring of the insects told them the day was still far from over. As though in response, Saoirse's stomach rumbled. A sliver of mirth shone through, and she snorted. Kaylem smiled and shifted himself, moving his arm around her.

"Aren't you tired of this yet? I am."

"I'm prepared to wait with you until you no longer have need of it, Shaji."

"I don't even know what I'm waiting for."

Kaylem shrugged and gave her a little smile as though to say it didn't matter. They sat, breathing together in the silence. A glimmer of gratitude flashed through the emptiness like a falling star. Saoirse blinked and smiled a small smile back. Maybe she wasn't completely dead inside after all.

With that thought, a crack opened up inside of her and through it poured a wave of sensation, of aliveness so strong she almost collapsed. Kaylem was there, solid as ever as she sagged against him, flooding the front of his robe as the heat, and tears, and sob after sob tore out of her.

Pain so strong it threatened to rip her apart was heaved out in her gasping breath, pouring out of her against Kaylem's chest. His arms, and hands, and body kept her steady as she raged and pounded the sleeping mat beside her, kicked at the hard earth under the rug, and shrieked into the close air, loud enough to momentarily silence the closest call of insects.

As the tone of the light around them changed to gray, Saoirse breathed and hiccupped, and allowed Kaylem to hand her his facecloth for her to drench in her tears, the runnels from her nose, and the sweat pouring from her body. Her own facecloth had been cast aside as useless long before.

As her breathing eventually calmed with only the occasional hitch, Kaylem brought his face close to hers and kissed her forehead. She felt dizzy, her ears buzzing, and body weak.

"I am honored to have shared that with you, my love," he murmured into her hair.

Saoirse took a breath and more tears formed at the corners of her eyes. She was surprised she had any left.

"Thank you," she whispered, her body and eyelids drooping.

"Sleep if you like. I can bring you some food and leave it by the bed in case you wake later. I can stay upstairs if you'd like to be alone."

"Come back and be with me, Kaylem, please?"

He nodded and kissed her again, his eyes sparkling. Saoirse was already spiralling into a different kind of nothingness, which was friendly and warm and welcoming, and which she sank into with relief.

CHAPTER 11

Saoirse woke to find her body melded comfortably with Kaylem's. It reminded her of the way she had seen a litter of village pups contort their bodies into strange positions to pile together in the closest way possible. She had always wondered whether their tiny bodies felt stiff when they awoke, but this morning she knew otherwise. Those pups had completely surrendered to the nearness of their litter mates. Their bodies had effortlessly fitted around each other and dissolved into the warmth and comfort such closeness brought.

There was no crick in her neck from lying on Kaylem's shoulder this morning, even though yesterday she had struggled to rise from the ache in her joints. Somehow this morning her body had softened and she felt totally relaxed, as though her solidity had somehow partially dissolved. Her eyes hurt and her body felt wrung out as though it had been mistaken for a robe by a village washerwoman on the banks of the river, but it was a different kind of sensation to usual.

Kaylem stirred and cracked open an eye, the corners of his mouth tugging upward as he moved forward to nuzzle her dry lips. He made the same moaning sound as when he was eating a particularly delicious meal. It made her feel warm and buzzy inside and her body softened further.

It was warm under their furs, and she shifted her leg lazily so that it glided upward along his. He responded by brushing his palm over her cheek, smoothing her sleep-wild hair from her face. She thought that her breath probably smelled revolting, and

CHAPTER 11

his wasn't the most pleasant in the known world, either. But, she let the thought fall away as he kissed her, dry lips, bad breath, and all. She ran her fingers over his beard, the bristly sound loud in the quiet of the morning alongside the rustling of their bodies and their small moans and intakes of breath.

She wondered, briefly, when the deathly emptiness would come to take the warmth of the moment away, and then allowed the thought to drift away as Kaylem ran his hand down her shoulder, her arm, and then her fingers. He moved slightly and sent his questing hand on a new course— to make small circles around her navel which made her giggle and her core liquefy.

The wanting of him became a violent ache, a different kind of emptiness that needed filling immediately. In her urgency, she grabbed his face and pulled him closer, deepening their kisses until both bodies strained toward each other, striving to be closer, and even closer still.

Kaylem lifted her to straddle him, and she looked down at him, her eyes widened and blinked. She froze for a moment, at a loss to know what to do with him. Kaylem stroked her thighs, her calves, her hands, the flat plane of her abdomen. He reached up to stroke her arms, and interlaced his fingers in hers, pulling her gently down so their bodies and lips met.

Her mouth found its rhythm once again with his, which spread to the rest of her and soon they were effortlessly joined, bodies moving together like they had known each other forever. For a moment, Saoirse forgot about everything except Kaylem's body joined with hers; his eyes, his warmth, and his musky smell that made her want to rub herself all over him.

Still, in a far corner of her consciousness she could sense the nothingness creeping back. Try as she might to hold onto the delicious closeness, she found herself watching her fingers thread themselves through Kaylem's hair, as though from a great and ever increasing distance. Kaylem moaned and stroked her body, which should have sent thrills through her and instead she could hardly feel it. Kaylem began to move faster beneath her, and she watched him, her body moving automatically. He finished with a shudder and reached for her, his breath heaving. He kissed her passionately and caressed her face, his wide smile gradually fading as he took in the blankness of her eyes and the passivity in her body.

"Shaji... Oh, gods, I didn't notice, it was so..." He was still panting, his body beaded with sweat.

"I am well," she told him, her voice sounding like it came from far away. He looked at her in concern and she felt a rising discomfort in her gut, her nakedness suddenly making her feel exposed.

"I have to use the..." She tilted her head toward the bathing room. It wasn't a lie, since her bladder was about to burst, and she could even feel it through the terrible numbness that spread its cold fingers through her chest and abdomen. Pulling on her robe, she forced herself to walk from the chamber, jogging the rest of the way to the rear of the household, hoping to avoid master Hos.

As she squatted over the hole, its stench far less offensive than the servants' latrine, she watched as the blowflies dipped and swooped... dipped and swooped, until her hips ached and she heard Kaylem calling for her. Even then she hesitated, rising only when she became worried she might fall into the hole from weakness after staying for so long in one position.

As she washed and freshened herself, she wondered where all the life had gone from her body, and whether it would ever return.

CHAPTER 12

"Shaji, the master asked you a question," Kaylem murmured into her ear as he gently caressed her arm, bringing her out of her stupor.

"A thousand apologies, master. I didn't hear you."

"Actually, Kaylem, it was a question for you." Kaylem narrowed his eyes at master Hos, who waggled his eyebrows up and down. Saoirse felt a moment of confusion before sagging back into the numb fog that had permeated her days since their last failed attempt at lying together.

"I see. Well, master, I don't know whether to believe in curses or not."

Saoirse idly wondered if what she was suffering from was a curse, and a part of her perked up to listen to the conversation, even as she suspected that the master was likely directing some kind of covert lesson at her.

"What do you know of curses from our previous lessons?"

"That the word has many meanings, and there are different types of curses. The most common forms either originate from the gods, or from other people."

"That is correct. I'm glad to know you were listening to your previous lessons. And when a curse originates from other people?"

"It is an abomination used to inflict pain and suffering onto an undeserving person."

The master nodded. "And when from the gods?"

"It's usually a reflection of the gods' system of judgement

in order to atone for a previous wrongdoing of ours," Kaylem intoned, as though by rote.

"And what does this involve?"

"A tragedy, or series of tragedies that happen to an individual who to all outer appearances does not deserve such cruelty of fate. This is to balance right and wrong in a larger scheme of Life, since the gods are immortal and can see the entirety of past, present, and future." Kaylem's voice had little inflection as though he was stating words learned from rote.

Saoirse glared at master Hos. "Are you implying that somehow I deserved to be cursed by the gods? To be sold to a brothel, for my body to be violated multiple times a night against my will by stinking, violent imbeciles who didn't care what injuries they inflicted onto me?" The words barely made it out of her as her breathing whistled through her suddenly constricted throat, her chest heaving. She could feel the flush of her skin and the grind of her jaw as she forced herself not to launch at the master.

"To deserve or not to deserve is the wrong way to see it, Saoirse, as nobody deserves this treatment. Not even the most evil person in the world deserves to be treated this way, and you are not evil. What you have been through, to be on the receiving end of one of the direst of cruelties imaginable, is far from what you deserve."

Saoirse sat back and forced herself to breathe, to calm the fire of her rage that had sweat pooling between her breasts and running rivers down her body. She forced herself to relax her fists and sat stiffly back on her heels. "Then please, master, I must hear your interpretation of this statement."

"The statement itself is loosely taken from one of the tablets, the words handed down from generation to generation, its origin lost in the mists of time. Its meaning… well… You, Saoirse, of all people know that this body you inhabit, this mind you use to understand our known world, and this tangle of feelings that binds you to your flesh are only outer coverings for who you really are."

Saoirse sat silently, knowing there was no point to answering.

"Have you ever wondered what other bodies, other minds, other tangles of feeling you might have clothed yourself with in previous times?"

"I have seen many of them in visions," Saoirse said in a small voice, suddenly cold after remembering her meeting with the

Anzu. She had even worn the flesh of the Anzu long, long ago.

"Could it be possible, Saoirse, that there might have been—"

"No, master, there is no possible way that I, in a previous skin, could have put somebody else through what I went through. I would have remembered that. The Anzu would have shown me. I would never do something like that—" Her last words became lost as Kaylem rubbed her back. She shrugged his hand away, the last to deserve such comfort if what the master said held even a glimmer of truth.

"Saoirse, we've all done terrible things in previous times. All of us. This is because we are so far from our true selves once we are packaged up in these bodies of flesh. We can no longer know the truth and wonder of who we really are. There is nobody here in the known world who is blameless." The master's tone was comforting and filled with regret.

"How is this supposed to make me feel any better about what I might have done?"

"Not you, Saoirse. It was another pile of flesh from long ago that did not feature in your memories with the Anzu. And we don't know what we do when we're not hearing the messages from the gods. Perfection can only be a reality for us once we are able to hear the gods always."

Saoirse sniffled loudly, wishing she could sink into the earth and never return to the surface.

"The only option, aside from self-flagellation like the desert fathers did, is forgiveness. And I truly can't see you living alone in a cave whipping yourself with sword-grass for the rest of your years, Saoirse. Besides, what good would it do for the world if you walked away from your duties? Who would guide the people of Ur once it is rebuilt?"

"Who am I to imagine I can do anything but flagellate myself if this is what I'm suffering for? What kind of guide would I be anyway?"

"It has already happened, Saoirse. What you choose to do with your lot is up to you. Would you inflict further suffering on yourself in order to somehow try to appease your guilt, now that you know?"

"Why is that not the obvious thing to do?" Saoirse decided she would walk out into the desert and allow it to swallow her whole.

"There's a reason why we don't easily remember the experiences of the skins we previously wore. To acknowledge that we were wrong and then do our best to help others now is enough, Saoirse. And remember who else you will consign to hardship if you choose the path of further suffering. It's not only yourself you drag into this morass of guilt you would create for yourself."

Saoirse imagined Kaylem alone, Anan and the other Temple elite gleeful that she was out of their way forever so they could torment the people of Ur without opposition. "So, why then? What's the point of it all then? Why are we even here?" Saoirse swept her hand in an irritable gesture meant to encompass herself, Kaylem, the master, and the rest of the known world.

"I would say *that* is the most important question you will ever ask yourself in your heart of hearts, in the darkest hour of the night," the master answered and then fell into a silence so profound they both knew there would be no more words forthcoming that lesson.

CHAPTER 13

The heat was a mere fraction of what Saoirse remembered from her childhood, even for mid-winter. A breeze sighed its way over the expanse, ruffling the tops of the dunes and setting the dry branches of the bushes clicking against each other. Once again, Saoirse was outside the walls of the compound, watching the eagles perform their dizzying dance, while her eyes ached from the glare.

The desert lured her, whispering that she should keep walking, and this time give her life to its dry expanse. It would certainly be easier than what she faced if she chose to turn back to the compound and its lessons, and far preferable to what awaited her in the city of Ur.

They would have to return to the city sometime soon. Given that it was the middle of winter, there would be less than an entire moon cycle remaining until the days began to gradually lengthen again. Saoirse wondered, yet again, how the people were faring and how quickly the rebuilding was progressing.

A thousand doubts pressed heavily upon her. Perhaps they would be better off without her, given how she still couldn't even figure out the answers to her own problems. Maybe she should just stay here, hidden away from the world so nobody would ever be able to look into her eyes and intuit the dreadful things that lay beneath her skin, not to mention the skins of her past.

She allowed the sun to warm her and infuse life into her body. For a short moment she forgot about her cares while she contemplated the source of that warmth. Unable to look directly at it, she shut her eyes and allowed the sun's rays to make the inside of her eyelids pink as she turned her face upward. The sensation made her smile. It was just a small smile, but she smiled, nevertheless. No matter what dreadful deeds humanity had committed, the sun would always shine, and its rays would fall upon everyone equally to warm them and offer life in abundance.

She wondered if it might, after all, be possible to find a path toward allowing herself to turn away from the past. Or maybe, more accurately, to turn toward whatever was before her. This was something she could act upon, instead of seething about her powerlessness and obsessing over what had already been and gone.

She could express her appreciation for master Hos, despite the many things he told her that she didn't wish to hear. He had proven, time after time, that he had the highest of intentions and she had often reacted with anger and distrust. She could show her love for Kaylem in many ways other than lying with him, and she could learn as best she could how to be useful to the people of Ur in the remaining time left at the compound.

She realized suddenly with a gasp, that it was a kind of selfishness to brood on how she had been wronged, and how she had wronged others. Especially when there were things she could do which would result in life being better not only for herself, but also for those around her. As though in answer, a warmth grew within and spread through her, matching the intensity of the sunlight.

After basking for a few more moments, she turned and ambled slowly back the way she had come. When Kaylem passed her in the courtyard, she smiled at him. Kaylem stopped short, blinked in confusion, and then smiled a tentative smile back at her. Had she really been that surly that even a smile surprised him? Their hands met, and Saoirse allowed him to pull her gently and slowly toward him.

There was a question in Kaylem's eyes, an unspoken glimmer of hope, and Saoirse answered him with a glimmer of her own. Together they made their way to their shared chamber and sat facing each other, knee to knee. Kaylem reached out and Saoirse allowed him to enfold her hands into his. He massaged her palms, then brought one of them up after the other to kiss on the sensitive place on each wrist, bringing to her a shiver and a little smile.

CHAPTER 13

Still silent, Kaylem began to lift the hem of his robe, bringing it slowly up his body until he sat unclothed before her. Saoirse slowly did the same, trying to keep her breathing even and unhitched. Again, they sat knee to knee, hands gently clasped and faces intent on each other. The everyday sounds of the compound were faded here in this chamber, where only the two of them existed and a world was growing between them.

It seemed like forever that they sat motionless save for a tiny caress of a hand, or the blink of an eye. Saoirse found herself wanting to grasp the warmth of the moment, to hold on to the tenuous connection between them. At the same time, a growing discomfort made her want to shift, to move, to say something that might break the moment and shift it into something less unpredictable.

As she took a breath, Saoirse noticed that their chests had both begun to move in and out at the same time and something dislodged from the wall of stone around her heart. It was only a small crack, a pebble falling from its previously impervious place, but it was a start.

As though Kaylem noticed that tiny crack, he took a deep breath and began to massage her arms, running his hands gently back and forth across her skin. The quiet rasping noise was hypnotic, and she watched as his palms made their way across various parts of her body. First her wrists, then upper arms, then down the sides of her torso, sweeping from her hips to her knees.

Saoirse traced a finger down Kaylem's cheek and then reached out with both hands to cup his face, allowing the tangle of his beard to tickle her palms. She caressed an ear, marveling in its complexity and how soft and pliant it felt under her tentative fingers. Kaylem brushed back her hair, running his thumb across one of her eyebrows and then down the side of her face.

Saoirse pressed both of her hands to Kaylem's chest, seeking for the reassuring beat within. She moved her hands around, allowing them to merge with the curve of his pectorals, down through the single trail of dark hair that descended to his navel. He raised an eyebrow and Saoirse fanned her palms out, running them up his torso and away from his swelling manhood.

Closer and closer they inched toward each other until the desire to lie skin to skin became overwhelming. Soon they were moving their bodies in a dance that felt entirely new, yet ancient and deeply familiar at the same time. Mouths moved together, tongues providing silver trails leading to an ever deeper desire to be within each other's skin.

Eyes locked together, Kaylem moved his body and Saoirse opened for him. Joined, they touched foreheads and stared with wide open eyes, bodies motionless for an eternity, seeking themselves in each other. Another shift and crack, almost audible to Saoirse. Something in her chest loosened further, enough for her to draw a breath so deep it felt as though she breathed Kaylem into herself, as well as the air around her.

He moved just a fraction, and Saoirse drew in another breath, a hiss this time as glorious sensation flamed through her, lighting up a place in her that she thought was dead forever. They made tiny rocking movements together, their bodies taking over with the knowledge of how to move as one, leaving them to commune silently through their still-locked gaze. Soon all was not so silent as Saoirse found it more difficult to breathe without small gasps, which grew to sighs and then to moans.

She wished for Kaylem to make larger movements, and yet the small moves he made slowly wound something deep in her core tighter with each stroke. As it built, Saoirse smiled and laughed with joy. The feeling reminded her of the place of the Knowing, the home of the gods which she thought she had been locked out of. She could have sworn that a sliver of a whisper wove itself through her inner hearing, a mote of golden light which flowed from the silent place and grew to a bright glow.

As her moans increased in pitch, Kaylem began making sounds of his own which brought Saoirse's hands wishing they could sink further into him. They found purchase in the thick muscles of Kaylem's shoulders. Her body was not entirely her own any more, a greater force turning it to a delicious, sinuous liquid that merged entirely with Kaylem's as though they had shed their skin and danced freely among the stars.

Kaylem grunted, shuddered and then whimpered, and the sensation of his seed rushing into her deepest of places brought a shuddering moan from beyond her throat. She allowed for just an instant for everything to slip away. There was a different kind of nothingness for a wonderful, fleeting moment, full to the brim with a fizzing kind of brightness.

She laughed in delight as the fizzing exploded in her core and the laugh ended on a shriek. The feeling dispersed and Saoirse wished she could to hold on to it for longer, maybe forever. Then there were the two of them again, panting, Kaylem above her dripping sweat, both hearts racing with the same beat.

"I guess I failed again," Kaylem said ruefully, but his eyes sparkled.

Saoirse just smiled at him and cupped his cheek. "There's always tomorrow. We can try again then."

Smiling, they untangled their limbs while he flopped onto his side, then re-tangled more comfortably to lie, sated, in each other's arms until the morning light drew them reluctantly apart once again.

CHAPTER 14

Saoirse was certain that the handservant was smirking as she brought their morning meal. A part of her didn't care, and she ran the tip of her big toe up the skin of Kaylem's calf as he dug into his bread slathered in besan paste. Kaylem stopped shoveling the food into his mouth for a moment and flicked his eyes to her, narrowing them to cheeky slits as his hand that wasn't holding his bread made its way under her rear and gently squeezed.

With a small squeal, Saoirse grabbed his thigh like a vice and Kaylem jumped, dropping his bread and smearing besan paste all over the small mud-brick platform beside the hearth that they used to spread their repast. Dropping her uneaten egg back onto the platter, Saoirse moved closer to Kaylem with a predatory gleam and readied her hand for a further onslaught.

The sound of the master's throat clearing, and scuffled step, brought them apart as though stung, and they sat like chastened children as Hos lifted the sides of his mouth in an obvious smirk. "I can always break my fast in the courtyard where the sun is pleasant at this time of day, if you're in need of some privacy this morning."

"No, please join us, master Hos," answered Kaylem with a face that was suddenly beet red. He moved to make room for the master.

Saoirse nodded her agreement, hastily reaching again for her egg and biting into it while keeping her gaze fixed on the wall vent. She was certain that the master's face radiated amusement even though she couldn't bring herself to look. Kaylem nudged

CHAPTER 14

her and she nudged him back. He poked her in her side. A giggle forced its way out of her, and she almost choked on her mouthful.

"I think it's the perfect day to begin something new in our lessons today," master Hos said as though Saoirse wasn't about to launch herself at Kaylem in retaliation. Both Saoirse and Kaylem eyed each other carefully for a moment then turned to consider what the teacher had said.

"Let us move to the shade, shall we, and continue there." As serene as an eagle gliding in the sky, the master plucked the last remaining egg from the tray. He dipped it in besan paste and floated from the hearth, leaving Saoirse and Kaylem to hastily finish their mouthfuls and stumble and nudge each other as they made their way to follow.

"What thoughts have you had about your return to Ur?" the master asked as Saoirse and Kaylem were fidgeting around with their cushions. They became engrossed in trying to get comfortable without spilling their ale, still letting out the odd occasional guffaw from their previous rumbling. Sensing the master waiting all of a sudden, Saoirse looked up guiltily and forced her body into stillness.

"In truth, I don't know what to think about Ur, master, beyond how I could possibly help them recover from the tragedy."

The master made a grunt which set Saoirse to wondering whether thoughts about Ur were desired or not.

"Actually, I have plenty of feelings about going back to Ur," she clarified, "most of them full of guilt for being here and living in such comfort. Not to mention terror of what we face when we return," she answered, knowing by experience that it was ultimately less painful to be truthful up front. Otherwise, she knew she would have to endure the master's questions designed to draw the truth from her in smaller, more tedious threads.

The master nodded silently. "What have you considered about the tasks and situations you may face as Oracle?"

Saoirse blinked at him as an eagle screeched overhead and the wind sighed through their shade screen. "I…" She looked down and her eyes found the mug of ale, which she took a large sip of and then realized her bladder was suddenly uncomfortably full. An urge to run away from the shade and squat for a very long time in the servants' latrine suddenly overcame her.

She swallowed and searched her mind frantically for

something that might pose as an adequate answer. "When I have needed to provide comfort, or help for the dead to pass, it has come to me from within. I haven't needed to think about it at all."

The master grunted again, followed by sitting for a long time in silence. Saoirse wondered whether she should say anything else and began to shift uncomfortably on her cushion.

"It is quite true that the Knowing is brought into the heart in the exact moment it is needed," the master said slowly. Saoirse nodded in agreement and smiled, hoping she wouldn't have to think too much more about being an Oracle. There was more silence, where she couldn't help but think about being an Oracle, and she wondered for the thousandth what it might be like. Would she sit in a big stone chair above people bowing before her like the stone tablet the master showed her recently? Just the thought of it made her feel even more like running away and hiding. Her bladder throbbed painfully.

"In your position as Oracle, you will be expected to conduct yourself according to the laws and doctrine of the Temple. How familiar are you with these?"

Saoirse felt her heart sink to her feet and her body became so heavy she could barely hold up her ale. "I know nothing about these things, master. Surely, I can just allow the Knowing to guide me."

The master was silent for a while longer. Saoirse wanted to yell and scream at him as she sat there waiting for him to speak again. She willed him to say that it was fine, and quite acceptable, that she didn't know the first thing about the ways of the Temple or its people. A part of her knew this would not be the case since she was about to become intimately involved with both when she returned.

"When the Knowing surges through you, Saoirse, whether it be through dreams or through your heart, how has it usually been received by those around you?"

Saoirse opened her mouth and closed it again. She decided in that moment that she would stay here and enjoy the bounty of the compound for the rest of her life. Maybe she would send a messenger to act as an intermediary between her and the people, or an army of messengers even. Kaylem was sure to agree. The master sat patiently but with an air of expectation. She wanted to growl at him, for he knew exactly how every single one of her proclamations of truth had been received.

"Then I'm destined to fail before I even set foot in Ur, master." Heat prickled at the corners of her eyes, and she caught herself biting her lip so hard she tasted blood.

"How have you come to that conclusion before we are even close to being done asking the questions?"

"Oh, gods, there are more?"

"There are always questions, Saoirse, and this is as it should be. Imagine if you were to arrive in Ur without first having asked these questions?"

Saoirse wondered about what life might be like if she joined one of the entertaining troupes that traveled the land and gave people relief from the dreariness of their lives. She couldn't dance, or sing, or contort her body into strange shapes. Nor, could she be trusted to accurately throw blades, or fling her body around into heroic tumbles. Yet she could be a mere fortune teller instead of the Oracle, and then she could assist the people from a small tent far away from the clutches of the Temple.

"I don't know how to answer any of those questions," Saoirse said in a voice that reminded her of a child. Kaylem, who had been sitting silently beside her, found her hand and gave it a reassuring squeeze.

"Up until now, you have been needing to focus on bringing yourself back into balance. Now, the time has come to prepare for your service to the Temple, and to the people of Ur."

"What if I'm not ready?"

The master nodded. "Does the mother truly feel ready to give birth and care for her baby? Even after seeing her aunties and older sisters with babes at their breasts, after caring for babes not of her womb, she will not be truly ready to be a mother. When she is looking back in hindsight once her babes have left the nest, she may have some idea. The grandmother has much wisdom only because of the experiences and many mistakes she made as a mother. This is the nature of all trials."

"But why must we be so unprepared for these trials?"

"We are ever learning and evolving. And yet, you can prepare."

Saoirse wasn't so sure, but she nodded and smiled, knowing that master Hos and Kaylem weren't fooled for a moment.

CHAPTER 15

It was sometime between day and night. Saoirse wasn't sure entirely where she was for a moment, until she turned toward the cry of a child and noticed the river flowing benignly in the background. In the foreground was a wasteland of dried mud. In the strange light, Saoirse noticed there were people around her, standing around occasional cooking fires which were more smoke than flame.

The air smelled worse than the servants' latrine in the courtyard of the compound. As she stared in horror, a woman carrying a small, hollow-eyed child cooked what looked like a rat over their sputtering fire. As she watched, the woman pulled small pieces of barely cooked meat from the animal and fed it to the howling child, who writhed and thrashed about as though in pain.

Once the mother had coaxed the child to eat, she then gnawed at what remained, and Saoirse noticed that the woman's hands were nothing but skin and bone, as were the sharp planes of the woman's face. A pitiful piece of cloth tied to sit in an uneven triangle above them was their only shelter, their pallet nothing but bare earth.

The child's cries intensified, and the woman brushed away an insect with a listless hand, shifting her position in order to make her squat more comfortable while holding the child against her. As the darkness slowly settled around them, the babe's cries gradually faded into agonized sounding grunts punctuated with the odd wail. Filled with relief, Saoirse allowed herself to relax a little as the babe made its way into sleep.

Only a moment later, the mother's keening speared into Saoirse as the woman shook the babe's lifeless body at the sky. A wave of sorrow mixed with fury almost knocked Saoirse over as she allowed tears to stream down her face.

The babe's spirit, a gray slip of a thing barely visible in the gloom, hovered uncertainly. Saoirse called to it, filled with a sudden tenderness, and it drifted closer. A note, a mix of notes blending into a tune, wound itself around the space, and she and the babe's spirit listened to it for a moment. Words formed on her lips. It was a blessing, sung along with the tune. The babe's spirit drifted toward the slight brightening of the horizon, which proclaimed either the setting or the rising sun.

Calm filled Saoirse as the babe's spirit became an indiscernible whisp among the other threads of cloud adorning the sky, even though the mother's sobs still penetrated to the very core of her. Turning to the mother, Saoirse tried to comfort the woman, but found she couldn't touch her. Instead, Saoirse sang to the grieving mother, a lullaby remembered from childhood, and the mother eventually grew still.

A hand on her arm shocked Saoirse out of the dream and back to the pallet she shared with Kaylem.

"Shaji, are you well? You were sobbing, but it sounded almost as though you were also singing. Are you having another nightmare?"

"The babe died," she cried into Kaylem's chest, and the mother's pained fury made her want to kick and punch something until it broke. "It died and it knew nothing but suffering. Nothing but cold, and hunger, and pain." Kaylem caressed her face and clumsily tried wiping her tears away. "Why would the gods wish me to save the people of Ur from the flood only to have them all die like this? Truly, it would have been a mercy if they'd all just perished straight away."

"Shaji, we can't know the reasons why. But surely, not all the people are dying." His voice rumbled from his chest and Saoirse allowed herself a moment of comfort in his arms. It wasn't Kaylem who had caused this, she reminded herself, and she breathed the fury from her body as best she could. The babe was now at peace, she reminded herself, and she held onto that to stop herself descending into madness.

CHAPTER 16

"The Temple Rite of the Dead must be memorized, Saoirse, down to the most exact tone of voice. This you will use more than anything, and the people expect it."

"I know, master" Saoirse answered in a tight voice, her throat already feeling the effects of an entire morning spent practicing the complex chant. "It feels empty, nothing like when the Knowing comes… Why must I bother?" She gestured as though she would like to throw the Temple Rite for the Dead far away into the sky.

The master nodded in understanding.

"How do I do this with any kind of integrity knowing I'm not feeling anything? This isn't coming from the Knowing." She slapped her chest so hard it stung. "It's coming from me trying to remember all those… details." Her hand moved to her head and she tapped it in frustration. She refrained from saying the curse words she wanted to say. They would not have been appropriate to apply to one of the most sacred rites that existed; one which she would have been honored to learn under other circumstances.

"Dear Saoirse…" the master began. She sat back with a sigh. "When you sit for your morning meal which was laid out before you wake, what is it that keeps the food fresh?"

"Er… palm leaves? What has that to do with the Rite of the Dead?"

"When you see those particular leaves wrapped around something, what do you automatically think of?"

"Food, of course."

"And there are usually no surprises when you unwrap those

leaves."

Saoirse nodded her agreement, resigning herself for the lesson she knew was to follow.

"Tell me, what would you do if the meal was wrapped in... say... someone's robe instead?"

Saoirse looked at the master with a curve to her lip. "As long as it was Kaylem's robe and not some dirty old person's filthy cloth who never washed."

The master nodded to acknowledge the humor of her reply. "Still, would you expect there to be eggs and dates folded up in someone's robe if you came across it sitting by the hearth?"

"Well, of course not, I'd probably pick it up the wrong way and it would fall out onto the dirt and then we'd all go hungry. I'd also be having a word to say to whoever was foolish enough to put food in Kaylem's robe instead of wrapping it in..." Saoirse slapped her forehead and sighed deeply. "Oh of course. I see."

The master merely raised an eyebrow. Saoirse lifted the corner of her mouth, noticing that Kaylem was trying very hard not to smirk as well. "So, if I'm not expecting food because it's in the wrong packaging, I won't handle it the right way and then I'll get upset. Then, of course, we can apply this concept to the Knowing, and if it comes with the wrong packaging then the people won't appreciate it and will think I'm not properly honoring the gods and the situation.

"They'll want the traditional Rite of the Dead that they know and expect, even if they think they want something new, but when they're grieving for their loved ones, they don't want to be shocked and faced with something unfamiliar. They want the comfort of the known..." She sighed again.

The master smiled. "Again, then."

CHAPTER 17

"The rise of your voice there is not quite right, Shaji. What you're implying there is that you'd like to… erm… engage the person in a dance, rather than an invitation to guide them through their problems."

"Well, this is just ludicrous. How is this…" Saoirse raised her voice in a ridiculous parody of the phrase she was trying to make, "any different to this?" She slid her voice up again, which ended in a snarl.

"Now I think you're saying you'd like to take them hunting."

"Argh." Saoirse let out a shriek of frustration and smashed her fist into the sand. Kaylem sat before her, trying to look serious. She wanted to slap the almost-smirk from his face.

"Why is the meaning of what I say different when it's to the Temple elite instead of just an everyday person? This is so foolish. They'll understand what I mean."

"They might choose to be supportive and understand. Unfortunately, they're more likely to judge you as being below them and act insulted, just so they can make you wrong and bring you down."

"These people we're returning to… they are worse than the worst of humanity I've ever come across if they're that exacting about how one should behave, and then do the things they do. This is some kind of torture… or a foolish joke."

"I remember having to learn all this as a child and it was like being tortured back then. But it will eventually become second nature. Again…"

CHAPTER 18

"How can there be so many different words for mistress and master? This is ridiculous!"

"Again, Saoirse. They sound different depending on the level of seniority. For example, if you start with the lowest utterance of mistress, which is used for people like my mother, you can hear that slight tonal difference than if you use the Mistress version to denote someone like the high priestess. Then there's your honorific *Mistress* which is different again…"

"They all sound the same to me, Kaylem," Saoirse said in despair.

"Wait till you hear the different words for master," Kaylem answered, giving her a sympathetic look that made her want to throw her ale in his face.

"Run them through again for me, slower this time…"

CHAPTER 19

"I am officially giving up. Let's just stay here for the rest of our lives." Saoirse threw her scarf at the wall with a grunt. "They're all going to hate me anyway. They all know I'm a prostitute. Why are we even pretending I could be anything else?"

"There are those who will adore you and worship you, Saoirse. You'll have plenty of supporters too, never forget that."

"This is what I've always dreamed of... Literally, I've dreamed of it so many times, especially back when your mother was alive and I was here as a servant." Saoirse answered, looking at the shadow of them both on the wall. "Returning to Ur together with you, no longer a servant, no longer a prostitute. No longer a slave and equal in my own right. But I don't feel like anything but my old self, just the same as when I was a prostitute. Just the same as when I was a servant here, slaving away out back." Kaylem turned to her and brushed her hair out of her face.

"I'm not their savior, Kaylem. Ur is a complete mess, it's beyond saving. I've seen it in so many dreams. How can I fix it when I'm just me?"

"You don't have to fix anything, Shaji." He brushed the hair even further back and planted a kiss tenderly on her cheek.

"Why are we going back then? What can I possibly do aside from annoying a bunch of horrible people and have them hate us even more than they already do?"

"Why do you think they hate us so much?"

"Because they see me as an imposter."

"Because they see you as a threat. They're the imposters,

CHAPTER 19

Shaji, and they know they are lying. In fact, even the people of Ur actually, deep down, know they're lying, too. But somehow everyone plays their part in keeping the entire Temple of lies standing because they feel powerless to do anything else. You threaten to bring them down, Shaji, if you can only be there for the people and help everyone unite at the right moment."

"But the people are dying and weak. They've been preyed on for so long, and then after the flood—"

"They are weak because the elite have made sure they're weak. But they haven't worked out that together they're strong. They've always competed with each other; for food, shelter, because the elite keep them poor. But with your help they may be able to see who the true enemy is."

Kaylem took her hand and put it against his chest. "We may die in Ur, but as long as I'm beside you, Shaji, fighting for the freedom of our people, I'll consider it a life worthy of those dreams I shared with you. Even if you didn't know I did."

Saoirse turned and looked at him, her eyes wide. "You dreamed of us, too?"

"Well, what else do you think I did on those long, lonely nights when all I had was a pile of stone tablets to keep me company?"

Face to face, hand to hand, forehead to forehead they sat, staring into each other's eyes until their vision blurred. Saoirse wasn't entirely sure who started stroking whom; long, sensual strokes along arms and up spines. The hiss of intakes of breath, small moans and rustling of robes was followed by a moment of silence as they lay skin to skin, breathing together and tracing shapes on cheeks, shoulders, and throats. A hum built in the air around them, between them and Saoirse's body felt as though it was softening and disappearing as she aligned the length of herself next to Kaylem.

As her need built, she gently pushed him onto his back and moved so that she was above him, stroking his chest, his belly; leaning down to maximize skin contact with him. She encircled her arms around the back of his neck, rubbing her cheeks along his, and she swore she could almost hear him purring like a mountain cat.

Whatever it was, the sound built until it became a subtle roar, the air beginning to almost crackle between them as though before a lightning storm. Moving herself along his body, Kaylem kept his eyes glued to hers, just the way he knew she liked it. His hands trailed and roamed, caressing and stroking wherever they happened to be.

As they joined, their breath also became one, along with their movements. Saoirse lost all sense of her body as she felt her essence expanding and sinking into Kaylem. Both of them surged like a wave of power upward into the heavens. The wave built until there was no more Saoirse, no more Kaylem, and no more separation between them.

Still upward, the wave that was once two, surged as one. It swept away the veil between them and the home of the gods and they became one with the source of the Knowing. Saoirse wept in recognition as she allowed what remained of herself to be intertwined in blissful reunion among the other presences, alongside what was left of Kaylem.

Soon, there was no difference between herself, Kaylem, or the swirl of life containing too many beings to count, as it was herself which spread infinitely from her center throughout the entire space. And yet, it was also Kaylem and all the others with them in that dazzling, golden light which pulsed with nothing but bliss.

Their bodies became still, limbs and torsos slick with sweat as they lay entangled together. Chests rising and falling, they fell asleep with their faces barely apart.

CHAPTER 20

The journey back to Ur was fraught with tension and silence. Saoirse and Kaylem sat side by side in the old cart, pulled by the two aging donkeys. Bo sat in the front, gently tapping the donkeys occasionally on their haunches with a long stick and clicking his tongue at them encouragingly.

Saoirse wished for a moment that she could be a donkey. It seemed such a simple life. She made small noises constantly under her breath to practice her tonal endings, fiddling with the longer sleeves on her robe. The sleeves covered her wrists down to her knuckles, as was proper for one of the Temple elite. She found them irritating.

At least nobody would notice if she made a rude sign, she thought wryly. Kaylem looked over with what looked a little bit like an encouraging smile, betrayed by the tightness at the corners of his eyes. He'd oiled his beard and donned a fancy turban, which made him look so different, especially along with his more formal robe that also fell past his wrists, hemmed with gold.

For a moment Saoirse worried that he might not be in there anymore, until he poked the tip of his tongue out at her. She allowed the sleeve to fall back just as she made a sign she'd seen a fisherman once use at the inn before being set upon by a bunch of traders. Kaylem's eyes widened, and he blanched.

"Don't worry, I won't be bringing that one out on any formal occasions."

"Do you even know what that means, Shaji?"

"Of course... Do you?" She didn't, and she could see that he saw through the lie.

"It's to do with a very unholy union between a donkey and a human, with the human being on the receiving end," Kaylem whispered into her ear.

"Oh gods…" Saoirse stared back the way they had come for a moment. "How do you actually know that?"

"Anan used to use it on a regular basis during morning blessing, but only when he'd angled it so that his cronies could see. They thought it was so funny, it was like they were still in scribe school, with all their sniggering. I wonder if he still does it or if he's moved on to something else."

"Thanks, that's just ruined it for me. And I can only imagine what might happen if a woman was seen using it instead."

"She'd likely be sent to the stoning pits… Or sacrificed on the altar." He rolled his eyes. "Apparently we are the most advanced civilization in the known world."

"Who told you that?"

"Merchants. They've been all over and they say here is so refined compared to everywhere else they go."

Saoirse rolled her eyes back at him. "Kaylem, they'd tell anyone that anywhere, no matter how backward, just to get a sale."

"I guess so," Kaylem said glumly. "I didn't miss Ur when we were home. Not for a moment."

Saoirse wanted to answer that the household wasn't her home and that she'd had a home before her parents died and left her alone in the world. But she stopped herself because it wasn't true. She had stood at the well for a long moment this morning, staring down at the shining disc of water. Even though no beings had appeared in the water's reflection, she had still watched as her tears fell and broke the still surface so far below.

For the past winter it had become her home. Thinking back to her childhood of toil, with Marsi, and Deni, and Bo, even then it had still felt like home. Seeing Bo's more grown-up profile as he turned to watch an eagle wheeling in the sky, she felt a smile come to her face and a warmth in her belly.

The warmth grew until she remembered her dream from back before the storm destroyed her home and her servant family; back before she was sent from the compound by the mistress, Kaylem's mother, and sold to the brothel. In the dream, she had been holding twin babes as her and Kaylem walked to the market in Ur. It was just as vivid in her mind's eye now as when she had awoken from it back then. The memory made her gasp, and she grabbed Kaylem's arm.

"I haven't been feeling so well in the mornings since the last ripe moon," she told him, and she saw his eyes widen.

"Do you think…" He looked down at her hand which sat over her lower belly.

"It's too early. I have so much to do. I never thought…"

"I had a dream last night," he said with a soft smile. "We were walking with two babes to the market in Ur."

Saoirse felt the blood leaving her face.

CHAPTER 21

When Saoirse and Kaylem arrived at the main gate of Ur, where the flood-damaged wall stretched away from them as far as the eye could see, the guards were standing in just the same way as Saoirse remembered from her previous entry into the city. Some were laughing, another was slapping a traveler on the back. When it was their turn, the guards merely nodded them through on their humble cart, not giving them another glance. They had not sent a messenger ahead of them to alert the Temple elite of their imminent arrival.

"Shouldn't we have told them who we are? At least to give some notice that we've returned." Saoirse couldn't help the hand that sat at her throat, or the tightness of her chest that made breathing difficult. A breeze sent a wave of rotting garbage and human waste their way. It made her want to void the nuts, bread, and hommous they had picked at earlier.

"Do you really want the official welcome, Shaji? I can go back and they'll arrange it for us straight away."

"Oh, I see. Maybe not then."

They made their way past the Temple and headed in the direction of Kaylem's old abode, now likely to be a pile of rubble unless something had already been rebuilt over it. The road snaked through half constructed buildings where skeletal men in filthy loin cloths toiled to the shouts of overseers who looked not much better than the laborers. Saoirse shuddered.

"Where will we go, Kaylem? We don't even know if we have somewhere to move into."

CHAPTER 21

"If I know the elite, they'll have made sure we have the most elaborate dwelling that they can build, with the most staff out of anyone, all of whom will be the most loyal to the Temple."

Saoirse cringed.

"We can work around that. Don't worry about that right now, Shaji."

As they neared the Temple, Saoirse noticed that the majority of new buildings were toward the rear of the compound, where future flooding would have the least impact. It had previously been where the poorer areas began.

"Oh, the irony that those now living in poverty might enjoy the breeze from the river, while the rich hide from it in relative, but stifling, safety," Kaylem remarked.

Saoirse, too overcome to comment, continued to drink in the sights of an Ur which was almost unrecognizable to her. Sensing movement behind them, Saoirse turned and noticed a small group had formed and was following them at a distance. Made up of street urchins even more skeletal than the laborers, Saoirse realized that she recognized most of them from her days at the inn.

Motioning for them to come closer, Saoirse gently tapped Kaylem, who asked Bo to stop the cart. The group of children stood where they were, nudging each other and whispering. She motioned again. The whispering and nudging grew more urgent and various members of the group turned to stare at her with wide eyes.

"None of you were scared of me before," she called out softly, holding out a large pouch of nuts and dates. One of the boys approached warily and she tossed the pouch to him. His friends crowded around the boy, and they demolished the food in seconds. Once they were done, they stood a little closer and Saoirse could hear the whispers.

"You looked her in the eye!"

"Well, you took food from her."

"You ate it."

"The gods will strike us all down then."

"She wants to talk to us."

"Well, you do it then, you ate the most nuts."

"I did not, you greedy hog, look at you still chewing."

"She's watching us now. I bet she can tell what we're

thinking."

"I don't need to know what you're thinking, even if I could. I can hear everything you're saying," she called to them. They all stopped and looked at the ground just in front of her, a sign of respect for a high-born woman. Saoirse sighed.

"I'm only wishing for information." She held out another pouch of food, one they'd packed for themselves for the coming days, and the group's gaze followed the pouch. One of them swallowed emptily.

"We are forbidden to speak to the Oracle," one of them whispered.

"I'm asking you to speak to *me*," she answered, a hard ball of despair forming within her. The one who had approached earlier, who seemed to be the leader, nodded and stepped slowly toward her again.

"What would you like to know, Mistress?" The leader bowed his head, although Saoirse could not help but notice that his gaze was firmly on the package of food in her hand. He hadn't quite given her the correct honorific, but it made her want to smile rather than chide him.

"What do you know of the dwelling made for us? I know you would have been watching as it was built. What should I be cautious of?"

"Your dwelling, Mistress, is the largest on the slope behind the Temple. Gibil and Kusu stand either side of the entry to guard it and keep it safe…" Saoirse shuddered at the mention of the angry looking gods she remembered from the room at the top of the Temple.

"It was one of the first to be finished in case you decided to return earlier," called another boy whose hair was so matted and filthy around his head it reminded Saoirse of a small mud-brick hut. She wished she could invite the lot of them for a proper meal and to bathe, and maybe to find some better clothes for them all.

"Just up the hill a little and turn that way," said another, pointing vaguely to the west.

"Watch out for the headservant, she's a snake."

"She took to Amir with a stick," said another who pointed at one of the boys with seeping wounds down his arms and face. Saoirse almost burst into tears.

"There's one you can trust. Her name is Asi. She's my

CHAPTER 21

cousin," said another.

"Kareem, she's not your cousin. There's no way they'd let anyone work for the Oracle if they were related to you," said another.

Kareem threw a fist, and they began to pile onto each other in the mud.

"Stop!" Saoirse shouted in the most commanding voice she could, and they all froze.

"You will take Amir to the healer as his wounds have festered and he'll die if you don't." At this, she threw a coin at the leader who caught it and stared at it like it might disappear. "And here is the food I promised. There'll be more if you can find a way to pass on useful information without making a spectacle of yourselves outside my abode." The ones who had been fighting looked ashamed of themselves and tried to dust off some of the dirt. The leader bowed again to her and smiled, and then without warning they all turned and fled.

Saoirse turned back to Bo and Kaylem who both stared at her open-mouthed. "You heard them. Let us go see our new abode, then," she said in a mock-imperious voice. Kaylem was wise enough to rearrange his features into neutrality. Bo turned away, but occasionally looked back at her with a speculative expression on his face.

It was not long before they pulled up in front of the most imposing abode Saoirse had ever seen, aside from the great Temple itself. Elaborate carvings entwined their way around the entire front entry which framed an enormous door. She wondered where in the known world the precious timber might have come from even at the best of times, let alone when materials were so difficult to come by. She suppressed the urge to order someone immediately to break it into smaller pieces and donate it to others who might not be able to afford to rebuild. Before they could knock, the door opened with hardly a creak. An imposing woman stepped out, smoothing down her scarf.

"*Mistress*, we welcome you. And yet, unfortunately no messenger has informed us of your imminent arrival, and we are unprepared for you. A thousand apologies, *Mistress*."

The language the woman used was the formal version with her cadences flawless as though she had been brought up as one of the elite. Her use of the word *Mistress* was exacting in its correctness, and it made Saoirse want to cringe away from the woman and run back to the safety of the desert household forever.

Instead, Saoirse forced out as much of a smile as she could manage. "Our messenger must have become waylaid. We will be satisfied with what is available to us." Already she belatedly recognized that the tonal ending was not entirely correct, and she was certain the woman would catch it.

The woman gave a small bow, showing no sign she had heard the butchered reply, aside from a slight stiffening around her shoulders and a thickening of the air around them. Saoirse swallowed what felt like a dry stone lodged at the back of her throat and hoped the woman didn't hear the agonized click in the sudden lull of the breeze. "I am named Maryam and will be here to tend your every need and desire, *Mistress*."

Stopping herself from giving the greeting of equals, Saoirse was momentarily flummoxed as she sorted through the many memories of how to greet one who was somewhere relatively high up in the social order, but below herself. It didn't come and just as she began to turn to Kaylem, she heard his voice and felt his steady presence beside her.

"Maryam, we are grateful for your loyal service and look forward to enjoying all that our new abode will offer. We have traveled far today and are tired. Well met to you, too."

Preventing herself from staring at Kaylem open-mouthed in much the same way he had stared at her earlier, Saoirse made a non-committal noise at the back of her throat that she hoped sounded imperious enough. Kaylem's diction was beyond flawless. His tone of voice was melodic and effortless, and she felt a moment of despair at how far she had yet to go with her learning. She watched as Maryam nodded deeply to Kaylem, an air of satisfaction to her stance that was completely absent when dealing with Saoirse.

"Please," Maryam said as she gestured formally for them to enter first. "I will arrange for your possessions to be brought to your rooms. There is water warming on the hearth and a meal being arranged."

Kaylem gave a shallow nod to his head and Saoirse followed suit, uncertain whether to thank Maryam or not.

The inside of the abode was overwhelming to Saoirse, who had thought the main dwelling at the remote desert household to be the height of luxury. This dwelling was something she imagined the great King himself in the royal province of Kish might live in. She forced herself to keep her mouth closed and her expression neutral.

Taking a peek at Kaylem beside her, she could see by the smoulder in his eyes that he was doing his best to control his fury. She felt it coming from him in waves. She might have felt the same way if she hadn't been so numbed by shock, and she suspected her own anger might surpass even Kaylem's once she recovered.

"There has been no expense spared for the great Oracle, *Mistress*," simpered Maryam in a voice that sounded so false, Saoirse could barely contain the urge to slap the woman across the face. Instead, she ground her teeth together and stayed silent. She was not able to stop herself from imagining how many people in Ur had gone hungry in order to build this excess.

"First, the sleeping quarters for the *Mistress*, as well as those for master Kaylem." Here, Maryam gave them both a look filled with speculation, making Saoirse feel like she was back in her prostitute's robes. She suppressed the urge to move her arms across her body and instead opened chest out, smiling benignly.

"Please, lead us on, Maryam," she said in a soft, sweet voice. If she truly was the *Mistress* of this household in the most formal connotation of the word, the first thing she would do once she understood the running of the place would be to get rid of Maryam.

The sleeping wing was just as palatial as the rest of the abode. Rooms upon rooms opened out as they passed them, one called a sitting room, another a receiving room, and another a viewing room with a large wall vent opening onto an inner courtyard where the beginnings of a fountain were being completed by a slightly less starved looking group of workers. Saoirse tried to picture the layout in her mind, but became confused as they finally came upon what was announced to be her own sleeping chamber, beside an equally enormous bathing room.

The sound of running water drew her attention to the bathing room and Saoirse blinked in astonishment as she saw the most bizarre sight. A small bowl sat against the wall at waist height. There was a hole in its lowest point and over the bowl was a small spout, out of which trickled a steady stream of water.

"You can stop the flow here, *Mistress*, see?" Maryam's voice was unnaturally high as though showing the wonders of the gods to a small child. Saoirse smiled sweetly again and batted her eyelashes.

"Just incredible, Maryam. It's a wonder beyond imagining, and seeing how it's already finished like this when the rest of Ur is still rebuilding…" She shook her head in mock wonder. "Such a miracle of the gods." Saoirse knew she was going too far but couldn't help herself. Maryam only nodded, no doubt tucking away the wrong voice modulation that Saoirse only just noticed she had, yet again, made on the final syllable. Kaylem's hand found hers and squeezed.

Kaylem's rooms were almost as spectacular, although Saoirse couldn't help but feel smug that the bathing room was closer to her side than his. Eventually they found their way back to the common area of the dwelling once the tour was finished. There, Maryam bowed grandly and swept her hand toward a cushioned area where a large meal was laid out for them.

"Unfortunately, the household stores are running a little low and there was not enough time to make anything more befitting the Oracle and master Kaylem. By tomorrow, we hope to have more appropriate fare for your meals."

Neither of them knew how to respond to that, aside from a small nod. They both sat and then waited for Maryam to leave. However, Maryam did not leave even after they thanked her profusely and gave the nod to release her from service. She stood in a slightly darkened corner at attention. Saoirse widened her eyes at Kaylem in a silent question. Kaylem rolled his eyes back at her and then turned to Maryam.

"Maryam, this repast is just what we needed. We shall not be wishing for anything else now, and we gratefully give you your leave."

Maryam blinked as though she would like to argue and then bowed to both of them, sweeping graciously out of the room. Before she was out of their sight, Kaylem put a hand on Saoirse's arm and looked at her warningly. Saoirse felt her whole being sag. There was nowhere in this dwelling that they could talk without someone listening in, and it was likely Maryam was standing just around the corner.

"These dates are delicious, do you not think, Shaji?"

"Quite," she answered mechanically, hardly tasting the food

CHAPTER 21

that she suspected should have been the staff's evening meal. Instead of talking with Kaylem, she spent the meal imagining what might have been their lively conversation about Maryam's attitude and how long it would take for Saoirse's temper to snap. As they ate in silence, exhaustion sat so heavily on her shoulders that Saoirse was almost grateful to Maryam for her help with readying her for sleep. Yet she found that as she lay without Kaylem's reassuring presence in the unfamiliar furs, Saoirse felt more alone than she ever had in her life.

CHAPTER 22

Saoirse awoke to the sun streaming through unfamiliar wall vents. Surprised that she had slept so well, she sensed a presence nearby and was on instant alert. A rustling sound made her turn toward the opposite corner, where a small figure stood.

"What are you doing?" she snapped at the figure, who startled and made a high squeak.

"*Mistress*," the figure breathed as she turned and stood at attention. "Good morning. I am Asi and I have been assigned as your handservant."

The name was familiar. Saoirse wondered how that could be as she sorted groggily through her mind, wiping the sleep from her eyes. Taking a closer look at Asi, the first thing she noticed was that Asi was very young and, judging by the way the whites of her eyes showed, was terrified.

"How many summers have you, Asi?"

"Eleven, *Mistress*," she said with a bow that had her head almost reaching her quaking knees.

Something wasn't quite right about the situation, even if it was a relief that the one servant she knew she could trust was standing right before her. Her sleep-addled mind refused to give Saoirse any insight into why this might be a problem. Shaking the sleepiness from her body, she arose and found that she towered over the child, who cringed and looked like she might burst into tears.

"Asi, what were you doing before you came to serve here?"

"My parents died in the winter, *Mistress*. When I went to the

CHAPTER 22

Temple to beg for food and shelter, I was told I must maintain the servants' latrine and keep their quarters clean. Before your arrival, *Mistress*, that was my work, and then last night..." Now, Saoirse could see that tears were leaking from Asi's eyes, her entire body visibly trembling. A terrible understanding clicked into place and Saoirse did her best not to let the outrage show on her face. Maryam was even nastier than Saoirse ever imagined, if she was correct.

"Tell me, Asi. Was it Maryam who brought you here to do this?" Asi burst into tears and could barely get her next words out. "I must not say, *Mistress*."

Saoirse sighed as she took a moment to gather herself. "Asi, do you have a cousin called..." She dug around in the recesses of her memory for a moment to extract a name bubbling up from yesterday. "Kareem?"

Asi's eyes lit up but then went dull again as the fear shuttered them down. "*Mistress*," she whispered in shame.

Saoirse nodded. Maryam had unwittingly done Saoirse a favor, even though it came cloaked in one of the most potent insults she might ever have devised. Asi would be considered permanently polluted by her work, and as far below the status of handservant to the Oracle as anyone could ever be.

Saoirse should have been screaming her fury to the world. As Asi stood before her with tears streaming down her face, Saoirse wondered how near Maryam was and whether anyone else might be listening in. Putting a gentle hand on Asi's shoulder to calm her, Saoirse spoke in a loud angry voice at the ceiling.

"I cannot believe this has happened. Maryam!" Asi flinched as Saoirse's roar made even her own ears ring.

Maryam arrived far too quickly for her to have been anywhere but very close by. She radiated smugness. "Maryam, there has been a grave error. Last night I was very impressed by your service, but unfortunately, I must hold somebody accountable." Saoirse frowned as ferociously as she could.

"As you told master Kaylem and I last night, you are in charge of the household and therefore you are responsible for this." Saoirse sent a silent apology to Asi as she grabbed the girl and pushed her towards Maryam. Asi's chest heaved, and Saoirse forced herself not to make any move to comfort the child.

"*Mistress*, please explain the problem." A knowing glint

showed in Maryam's expression even if she radiated concern. There was no way a servant who maintained latrines would be here serving the Oracle unless it was meant as an affront. But Saoirse did not know the exact way she should approach the issue. Only Kaylem would be able to help her with navigating what was to come.

"What is amiss?" Kaylem's voice croaked from behind Maryam, and Saoirse resisted smiling in gratitude over Maryam's shoulder at him.

"Kaylem," Saoirse said before Maryam could inject her venom into the situation. "I have awoken to this!" She shoved Asi forward again. "A latrine digger for the servants. How in the name of the gods is she now suddenly my personal handservant?"

Kaylem blinked at Saoirse and scratched at something on his abdomen. There was a long moment of awkward silence while Saoirse watched Kaylem muddle through the issue in his mind.

"Someone must pay for this insult," she said in a voice she hardly recognized and wished she would never have had to use.

"I'm certain we can all sit down over a small-ale and discuss the problem," Kaylem finally said.

"*Mistress*, a thousand apologies if you are unsatisfied with the staff," said Maryam at the same time in a voice that implied Saoirse was being hysterical and unreasonable. "I will have her sent away immediately."

Panic hit Saoirse. That was not where she wanted this conversation to go. "The girl herself is beside the point. This is your area of expertise is it not, to source the correct staff?"

"I often delegate those duties to others, *Mistress*."

Saoirse felt backed into a corner. Was it enough to fire the odious woman? If Maryam had even an inkling that this would be her downfall, she never would have done such a thing. Saoirse felt like she was playing a game of twenty-squares. To make a wrong move here may prove life threatening if it caused enough insult to the ones who hired Maryam. She looked at Kaylem, hoping her desperation didn't show.

"This affront is very upsetting for the Oracle," Kaylem huffed as he addressed Maryam. "May I suggest you run some errands elsewhere until we are all sufficiently calm enough to find the best solution?" Saoirse could have flung her arms around him and his perfect tonal ending. Asi stood between them, confusion and distress plain on her face.

Maryam nodded primly and made a curt summoning gesture to Asi. "Come along!"

Asi edged towards Maryam, cowering and shaking all of a sudden.

"No," said Saoirse firmly, pulling Asi back toward her. "She can stay in this position. Let this be a reminder to you every day that I don't take kindly to affronts. You will now just have to live with the fact that a top member of your staff, under your guidance, was formerly working the latrines." Saoirse made a little smile that she hoped radiated every bit of outrage that she felt, and then turned to Asi.

"Asi, I prefer my robes hung over a stand. Maryam, please see to it on your errands that something appropriate can be found to sit in that corner." Saoirse dimly hoped it was the correct tonal ending, and yet found that she didn't care quite so much all of a sudden. Maryam's face carried no expression, but Saoirse noticed a tightness around her mouth that wasn't there before.

As Maryam bowed and left, Saoirse listened to the woman's footfalls that were much heavier than usual. Kaylem was staring at Saoirse and Asi with wide eyes as Saoirse turned back to him with a tight smile.

"Well, I wonder what awaits us for our morning meal?" she said brightly as she took Kaylem's arm and dragged him to the first place she could think of that might have a little privacy.

"Why are we in the bathing room, Shaji?"

The trickling sound of the basin made Saoirse's bladder want to let go on the spot.

"The nerve of that woman," Saoirse ground out through clenched teeth.

"It might not have been the best idea to speak to her so strongly, Shaji."

Saoirse turned and looked daggers at Kaylem. Nausea rolled through her and for a moment she thought she might have to lean over the basin and void the contents of her stomach. She propped herself up with a hand on the wall and said, "What would you have done then?"

Kaylem looked at his feet.

"Do you truly think saying nothing would get us anything but ridiculed that I just accepted one of the worst insults they could throw at me?"

"I'm not saying you should have said nothing…"

"So, what would you have done in my place?"

"I'm still trying to work it out," he said eventually.

"How can we get that woman out of here?"

"It would have been catastrophic to fire her for this," Kaylem answered. "It had to have been a test."

"A test with no correct answer." The nausea increased and she swallowed.

"That may be, Shaji. But now you have even more of an enemy in Maryam. You've made a fool of her by keeping that servant girl."

"Kaylem, Maryam despised me to begin with, before even meeting me. I will not creep around my own abode terrified of offending the staff, especially ones who think they can—"

"Shaji, please, you must speak quietly."

"How is it that I must be the one—"

"Because this is only the beginning, dear one." Kaylem took her in his arms and ran his hands down her back.

Saoirse pushed away the prickle of tears, but they came anyway. "I don't know if I can do this."

"I am here by your side, Shaji. We both need to be shrewd about this. The worst is yet to come, and we must play the game. I wish it wasn't so. Gods, I wish we could turn around and go home. But that's exactly what they want us to do. That's why they're doing this."

"But there's no escape from it, Kaylem. If I can't let my guard down here for even a second, how will we even make it through? Will we have to whisper to each other in the bathing room forever?"

He huffed a quiet laugh into her hair. "We'll find a way, just like the way was found before the flood, and just like the way was found to get us to this point in time. I love you, Shaji. And to see you suffering tears me apart. I wish this could be easier for you… for us." He stroked his palms across her cheeks, brushing her hair back from her face and then his eyes widened in concern.

"Why are you so pale, Shaji? Are you sick?"

"You could say that," said Saoirse. "I need to—" She gulped and nodded her head toward the pit, a far cry from the servants' latrine that she remembered from her childhood and the ones that Asi would have been spending her hours digging out. At the thought of stinking latrines she retched, and Kaylem jumped as though she had stomped on his foot.

"A thousand apologies, Shaji. I'll leave you in peace." He squeezed her arm gently and shuffled past her in the tiny space, apologizing for every bump and brush. Saoirse only just made it to the intricately decorated brickwork surrounding the hole in the ground before her stomach forcibly ejected its contents.

CHAPTER 23

Just when Saoirse thought that she and Kaylem could enjoy their morning meal in peace without hovering servants, she heard Maryam clear her throat importantly. Saoirse suppressed a shudder at the sound she had already come to despise. She was certain Maryam was also suppressing a shudder at the lack of decorum before her. This meal would be far too relaxed for her liking. "*Mistress*, you have visitors!"

"Now?"

Maryam nodded with what looked to Saoirse like excitement. Saoirse stood from her cushion, still trying to swallow the remains of the last mouthful. "Who is here?" she asked as they made their way to the reception chamber. Maryam didn't answer but smiled like a star-struck little girl. Saoirse couldn't help but feel anything but dread.

Two women sat primly on a bench in the reception chamber. Everything about them was flawless, down to the ornately decorated robes and scarves they wore. Saoirse had thought that her own robe was richly appointed, but theirs made hers look like rags. One of them was older, darker-skinned and serious looking. The other was finer boned and possessed a fragility about her.

Taking a deep breath, Saoirse nodded as she had been taught by Kaylem.

"Fortune to yourself, *Mistress*," simpered the older looking one while somehow looking down her nose at Saoirse despite her smaller height. The hands that reached out to Saoirse were so soft, Saoirse uncharitably wondered if the woman had ever even had to clean herself after visiting the privy.

"I am named Kettel, and my dear companion is Ashira." Ashira gave an exaggerated bow, her face reminding Saoirse of a child's and yet the expression in Ashira's eyes seemed a thousand years old in its calculation. "We come to offer our friendship and assistance with anything you should desire."

As she discretely dabbed around her mouth and swallowed the last dregs of the mouthful down, Saoirse silently cursed herself for having rushed in response to Maryam's sense of urgency.

"It pleases me greatly to greet you, Mistress Kettel and Mistress Ashira. I thank you for visiting so soon upon our return." Saoirse hoped she had spoken voice modulations and their titles correctly as she answered with the traditional greeting to each. Was that a small twitch in the corner of Ashira's mouth? She pushed the concern away because Kettel was speaking again.

"I trust that your dwelling is in order, *Mistress*?"

"I thank you Mistress Kettel for your concern. I am so gratefully surrounded by such beauty and wonder it takes my breath away." Saoirse wondered for a moment if they were going to burst into guffaws at her flowery language and simpering tone. She forced her mouth into something resembling neutrality as she remembered rolling around with laughter with Kaylem during their many lessons in how to speak to the elite. "Is all in order for your home, Mistress?"

Kettel's lips pursed, not even a glimmer of humor in her expression. "Our dwelling is now complete. The servants have put it to order, yet I cannot tell you how traumatic it has been while the rebuilding occurred. Our children have become accustomed to playing in the mud outside those terrible, crumbling hovels we took shelter in. Now, even though we are housed properly, they still wish to become savages." Saoirse nodded in feigned sympathy, hoping Kettel and Ashira couldn't hear the grind of her teeth, or notice the narrowing of her eyes. She was glad the sleeves of her robe hid her fists which were tightly bunched. Those hovels had been previously occupied by peasants who were likely now perished from the harshness of winter after their unjust eviction.

Ashira spoke, a whine to her voice. "We have had to acquire new servants, and training them to do things the correct way is terribly tiresome. Most of our servants did not make it up the Sacred Steps as they were busy burying our supplies at the time the flood hit." She sighed deeply. "You cannot imagine how tedious it was to find all the jars afterward. There are so many valued possessions still buried beneath the earth, yet do you think one can find them?"

Ashira blew out a prim huff and Saoirse almost expected her to stomp like a young girl having a tantrum. "It has truly been a great trial; a great trial indeed. And the men we have had to replace as they tire in their digging..." Saoirse imagined men being forced to dig in the stinking mud until they dropped. She couldn't think of any answer that wouldn't seriously insult her guests, but she must have made some kind of sound in response because the two women nodded to each other and her in mutual aggrievement.

"Yet, dear Ashira," purred Kettel, "We come to express our gratitude to the *Mistress* for saving the city."

"Ah, yes, my greatest friend, of course!" Turning from Kettel, Ashira once again bowed exaggeratedly to Saoirse, who did her best to keep a straight face. "In our joyful gratitude we offer you this vase as a token of our fealty." Ashira nodded to one of the servants standing in the corner of the receiving room, who disappeared for a moment and then there was a scuffling sound from outside.

Saoirse looked toward the main entry, where four servants now appeared, heaving an enormous vase. They slowly made their way to an empty corner of the chamber, their faces almost purple from the strain. The vase was stunning, carved in incredible detail with many scenes of gods, goddesses, and animals.

"I... I have never quite seen anything like it," Saoirse stammered, berating herself for allowing Kettel and Ashira to see her rawness and lack of sophistication. Her ending was all wrong. She was certain she had offended them. It was all over before anything had even begun. They would know she was a fraud. She slapped herself mentally and forced herself to focus.

"You do not fancy it?" Kettel asked with a curl to her lip. Saoirse took another breath to try to steady herself. She had practiced and studied for so long. She knew how to deal with these people. She wouldn't let them get under her skin this easily. A wave of nausea rose into her throat, and she swallowed it down. There was only one reason a woman might be nauseous first thing in the morning, and she definitely did not want these women

CHAPTER 23

knowing about that.

"It is an incredible piece, Mistress Kettel and Mistress Ashira," she said in a breathy voice that she hoped conveyed joy, instead of how close her throat was to opening and vomiting the breakfast she had only eaten half of. "I love it dearly." She pushed her mouth into a smile, knowing that the tonal ending wasn't quite right, but would have to be close enough. She hoped there weren't any chunks of besan paste, or even worse, dates in her teeth.

"I am so glad you find it pleasing," Kettel murmured. There was a pause, and Saoirse hoped her smile wasn't slipping as they all stood looking at each other. She crouched before the vase and began to study the carvings, making small noises of appreciation here and there.

"There is also another matter which we have come to discuss, *Mistress*," said Kettel.

"Of course." Saoirse replied, nodding as though her head was loose on her shoulders. She pictured for a moment the desert stretching into infinity around Kaylem's home, the eagle flying through the air, and the silent sky stretching above her.

"It is the small matter of your wedding. Of course, the Oracle Ceremony is also imminent, although on a more personal nature it may be of benefit to... er... hasten the wedding; for the benefit of the moral standards of our great city." Both visitors delicately lowered their eyes. Saoirse could not help but blush violently.

"Er, Kaylem and I were married by master Hos in a private ceremony at the household only just recently."

"Master... Hos? Private... ceremony?" Shrilled Ashira with a pasted smile on her face that looked more like a grimace of horror.

"How... quaint," murmured Kettel, who looked pale.

"Who, exactly, is master... Hos?" asked Ashira.

"He is an eminent spiritual teacher..." Saoirse stopped midsentence, hoping that because the sentence wasn't finished, she didn't need some kind of tonal ending there. The chanting group would be decimated by the Temple authorities if they knew of it. She would have to tread carefully. "He harks from far-away Kish and—"

"Kish? An uncle on my father's side hails from Kish. I must ask him of this wondrous master Hos, *Mistress*."

Saoirse only tugged her mouth up in a smile and said, "How wonderful. What a pleasant surprise." She was certain Ashira knew she was lying and forced herself to keep her gaze steady.

"We must announce to the people at once that you have been wed in a lavish ceremony at the... desert household, then, *Mistress*," Kettel said in a smooth voice, as though to step a foot in the desert household would invoke her death. "Invitations were very exclusive, as one can imagine for the gravity of the occasion, and only a small number of important individuals were able to be present."

Kettel paused dramatically and blinked at Saoirse. "This may invoke some hostility from those of the Temple. Yet it is necessary to ensure the people that you live here in respectability... I am certain you understand, *Mistress*?"

"Er..." Saoirse did not understand and was filled with alarm at the prospect of being the target of even further hostility from the elite. "Might there be another way, perhaps, Mistress?" she asked, resigning herself to the fact that she was stepping directly into their snare.

Kettel and Ashira looked to each other and nodded in a way that confirmed her greatest fears. "The people await with anticipation the formal Oracle inauguration ceremony. Yet this must not occur until repairs to the Temple are somewhat further along. Your wedding to Kaylem would be the most perfect celebration for the people to anticipate and focus on in their many challenges," Kettel said, eyes unreadable.

Saoirse, unsure of what to say, looked at the two women helplessly, praying one of them would speak first. The silence grew until, desperate, she spoke. "I see, Mistresses, and I thank you for your wisdom in this situation. And yet, planning such a celebration while the city is rebuilding... and so short on supplies..."

"With your pardon, *Mistress*." Ashira's lip curled upward in what could have been an eager smile if she hadn't noticed a hastily suppressed flash of contempt, "Wedding preparations are by tradition arranged together by the women of our great Temple, and there will be enough supplies for a grand feast."

Saoirse wished she could hurl obscenities at them, to shriek at them to leave and never come back. She doubted that any of the people of Ur, aside from the elite, would be permitted to join in

CHAPTER 23

whatever feast they arranged. Under the generous sleeves of her robe, her fingernails pressed painfully into her palms.

"Now, if you so desire, *Mistress*," Ashira continued, "I am in a position of influence to arrange the best of everything for the celebration. A short ceremony acknowledging the prior... union... may be advisable. It would give me great pleasure to assist, or even take from your hands, the wedding preparations, leaving yourself in peace to become better acquainted with your new abode."

Saoirse hoped the smile she gave Ashira was acceptable. There would be no way out of this. "Mistress Ashira, your generosity astounds me. I could never bear to burden you with such a tiresome task when you have so many other concerns at this time." An evil widow spider organizing her wedding would be preferable to Ashira.

"Please, *Mistress*, consider it a pleasure to take my mind from the present trivialities," crooned Ashira. "I would desire nothing more than to serve our new Oracle in this way."

"Of course, Ashira possesses true flair for creating memorable occasions," said Kettel in a voice that sounded ominous to Saoirse.

"I am honored and filled with gratitude for your offer," she choked out, hoping they would leave soon so she could hide from the world for a long time to recover.

"It is agreed then!" Ashira clapped her hands in glee, her eyes gleaming. "All you need do, *Mistress*, is find yourself a wedding robe. I myself will accompany you to the markets tomorrow to seek such a wonder, which will reflect the sacred glow of the moon in its full ripeness." She made a little squeaking noise which Saoirse assumed must mean joy.

"It is fortunate that the merchants have returned to Ur," Ashira continued. "It must be ordained by the gods that the first market day since the flood just happens to be tomorrow, of all days! Such wonders as you will find there. I tell you, *Mistress*, it is a blessing to have been born in Ur and not some backwater like Erech where I have heard the markets are pitiful."

Kettel nodded. "It is of utmost importance to return the great city of Ur to the way it has always been. This will comfort the people in their great loss. The markets assist us all to restore our faith in the gods and their mysterious ways..." Saoirse almost allowed her mouth to hang open but remembered to keep it shut and nodded instead.

"Bless the gods." Ashira assumed a dramatically worshipful pose, eyes skyward and hands splayed on her chest.

"And now we must take our leave, *Mistress*," Kettel said just at the moment when Saoirse was sure she could no longer hold back her scream. "Please forgive us for not staying longer, as we have many humble dwellings to visit. It has been such an honor to finally meet our new Oracle, even if so informally. Yet, once the wedding ceremony occurs there shall be the chance for us all to meet as deemed appropriate."

"I anticipate the day with such joy in my heart," Saoirse answered, filled with a new enthusiasm now that she knew they were leaving. "I thank you deeply for your visit, Mistress Kettel and Mistress Ashira. May the gods bless you both."

After they left, Saoirse allowed herself to collapse onto a bench in the reception chamber. She watched specks of dust float in a beam of sunlight and land silently on the vase, which dwarfed the room. The light slowly moved across it, bringing out different carvings across its surface.

Oxen were driven by a farmer. Two men bowed to an Anzu, his wings spread impressively behind him. The shape of his wings and the length of his torso were all wrong, she noticed uncharitably. She brought her gaze instead to a woman playing a harp who sat beside a scribe carving letters into a tablet, and then another woman feeding a babe from her breast. Then she stared at the dust motes again and how the sun played with them. Footsteps approached and Saoirse looked up as Kaylem peered timidly into the room.

"Have they gone?" he whispered, and Saoirse felt like laughing hysterically at him. It would have been the worst of social blunders if Kaylem had appeared in such a way in the midst of their visit. Instead, she gave a tiny nod. He sank down on the floor beside her.

"Oh gods," he whispered into her ear, shaking his head. "Those two are the worst of them all. You did well, Shaji."

"Did you hear it all?"

"This place carries the spoken voice even more effectively than we ever imagined, but I could not come for you until our favorite servant finished her oration about what wonderful pillars of our society those two are," he said with an eyeroll that made

CHAPTER 23

Saoirse growl.

'Kaylem, this is madness. We're already married, this is going to turn into a nightmare," she whispered back.

"Er... um..."

Saoirse waited for more. "Is that all you have to say? Er... um?"

Kaylem winced and held up a finger to silence her. He moved closer to her ear, and she flushed as his lips tickled her skin. "I don't know enough about the ways of the female side of the Temple, but it would have been considered a great honor for them to visit you, Shaji. Kettel is married to Anan, remember, and he is the Temple leader, after all."

"I'm not deluding myself that the meeting was a success," she mouthed.

He wagged his head back and forth. "You did your utmost. They are very skilled at making people feel small. There's no way you could have done any better."

"I've never felt so belittled by a gift, Kalyem! What were we thinking? That somehow, I could just walk into this dwelling and this new life, with a little bit of voice training, and be more than just a prostitute?"

Kaylem set his fingers lightly on her chin and drew her face to his. "Shaji, look at me." Saoirse blinked the tears from her eyes as she looked up at him. "The day you feel equal to them will be the day I grieve a thousand tears, as you'll have become one of them." He smoothed the tears from her cheeks and kissed her forehead. "You need to remember the master's teachings on how to hold a part of yourself separate while you play their game."

He kissed her nose, her cheeks, and her forehead again, and she leaned into his touch for the first time in what felt like forever. It wouldn't be long before Maryam would discover they were alone. "What a shame such a thing of mastery was gifted by this pair," he said in a rueful whisper. "Imagine if we could somehow cleanse it from its source so we can actually enjoy its beauty."

"It is beautiful," she said as she allowed herself to be distracted by the carvings again. "It just felt like they could see right through me to the core," she murmured into his robe.

"Their art of seeing into people goes only as far as how much they can attack and belittle you. For what it's worth, it can only bother you as much as you allow it."

Saoirse sighed for what must have been the hundredth time and Kaylem stroked her again.

"You made it through the first introduction, Shaji. We always knew this would be difficult, but you've been chosen for this path, remember that. The gods have faith that you can achieve this."

"Can we walk, Kaylem? I have to get out of here, these walls are suffocating me, and I need fresh air or I'm going to go crazy. That will help me get my mind off it all."

Kaylem cringed for a moment. "Shaji, for someone of your position to walk aimlessly around out there among the rabble, just for the sake of walking… it's considered… coarse."

"What?" She wanted to yell and scream and rage. "You mean to say I can never just leave here to go anywhere without you or one of the servants? And then only for a good reason?"

"Things may have changed since the flood, but… well, the women of the temple are very cloistered and usually never leave."

"Scourge of the gods, Kaylem, you never told me that. I would never have come here if I'd known—"

"Shh, please Shaji." Kaylem's eyes were suddenly huge, and he flicked his eyes back in the direction of Maryam. His skin was suddenly paler than Saoirse had seen in a long time, and Saoirse had to suppress an urge to slap him. She reminded herself that the ridiculous laws of the Temple weren't his doing. "Let's take some mugs of ale up to the rooftop, eh?" he said hastily. It's so nice up there and has a great view of the city, and it's noisy outside so it's very private."

Saoirse knew when to admit defeat, for now. With a furious grunt, she followed Kaylem up the narrow staircase and out onto the roof top. The kitchen servant appeared not long after with mugs of ale, staring in an intently curious way at the tense silence between Saoirse and Kaylem. Saoirse sent the woman away with a tone that was possibly a little sharp, and then felt guilty about the flinch in the servant's eyes, which only made her frustration worse.

She tried to enjoy the beauty of the city from a distance, the prettiness of the cushions lying sheltered under a palm-shade. The ale was delicious, but it was difficult to make herself relish it, since there was a whole population of people below her slowly starving to death, while she sat up here practically a prisoner in her own home. She stared out at the bay, Kaylem equally quiet beside her, the water glistening benignly in the sunlight.

CHAPTER 24

"*Mistress?*"

Saoirse forced her eyes open and squinted in the torchlight cutting through the pitch darkness. Asi's silhouette stood above her, a cringe to her posture.

"What in the name of the gods? Has someone died?" Certainly, that was the only reason to wake her up in the middle of the night.

"I regret to awaken you so early, *Mistress*. Ashira awaits you in the reception chamber to escort you to the markets."

"Now?" Saoirse looked at Asi in despair. Surely this was a joke.

"She has been offered refreshments and is content to wait until you are prepared."

"But it took an hour to prepare me yesterday, and I still looked like a street urchin next to her…" Saoirse pushed herself up from the pallet, only to collapse straight back down from a bout of dizziness.

"*Mistress!*" Asi reached to support Saoirse as she arose. "Shall I tell her you are unwell?"

"I only wish you could, and then I could go back to sleep and pretend this is not happening," she grumbled as she forced herself up more slowly this time.

With Asi's faltering help, Saoirse dressed in record time, praying that the robe she had chosen was appropriate. Perfumed oil was applied behind her ears and under her arms as there was no time to wash properly. A rinse of charcoal and anise was used to freshen her breath, while Asi tamed Saoirse's long, thick hair to sit properly under the head scarf.

Saoirse looked critically at her reflection in the polished piece of bronze in the gloom. Even despite the lack of clarity in its reflection, she could see creases in her skin from the sleeping pallet. Her eyes were puffy and showed her exhaustion, especially after tossing and turning for so long the night before. While Asi finished the remaining touches on her hair, Saoirse applied a line of the charcoal and oil mix to the delicate parts under her eyes and over the lids, praying for a steady hand.

Her stomach growled and she hoped one of the other servants had prepared something she could eat in a hurry, otherwise the nausea would hound her for the rest of the day. Asi followed along silently behind her. Still lightheaded, Saoirse made her way carefully down the steep steps, heart palpitating at the stress of the sudden awakening at such an early hour.

Today, she would be choosing the fabric for her wedding robe if Ashira had spoken true yesterday. The whole area around her chest tensed convulsively at the thought. She couldn't even bring herself to think about the actual wedding day, let alone the consecration ceremony a moon later.

She pushed the thoughts of both to the back of her mind as she passed the hearth. Asi was rustling around in the store and then passed her a pouch of nuts and dates, and a mug of ale. Saoirse paused for a moment to smile at her in appreciation. Asi blushed and turned rapidly away. Crunching as fast as she could on some nuts, and washing them down with the ale, Saoirse paused outside the entry to the reception chamber, heart jumping frantically around in her chest, before rounding the final corner where Ashira impatiently awaited.

"Ashira! I am so grateful to see you this beautiful and early morning," Saoirse said through a constricted throat, hoping there was no flecks of nuts in her teeth.

"Ah, *Mistress*, I regret to have awakened you from your slumber. Please, allow me to straighten your scarf which lies crooked. Such a fine one it is, too. Was it from the markets?" Ashira was immaculately dressed in a far finer outfit than her own, and Saoirse told herself she would not allow herself to go down that same pathway again. She moved her mouth in a smile that felt like armor.

"And likewise, your scarf is delightful, Mistress Ashira. You must show me where at the markets you find such pieces, as I have never found anything to match it."

"I have a merchant who brings me more than just the usual offerings, *Mistress*. I do tire so of the same things displayed month after month. This merchant makes special trips to exotic regions. It is worth the interminable wait, and he informed me he would be back by today. It is imperative we are early as the exceptional pieces will be gone if we tarry. We must leave immediately."

"I see. Would you like to join me for the morning meal before we go?"

"Why, it would be impossible to force myself to eat at such an early hour. Shall I keep you company while you avail?"

Saoirse imagined attempting to eat under the gaze of Ashira and her belly shriveled. "It is of no matter…" The tiny handful of nuts would have to do until later, and she hoped she would find something to eat once they arrived there. "Very well then. Shall we?" Saoirse smiled brightly, pulse thundering in her ears. She blinked away the vertigo and forced her limbs to move.

"Would your manservant be coming, *Mistress*?" Saoirse looked down at Asi, ready to go. "To carry for you," Ashira said meaningfully, while looking on in scorn at Asi.

"Ah, yes. Forgive me. I am not quite awake." She turned to Asi, who bobbed and then melted into the darkness.

"The manservant will be here shortly, mistress." Asi bobbed once again as required and Saoirse noticed she trembled.

Ashira gasped. "Servant girl! That is not the correct way to address the great Oracle," snapped Ashira, no longer so reserved away from Kettel's presence. "Such insolence you should never stand, *Mistress*." Ashira shook Asi roughly by the shoulders who stared wide eyed up at her.

"Who is this child? Where is the handservant?" Ashira slapped Asi's face. Saoirse looked on, almost as shocked as Asi.

"The correct address for the Oracle is *Mistress*, and only the head priestess of our great Temple shares that great honor. Do you understand? I do not know how you came to be calling our revered Oracle something so lowly as mistress." She spat the word as though Asi had flung Saoirse a hideous insult. Asi cringed away from Ashira.

"Servant girl. Your apology to the Oracle. Now!"

"*Mistress*," Asi sobbed, "A thousand regrets for my misdeed.

May the gods forgive me and bless the Oracle." Asi's thin chest hitched, and Saoirse resisted a guilty compulsion to comfort her, which would surely have resulted in even more grave insult being taken.

"Shall we, *Mistress*?" Ashira smiled at Saoirse as though the moment before had never happened. As they left the dwelling, Saoirse noticed an enormous looking maleservant who bowed deeply to them, as well as a handservant who looked better dressed than Saoirse. They followed behind, the male looking somewhat disheveled as he had emerged blearily at Asi's summons. They made quite the procession as they headed off, and Saoirse couldn't help but feel a small amount of excitement if only because she was finally allowed to leave the dwelling. The markets were not far, much to Saoirse's relief. The nausea was especially bad this morning for some strange reason.

"*Mistress*, you look pale. Are you unwell?"

"I do not do well in the mornings. Some dates and yogurt at the markets will suffice."

"I see." Even through the exaggerated sympathy brimming from Ashira's eyes, Saoirse could see the calculation behind it. They walked in silence for the rest of the way, Ashira looking as though she was considering something vitally important.

As they rounded the destroyed foundations of a deserted building, the market square opened before them in the wan light. Already the markets were thronging with people who haggled vigorously and laughed with their companions, and Saoirse couldn't believe how busy they were. The first rays of the sun had not yet even made their way to the horizon, and everything was still in gloom.

"The food stalls are yonder, *Mistress*. Have you your coin ready?"

Saoirse's heart sank. In her haste she had forgotten her coin. Ashira laughed with no amusement in her eyes.

"I have more than enough. If you send the servant back, I am sure that Kaylem will provide you with a pouch."

"Yes, of course, Mistress. Many blessings. Asi! Tell Kaylem I have come without coin, and he must give you enough for a noteworthy purchase." She prayed Kaylem would read into her request enough to provide Asi with more than just one pouch of coin, as she had the sense that this trip to the markets would be

CHAPTER 24

far from a bargain.

"*Mistress*," Asi said perfectly, and bowed deeply on knees that still trembled. Saoirse forced herself to turn away and Ashira pointed at a stall overflowing with food. Saoirse forced down dates, bread and yogurt, glad that Ashira and her servant were tactfully appraising a stall selling bread instead of watching Saoirse's indelicate manners.

The sun began to throw its light and as she ate, Saoirse looked over to the distant Temple, its soaring tip now illuminated. She turned away, unwilling to be reminded of the trials she would soon be facing in order to be part of its toxic workings, its false beauty mocking her. Scooping the last of the yogurt onto a date, she prayed that the meal had come soon enough to quell the nausea. It wasn't often that she was actually sick unless she waited too long to eat.

As she gingerly drank another cup of morning ale, she sent it down with a request for her stomach to behave, then sat on a bench next to the stall. Mentally telling Asi to take her time so she would have the chance for the food to settle, Saoirse watched Ashira haggle with the baker nearby, in her high, brittle voice. Ashira was busy accusing the baker of wishing to bleed his customers dry.

Saoirse allowed the gentle morning sun to warm her face, and she would have liked to fall asleep right there, to relax like some of the others who sat next to her. With a start, she realized that Ashira would be horrified to know she sat on this bench with any manner of people beside her. With a sigh, she got up and headed toward Ashira, who was pulling coin from a pouch to pay the baker. Saoirse was sure Ashira would make some kind of comment later about the spectacle of the Oracle sitting with the good citizens of Ur.

"*Mistress!*" A whisper in her ear surprised her, and she looked up as Asi stood before her. The towering form of Kaylem's most trusted manservant carried a sack, and Saoirse felt a wave of relief that Kaylem had understood.

"Bless you, Asi," she whispered back, hoping Ashira was far out of hearing range. Asi blushed again and looked to the ground uncomfortably. It was undoubtedly a grave social error to express appreciation to a servant, especially after that servant had been so harshly disciplined by such a high standing member of the

Temple elite.

Saoirse rejoined Ashira and they walked in the direction of the women's stalls. They all craned their necks to see the incredible sights of multicolored fabrics, gaudy scarves flapping in the breeze, and everywhere the hubbub of women haggling vigorously with merchants.

Ashira noticed the newly arrived manservant with the sack of coin who stood next to Saoirse, and her hand fluttered to her chest. "Blessed gods, *Mistress*! I do pray we will not be needing quite *that* much coin. It is dangerous to be seen carrying such riches. We must hurry. Come and meet my merchant. His name is Abdul."

"*Mistress*!" Abdul simpered, bowing low and making Saoirse feel somehow cheapened. Abdul stood like a petty king in his stall filled to overflowing with all manner of fabrics, trinkets, and other objects Saoirse would never have recognized. She suppressed an urge to run her hand over a statuette of some exotic foreign god that sparkled with gold and jewels that jumped out to her from the corner of her eye. "May a thousand blessings rain down upon the Oracle." Abdul's eyes flicked to the sack the manservant was carrying, widened slightly, and then his face became smooth again.

"I have heard of your wedding plans, *Mistress*. Such an honor you would bestow on the humble citizens of Ur. I have been travelling in far and mysterious lands to bring with me some extraordinary wares, many the likes of which even the high priestess has never laid eyes upon."

He gestured for them to enter deeper into his stall, and Saoirse turned this way and that, finally allowing herself to pick up fabrics and bend to look more closely at the wonders piled so artfully on the tables. Everything smelled exotic, like perfumed herbs.

"A piece befitting the new Oracle." He opened a chest studded with dazzling specimens of lapis lazuli, gold, and a shining, white crystal Saoirse had never seen. She forced herself to appear as nonchalant as possible, wishing she could reach out and trace her finger over the incredible workmanship of the pieces.

"The Oracle possesses a keen eye for beauty." Abdul glanced sideways at the sack of coin once again, and Saoirse suppressed a sigh of exasperation. Everything felt wrong. This was not how she should be preparing for a wedding celebration. She considered just calling to the servants and walking out of there, insisting that she could choose her own stall and her own robes.

Abdul, possibly sensing her attention wandering, jumped into action and opened another chest. She couldn't help but look, and almost regretted that she had. Inside the chest was the most amazing material Saoirse had ever seen, lying in folds inside the polished wood of the box. She reached out to run her hand over it.

"It is silk, *Mistress*; from the lands of Chin. My men have braved many dangers to bring this material to your sacred gaze, and it is one of a kind." Abdul handed the material to Saoirse, who received it with shaking hands. The silk fell in smooth, shining folds and the feel of it on her skin caused her to forget all attempts at composure. Its pattern was exquisite, with hand painted birds and other animals on a delicate green background.

Blinking back tears, she returned the material to its resting place inside the small chest, overwhelmed. Since the nausea in the mornings had started, she found it difficult to hide her emotions, and could feel a deep blush creeping up her cheeks. Both Ashira and the merchant had seen her moved. She should be aloof like Ashira if she was going to have a hope of getting this fabric for anything less than a king's fortune.

"I thank you Abdul for showing me such beauty, yet now I must gather myself. May you give me pardon to discuss with my companion?"

"It would delight me, *Mistress*. Please, take as long as you wish. I am here to serve." He bowed in such an exaggerated way he almost overbalanced and Saoirse could not stop a smile tugging at the corners of her mouth at such a ridiculous sight. Glancing at Ashira's expression stopped her cold.

"It is a charming piece, *Mistress*." Ashira's voice was cutting in a way that Saoirse was certain the merchant would hear. "Yet I have seen this many times before. Your mundane items are exasperating to the eye, merchant. What other pieces have you?"

Abdul blinked quickly, and Saoirse could have sworn that tears glimmered in his eyes. "Longer than a full year it took to travel to the lands of Chin, Mistress. My best man met his untimely end at the hands of the dreaded Mongols, and the other died of a mysterious illness. He was yellow as the sun from head to toe, even his eyeballs, as he handed me this precious bundle. Surely your accustomed and expert eye can attest to its extreme value."

"Oh Abdul, how you do expound. Your words are like the juice of the onion bulb; enough to bring tears of misery to my eyes. How I feel for your loss. Now, what of the other pieces?"

"Yes, very well, Mistress," he said offhandedly, suddenly back to his usual self. Saoirse was thoroughly astonished by the exchange, now grateful for Ashira's experienced presence. Again, the merchant's soft skinned hands reached into yet another chest, larger this time. When he opened it, she smelled the contents before seeing what was inside. The aroma spoke of delicate spice with a hint of smoke behind it. It was reminiscent of the faint, perfumed wafts emanating from the sacred areas of the Temple during ceremonies, although this was far stronger, and the scent was completely unfamiliar.

"It is sandalwood, *Mistress,*" whispered the merchant in reverence. "The priestcraft of the Indies burn it in their sacred rites. I invite you, great Oracle, to peruse what lays within."

"Sweet mercy of the gods." The exclamation escaped her before she could prevent it. Even Ashira was looking over her shoulder in awe. The fabric was inlaid with tiny threads of precious metals, jewels, and crystals, many unfamiliar to both the women. Abdul drew it out of the chest theatrically, evincing another gasp as it was displayed to its full length.

"I have been awaiting a moment such as this to uncover this most stunning cloth that even I have ever seen in my life as a merchant. I have carried it with me for many moons."

"Very well, Abdul. Name your coin and we will relieve you of your burden." Ashira had recovered from her momentary lapse of composure, although not before it was noticed by the merchant.

"I am reluctant to sell as I happen to have become extremely attached to it. I do not think I will ever make the journey back to the Indies. It was such a perilous journey, full of hardship and suffering. I went myself, unable to trust even my most faithful men. Almost did I not return, and as it was, I very nearly sold myself to bring this back. The things I was required to do in order to gain possession of this piece of magic filled cloth."

It sang to her. Saoirse could almost hear its siren call. For that moment she was almost willing to sell her soul to possess the gleaming treasure now folded carefully back in its place, and she was acutely aware that Abdul knew.

CHAPTER 24

"A thousand coin and the girl slave." Abdul's eyes were now hard flints of steel. The bargaining process had begun, and Saoirse almost collapsed with shock at the thought of allowing Asi to be purchased like an animal by this man.

"Five hundred coin and no girl slave. Abdul, shame on you." Ashira scolded.

"I have my eye on her to sell, not to take my own advantage."

"I will not sell the girl," Saoirse answered, the spell suddenly and violently broken. She turned to leave. Asi looked ready to collapse.

The bargaining continued back and forth until the sun was shining directly into the stall. Saoirse, feeling lightheaded again, was ready to turn and walk away, and the merchant paused a moment in his banter, suddenly aware of her loss of interest.

"Alternatively, *Mistress*, I have a unique proposition." The merchant's voice was almost pleading now. Saoirse turned reluctantly back. The fabric glittered and shimmered, almost blinding her now that the sun was shining directly onto it.

"*Mistress*, I have a matter that must be settled, and I have thought long about it over many a sleepless night. If your wise self can assist me in my conundrum, I will sell you the cloth for five hundred coin and no slave girl. If you cannot give me aid, I will take the girl and the five hundred coin. Is that a fair bargain, great Oracle?"

Saoirse couldn't even look at Asi as she listened to her fate being discussed, and nausea rose again, burning the back of her throat.

"I will not trade in human flesh, Abdul. Take a thousand coin if I cannot assist you and the deal will be equal to the servant girl." Her voice was trembling, and she forced the emotion violently away, stomach churning.

Abdul looked at Saoirse cunningly, with a gleam of amusement. He traded a look with Ashira, which Saoirse could not read.

"As you wish, *Mistress*. Your servant must be very valuable to you."

"I abhor the trade of human flesh," Saoirse snapped. There was a charged silence while the markets around them roared and throbbed with trade. Ashira was too knowing in her look as Saoirse simmered where she stood.

"Very well, *Mistress*." The merchant bowed again. "A great and rare privilege it is, to be one of the first to receive counsel from your eminent self. Would you do me the honor of accompanying me behind my curtain to give your advice on my situation?"

Saoirse nodded, regretting that she did not simply offer the extra coin. She was aware that this was a dangerous game the merchant and herself were playing. She was not even formally consecrated as Oracle, and to counsel a merchant would surely be considered to be lowering herself.

Ashira would probably be desperate to tell Kettel all the social crimes Saoirse had committed just in the past morning. The merchant held open the curtain for Saoirse and they sat on small stools in the cramped area, Asi standing behind her as chaperone and the large back of the manservant guarding the opening.

"Hand me something you are attached to so I can hold it while we talk. Your ring, it looks well worn; that will do. What is it that concerns you, Abdul?"

"*Mistress*," he said as he bowed deeply and handed over his ring, "I have heard of a treasure so vast the known world has never seen such riches. Of course, a merchant such as myself would roam far and wide to seek such a thing. Yet I am nearing the age where I yearn to settle and enjoy the modest fortune I have created for myself. Here is my dilemma. Would it be in my best interests to seek out this treasure, or is my fate leading me down a quieter path now that I near the sunset of my life?"

Saoirse, initially nervous, sat with her eyes closed and quieted her thoughts, focusing inside herself. She found herself listening to something the man said behind his words. It was concealed in the tone of his voice; a wistfulness, a desire beyond merely the treasure that might be found at the end of the journey. There was something else in that wistfulness; something she could relate to within herself.

With a start she realized it was loneliness. The man was nearing a time when he would no longer be able bodied enough to travel. It was the need to travel as a merchant that had reduced his prospects of establishing close ties with anyone. She could sense him sitting opposite her, his breathing suddenly loud in the small space. Understanding flowed through her. A powerful sense of steadiness and certainty filled her, and she opened her mouth without knowing quite what she was going to say.

CHAPTER 24

"I wonder, Abdul, whether you are asking the right question. What I am sensing is that you are uncertain whether you will ever find one to share your heart with. And, if you stay in the one place and do not find a suitable wife, will it be too late to embark upon that final adventure?"

Abdul drew in a great, surprised breath and nodded. "I do not just want to marry any woman. Most I've met have been dreadfully vapid and would only infuriate me."

Saoirse nodded and sat quietly again, touching on the place of the Knowing, sensing it stir. Focusing inside herself, she almost gasped. It was as though an eye had opened inside her head and she watched in fascination as two paths formed before her. The sounds of the market dropped completely away. "There are riches awaiting you on either path," she told the merchant in a halting voice as she followed the paths to their end. "No matter which you should choose, there lie many tests and trials…"

"What do you see, *Mistress*?"

Her stomach lurched. It reminded her of a gentler version of when she had touched Thar before the flood, and she forced herself not to retch, instead bringing her attention back inward. Drawing deeper into her vision, she drew her breath in sharply. "I see Temples; sacred Temples different to that of Ur. Not built with steps, as their sides rise straight into the sky to form a point…" Saoirse shook her head in awe, eyes still closed.

"Astounding! All worship occurs deep within rather than at the top. Their shape serves to magnify the sound of prayer to the gods, and the Temples sit, not alone, but in groups together in the sandbanks of a great river. The Temples are placed in the configuration of the stars above! To this day they have not been pillaged by godless ones…" Saoirse's voice became harsh, and she opened her eyes. The merchant was trembling, looking at her in awe.

"The second path… many perils lurk of a different nature. The direction is one that no feet may tread, even though the distance is great. This path holds instead the possibility of seeking riches within, as you seek to satisfy the longings of the heart. For this you must work even harder than you ever did to broker a deal. What you yearn for more than anything in the world is the greatest treasure of all." Her voice dropped to a whisper and the merchant leaned forward, captivated. Saoirse could smell his sweat, and a spiced hair oil that wasn't nearly as nice as Kaylem's.

"This treasure," she continued, "cannot be found anywhere in the world, no matter how far you travel. This road will not be easy. You must also wait long before you conquer the hunger within to satisfy only yourself. Once you learn to place another's needs before your own, and I mean truly from your heart, then you will find what you are looking for most of all." The merchant sighed like a young girl.

"That is all I need speak of for this path, and all I must say in order for you to make your choice…" Her vision cleared and the merchant was bulging-eyed, sweating, and a strange shade of gray. She handed his ring back and he took it with a trembling hand. "I wish you all the fortunes of the gods that you find your treasure no matter which path you choose."

To her surprise, Abdul suddenly lowered his head and began to weep like a child. Asi stood watching with a gaping mouth and Saoirse gave her a small, subtle nudge with her toe. There was a tiny click as her mouth snapped closed, which spurred the merchant to collect himself with a vigorous clearing of the throat. He reached through the curtain with a meaty hand that still shook a little and held the magic cloth out to Saoirse.

"Take the cloth as my gift to you, *Mistress*, in return for the greatest gift you could ever have given. You are truly the Oracle and you carry the voice from the gods. I thank you for freeing me from my inner torment."

The merchant wiped fresh tears from his eyes, then turned away momentarily to wrap the sparkling fabric in a swathe of cheap, plain weave from a messy pile in one corner. They stood, too close in the cramped area, and the merchant handed the bundle to Saoirse, bowing as deeply as the space allowed. As he turned to make his way back through the curtain, Saoirse watched in awe as his face shifted back to that of the fawning, hard-hearted merchant.

"The great Oracle and I have come to an agreement, Mistress Ashira." the merchant said in a high, servile voice, bowing low over and over again. Ashira's eyes narrowed as she looked from Saoirse to the merchant, as though the exclusion from such a momentous occasion was a grievous and unforgivable insult.

Saoirse suppressed a shudder. She was sure that Ashira would tell the elite every detail of the terrible behavior of the new Oracle,

CHAPTER 24

ruining any remaining shred of empathy before even meeting them. Ashira nodded to the merchant, indicating for Saoirse to follow with a bow that spoke volumes of her silent wrath as she turned sharply on her heel and stalked from the stall.

Ashira set a return pace that was impossible for Saoirse to follow. Soon, flanked by the servants, she fell back so far, she could no longer make out Ashira's scarf in the teeming crowds. The servants guided her into a reeking side alley away from the jostle of the people which made the nausea peak in an urgent wave. Leaning against a wall for support, she surrendered to the rising tide that had been so narrowly kept at bay for the morning.

Her stomach convulsed and she expelled its contents onto the stained yellow-brown earth. The manservant stood to block the view of those passing, and Asi wiped her brow and offered a sip from a bladder. Soon she felt strong enough to continue, Ashira nowhere to be seen. As they trudged back to the abode, Saoirse was relieved, but at the same time aware, that Ashira had delivered a grave insult in not formally taking her leave.

Her thoughts turned to the strange turn of events this morning which sent her hands digging into the package to yet again feel the texture of the incredible fabric that she couldn't wait to show Kaylem. At least that part of the morning had been successful.

CHAPTER 25

Saoirse turned over yet again in her pallet, lined with furs so soft it felt like she was sleeping on a cloud. It was late. The moon was shining brightly through the wall vent— not yet in its full ripeness which would happen soon, but on its way. She would marry Kaylem for the second time at the full moon, which still made her want to scream out her frustration that she wasn't permitted to spend any time with him at all until then, unless one of the servants were present.

Only very occasionally were they allowed a moment together on the roof, but too soon Maryam or one of the other servants would be breathing down their necks to ensure nothing untoward was happening. Saoirse would have laughed hysterically at the irony if she didn't miss him so much.

She could almost feel the time trickling away until she would come face to face with the rest of the Temple elite and formally meet them all. It felt like counting the days to her execution, even while she desperately wished for the wait to be over so she could spend intimate time with Kaylem again. Weddings were usually to be celebrated with close family and friends. Saoirse had only Kaylem.

It had been growing silently inside for a while now; an ache, a yearning for the solace only female friendship could bring. The moon sat like a silent eye, pinning her beneath its glare as she turned over once again. Winter had begun to lose its grip on Ur, but she still had her covers pulled to her throat. She wondered if it was only the covers that kept her lying there, watching as the

CHAPTER 25

moon made its way slowly across the sky.

Soon it would be morning again, and that made Saoirse's throat close over. She could look forward to yet another day of continually putting Maryam in her place, silently tensing against her subtle insults with absolutely no escape at all. Close to tears, Saoirse turned over once again. The moonlight brought out the shadows in the corners of the room. Her chamber was ridiculously large; the largest room she had ever been in. She should have been filled with gratitude to be sleeping in something so grand and yet it was wasted on her. All she could think about was the desert sky, where the hoot of the owl and the night insects would give a calming lullaby that she missed like her own limb.

And when she had last been in Ur, she had had the girls to sleep beside at the inn. Their sleep noises were the lullaby she had fallen into slumber with. She had become accustomed to Kaylem nearby after they were married at the household. Now, Kaylem slept somewhere else, and she had hardly seen him for days. There was nobody except Asi who was a servant, a child.

She threw the covers from her body and strode to the corner where her robes hung over the new clothing rack. There was the robe that Kaylem had strongly recommended she throw out, hung partially hidden right at the back against the wall. The robe's sleeves were too short, the cloth too coarse, and the elite would be scandalized if they ever saw her in it.

She didn't know why she was still attached to it after all this time, given that it was the one she had worn the fateful night that everything changed after the flood. That and the dagger were the only things she had kept from her life before, and she dug into a small niche beside her pallet to find it. Then, she hugged the robe to herself as though she was a small child comforting herself. It would be perfect for what she was about to do.

Pulling it over her shoulders, Saoirse tied the plainest of her scarves over her hair while contemplating how best to make her way out onto the street. She had been watching closely the past few days, observing where the servants slept, making sure to wander now and then in the dead of night to ensure her presence at this time was not unusual.

She wrapped a shawl around herself, hoping that if one of the servants did happen to catch her out, she could pretend she was just wandering the abode as usual. So much for this place being her home, she thought as she nervously tiptoed her way through room after room until she found the small back entrance. The door let out a squeak that she was sure would awaken every person in the entire neighborhood. She winced as she shut it slowly, hardly able to breathe, and scuttled away as fast as she could.

Peeking back from around the corner, she saw that there were no wall vents glowing with newly lit candles, and no other sounds or sights of anyone stirring. With a sigh of relief, she disappeared into the night, the partially swollen moon all she had to guide the way. In the pre-flood days, Saoirse would have had no trouble finding the way to her destination. Now, there were no familiar landmarks and she had to go on her sense of direction alone. She stayed in the shadows, freezing at every skitter and screech of rats and other night animals of the city.

The mud, now dried into cold, stinking hardness, was uneven beneath her feet and she frequently tripped as she made her way further into the poorer quarters of the city. It was around midnight. Of that she was somewhat certain, with the velvet quality of the darkness and the height of the moon which was her only company. Still, she felt the pressure of time heavily on her shoulders and it was with a sense of urgency that she moved, heart in her throat.

At last, she came upon some skeletons of buildings that looked familiar. Far enough away from the river to avoid the worst of the impact, the buildings had merely been waterlogged rather than crushed by the force of the water. Somewhere around here would also be the building where the chanting group had met. For a moment she stood in the wreckage of the place she thought it might have been.

A ghost of a tune flitted into her mind, the one which had traveled to her ear the day she had been reunited with master Hos and seen Kaylem for the first time since being banished from the household. Saoirse allowed a smile as she remembered being ushered by Jivan into the tiny hall, filled to the brim with people swaying and singing to the gods.

Heaviness that she wasn't even aware of loosened its stranglehold on her for a moment, and she breathed out a sigh. The day she discovered the chanting group had completely changed the course of her life. She wondered what might have been if she had ignored the urge to follow the music that day. Would everyone have died in the flood, including her? Would Ur

CHAPTER 25

now be an abandoned wasteland, never to be rebuilt?

And, where were Raya and Jivan now? Surely, since they were the first people who she told about the dream warning her of the flood, they must have made it to safety. She would get Kaylem to help her find them somehow and give them coin to rebuild the chanting hall. No matter how much the Temple forbade unsanctioned worship, she would give anything to be sitting next to Kaylem in a ramshackle room, on a threadbare cushion, with master Hos' reedy voice, than anything the Temple could offer.

A screech and frantic scrabbling jolted Saoirse out of her reverie. It was likely to be rats fighting over a morsel, but just in case a starving person might have been on the hunt, she did her best to silently sneak away from the place.

It didn't take her long to find the inn of Ur, and to her surprise the closer she drew, the more sign of life she found. A fire was burning, its flames dancing merrily on the surrounding pockmarked walls, and familiar voices sounded. She smiled silently to herself. As she rounded the corner, she saw six figures sitting around the fire and they were laughing. Saoirse smiled as she approached, aching now to be closer.

Near enough now to see their individual faces, Saoirse made ready to call out. As she took another step, her foot sank into a hole, and she fell with a loud clatter of limbs and swearing. The people around the fire fell silent. Cautious footsteps sounded close to her ear.

"It's me," she mumbled as she did her best to push herself back to standing. Her elbow hurt where it had knocked on something. Her knees were shaky, and she was sure she'd be covered in bruises the next day, not to mention mud.

The footsteps stopped and she heard an intake of breath.

"It's me," she said, more loudly. "Nergal's back end, how do I get out of this rutting hole? Bring me a gods-damned torch, I can't see a thing." She held up a twisted piece of something that felt like mud-stiffened fabric. "What is this junk? I'm all tangled up now, scum of the underworld, get this off me—"

"Girl?" Zara's voice was a sob. Beside Zara was Asher's silhouette. "Help me up," she instructed the innkeeper who had taken them in after they had escaped from the brothel in Erech and made their way to Ur.

"I figured as much," Asher said as he hoisted her out of the hole and helped unwind what looked like an old, rotting fur from her legs. "Nobody else has such a creative repertoire of curse words." He turned her way and called, "Careful there as you walk, *Mistress*." His voice was loaded with what to Saoirse sounded like amusement and irony. "The ground is full of holes."

"So I noticed," she grumbled, her chest suddenly overflowing with warmth as he held out his hands in welcome. "And call me Girl tonight please, Asher."

"Girl it is then," he answered after a pause. She approached the fire where the others squatted. Sybel and a couple of the servants from the inn of Ur stood as she neared. The servant boy who had saved her life after Milar tried to choke her to death, had grown taller, she noticed. His eyes were popping out of his head as she drew level with Sybel. Everyone went quiet. She endured it for an uncomfortable moment, the fire crackling behind them and the night insects the only sound.

"So, I don't see you for an age and all you can do is stare at me?" She prayed that the humor lacing her tone and the crooked smile was enough to defrost their shock.

"*Mistress*," whispered Zara, and Saoirse's shoulders drooped.

"No, Zara, please, not tonight" she breathed. "Tonight, I'm just Girl," she said in a stronger voice. "Nobody else. Just Girl. Just for tonight. Please!"

Another pause, a beat of silence until Sybel let out a cry and embraced Saoirse. Zara moved closer too, and soon the three of them were dancing around in an awkward three-way hug which threatened to trip them all into the fire.

"Watch it!" Asher called to them as they separated, and all began to talk at once.

"You found us on a good night, Girl. This is a good night, one of the only good nights since the flood. We found the biggest bundle of the supplies we'd buried. Right where you fell, I think."

"I can't imagine how things have been for you," she answered, ashamed. "I've been thinking of you all for so long, and we've only just returned."

There was another silence at that, as she could almost hear their thoughts wondering about where she had been, what she had been doing while they had almost starved or frozen to death over the winter moons.

"I am so sorry—"

CHAPTER 25

"No, Girl. We don't go there, just as you asked us to not call you by your title now." Zara took her hands. "See? We even have ale tonight. The well is fortunately still in operation, even though the water tastes like latrine run off... but tonight, we are celebrating our find. Come and join us, tell us everything and we will, too."

Saoirse allowed herself to be drawn closer to the fire, into the ring of the only people remaining of her old life, and for a moment felt like she had come home.

"I've thought of you all so much," she murmured as Asher himself pressed an ale into her hands.

"We've thought and spoken constantly of you too, Girl," Sybel answered, her voice still holding a measure of reserve that made Saoirse's chest feel heavy. They all fell silent again, and Saoirse watched the flames as she sipped her ale.

"How did you know?" Zara finally asked into the silence with a voice filled with wonder. "How did you know about the flood?"

"I had a dream," Saoirse told her, and she remembered back to that night, back to waking up in the shared chamber with the other girls, stomping around in a frenzy trying to find her robe. Still filled with despair after sending Kaylem away, resigned to the life she was trapped in. The flood had changed everything, and nothing, all at the same time she realized, as she smiled at them all.

"I thought we were being robbed," Zara said with a chuckle. "My head took a long time to recover."

"We found a spot," Sybel said softly. "At the top of the Temple. After we'd buried everything we could, we wrapped ourselves in layers and layers of shawls and scarves and we didn't wear one bangle or any charcoal on our eyes."

Saoirse smiled. "I'm so glad you made it to safety."

"Even while we had to take it in turns to half carry Lania—"

"She is at peace now," Saoirse told them, hoping they wouldn't look at her as some kind of monster. "I saw her in the innerworlds as she passed. She was happy to leave her body, happy to no longer be in pain..."

The silence around the fire was different this time.

"You never told us..."

"Zara, I hardly understood what was happening. I'm sorry I couldn't talk more about it with you. It was just a bunch of random dreams and images that would appear out of nowhere…" She took a deep breath, the fire smoke heavy in the air.

"The things I saw were small things that would happen later on… but they had no use in my life at the time, they didn't change anything. Like knowing a bird would be coming to peck at me at a certain time of day, in a certain place…" Asher nodded at her in recognition, "…or that I'd hear a snippet of conversation and know I'd heard it before. They weren't relevant to anyone else… or so I thought…"

"How long did this go on for?" Asher asked.

"Weeks, or even moons, I guess. Maybe longer. After I saw Kaylem again it became stronger."

"And nothing like that ever happened to you before?" Zara wouldn't stop until she was satisfied she had all the details. Saoirse resigned herself to being here for a while but was mindful of watching the sky in case it began to lighten. Then she would really need to race away.

"Well… it did… but I was always told to keep it quiet, not to tell anyone. And then my parents died even though I begged them not to go on that fishing trip. And after that, every time I opened my mouth to tell someone something, all I got from people was fear and hatred as though I was some evil daemon. As though it was my fault those things happened that I warned them about. For a long time, I just wanted it to disappear…"

"And now..."

"Now I'm to be married in a very public and, I'm sure, demeaning way within a few days, when the moon is next at Her ripest. Then, the consecration ceremony to name me Oracle is the month after."

"But you sound like you're not happy to be marrying the one you always called to in your dreams," Zara said.

"We are already married. It hasn't been recognized by the Temple, so at the moment, I can't even speak to Kaylem without someone playing chaperone. And, the women of the Temple are organizing my *true and proper* wedding," she spat. "I'm dreading what they've planned, to tell you the truth."

Zara laughed, a harsh sound which brayed into the night and echoed off the crumbling walls. "Oh gods, the irony of keeping you of all people from getting under your beloved's robes. They couldn't have found a more insulting way to keep you under their

CHAPTER 25

control."

"I know… they couldn't have found a better way to make me miserable if they'd tried."

There was a beat of silence again as the conversation lulled. Saoirse looked up at the sky again and noticed the darkness was beginning to thin. It wasn't just the smoke making its way into the air. That was a hint of purple. It must have taken longer than she thought to find them, and now all too soon it was time to take her leave.

"I have to get back," she told them. They all embraced her, one by one, even the servants. Zara told her to use her special powers to make all the evil ones regret the day they were born. If only she could do that, she replied. Sybel merely held her and wept. Asher insisted on accompanying her to the near invisible boundary of where the inn's walls used to be, guiding her around the many holes. She pushed a pouch of coin into his hands as he bid her farewell.

"Don't come back, Saoirse," Asher growled into her ear after nodding solemnly in thanks. "I mean it. Turn around and don't ever return. This life was never meant for you. I don't know how you managed to come tonight, but this was the only night we've even had something to burn for a fire since the flood, the only time any of us have had something to feel joyful for. Go out there and make our world better, and don't look back ever again."

Despite the darkness, she saw a small smile on his face, the hint of tears lining his eyes. She smiled back and nodded, turning only when his silhouette became one with the darkness itself, and then ran the rest of the way back to the abode.

A single wall vent was lit up when she returned. Swearing under her breath, silently cursing with every foul word she had ever heard, she shrank into the shadows as she pondered how she could get back in. The servants were more than likely all awake now that dawn was so close. She had left it too long. Without the fire to keep her warm, the night air made its way through the small gaps in the fabric of her shawl, creeping into her robe. Her teeth started chattering as she watched and listened, cursing herself every moment.

"Yes, mistress," came a voice Saoirse knew well. It was Asi's, and she sounded afraid. "I will clean it properly."

"And do not come back until it's perfect," Maryam called

after her. Maryam left the servant door open and yellow light leaked out of the crack.

"Asi," Saoirse whispered, and Asi jumped with a small cry.

"*Mistress?*"

"Quiet, Asi. Please, can you get me back to my chamber without anyone seeing? I can pretend I was in the bathing room or wandering on the roof. I don't want anyone to know I was out."

"I will try, *Mistress*, but the servants are up. Maryam is likely at the hearth." Asi's eyes popped out of her head as she took in the simple shawl, the threadbare robe underneath and the scarf tied to make Saoirse look like a commoner. They wended their way through the abode in the near darkness, Saoirse grateful for the small body leading the way, until Asi bowed and moved aside so that Saoirse could pass through.

"Thank you, Asi, I know you were supposed to clean something. You can let Maryam know I wanted you for something if it doesn't happen to her liking. And need I ask that you don't mention what you saw here?"

"Of course, *Mistress*," Asi stammered. "I must go." She bowed her head again and disappeared into the darkness. Saoirse removed her clothes, flattening them under her pallet to hide them. They smelled of fire and night and freedom, and she patted the small unevenness with a grin, returning the knife to its hole. Throwing on her sleep shift, she pulled her furs up under her chin, meaning only to lie there for a few moments before rising. Before she knew it, she was awoken by the sun pouring in hours later through the wall vents; to Asi bustling around in the corner.

CHAPTER 26

"*Mistress*, it is time."

Saoirse groaned. It seemed only moments ago that she had finally closed her eyes, which felt grainy and sore after a near sleepless night. She squinted away from the candle that left dancing spots in her vision as she blinked.

"Your wedding robe was delivered late last night, *Mistress*. Here, I hold the parcel!" Asi's entire being was tense with what sounded like excitement. She wished she could feel the same. At least the robe had arrived, but she wouldn't relax until she saw it with her own eyes.

"There is warm water for washing in the bathing chamber. Kasib is tending to master Kaylem to ready him for you."

Saoirse sighed and pushed herself up. "Thank the gods... I lay awake worrying that I'd be wearing the old peasant's robe instead," she joked. Asi's eyes widened and her mouth tightened. She hoped Asi hadn't been punished after the other night's wanderings.

As she tried to stretch the stiffness from her body, she could already feel her heart jumping around in her chest, and suddenly she was wide awake. She had deliberately refused to think about what she must do today until now, and along with her heart, her stomach threatened to exit her body through her throat.

There was no possibility of avoiding this climb to the lesser Temple Sanctum, half way up the Sacred Steps. She was grateful to at least have Asi as one of her attendants, who would help support her if she faltered. And, at least, she had the robe of wondrous fabric from the merchant to look forward to, she hoped. The parcel was in the corner, and she glanced at it as she made her way to the bathing chamber to ready herself for the day.

Ashira had insisted on arranging for the jewel-encrusted cloth to be sewn into the ceremonial garment Saoirse would wear for the occasion. Ashira had proclaimed to know the best seamstress in the known world, who must be appointed to such a sacred duty. Saoirse couldn't help feeling a little burst of dread on eyeing the package now, sitting so innocently, still on the floor.

She had spent a mortifying afternoon naked, aside from a rough shawl, while the seamstress measured her body thoroughly under the gleaming eyes of Ashira. A few times Saoirse had questioned Ashira as to why such close measuring was necessary, since ceremonial robes were by their very nature loose and flowing. The seamstress had told her that herself.

Shivering as she pulled a blanket around her, still watching the package as though it was a dangerous animal, Saoirse sipped at some warm water with lemon. She thought about the sweating, groaning men who would right now be dragging an enormous, bronze vat of consecrated river water to the Temple in order for her to purify herself before the ceremony. This would again be scheduled to happen a month later to prepare for the Oracle Ceremony, where she must walk up the entire Sacred Steps to the top of the Temple. For today, thankfully, the walk was much shorter. Saoirse supposed that the walk was the least of her worries, considering what else might happen today.

All Temple workers were required to undergo this cleansing sacrament on the day of their wedding, as well as for their consecration, although the lesser priests and priestesses were given unheated water. For the more important dignitaries, they would light a small fire underneath to warm it for her, and she was at least grateful for this small mercy. She was almost looking forward to an hour of solitude immersed in pleasant warmth, with fragrant oils and rare desert flowers added to the water. She hoped Ashira hadn't insisted the water be cold as part of her punishment.

Asi handed her the wrapped bundle containing her robe and stood nearby so she could see the finished garment for herself. Saoirse tore open the loosely sewn protective fabric with a slight shake of her hands, almost scared to look at what lay within.

"But what's this?" Saoirse dropped the package and it came

loose from its wrapping. Of course, she thought as she kicked it savagely. "A curse of the Alal on that filthy rat's spawn!" she hissed. Asi looked at her wide eyed. Footsteps sounded and Asi turned to shoo whoever it was away. Kaylem's rumble sounded, and she wished she could bury her head into his chest and feel his arms around her.

She looked back down at the now crumpled, yet beautifully sewn robe made of shimmering green, hand painted silk from the land of Chin. Picking it up with a snarl, Saoirse saw that the robe was far from the voluminous ceremonial garb she pictured. Instead, the garment was even more scandalous than the prostitute's robe she once wore. Asi made a small sound of distress.

"My fabric..." Saoirse whispered. "My beautiful fabric, given to me as a gift of gratitude from the merchant." Her eyes stung and she ground her teeth so hard they hurt. "I will today see it hanging on that disgusting, evil bitch from the netherworlds with the vile Kettel watching on in satisfaction."

She leaned against the nearest wall and slid down its rough surface, feeling the harsh scrape of mud-brick on her back through the thin fabric of her sleep robe. It was too late now to do anything about it, and the anger turned to despair. There truly was nothing else she could wear today. Still, the punishment was light considering Ashira had been furious to be excluded from closing the deal with Abdul. Kaylem had warned her to expect Ashira to retaliate, but there wasn't much that could have been done about it and now it was time for the next move. Ashira had played the game to perfection so far. Saoirse was even less eager to face the day now, given what other nasty surprises might be waiting for her.

Asi's hands were shaking as they reached for the offending robe. Saoirse held it up to her. "Maybe with scarves..." Saoirse's voice shook as she rested her forehead against the wall, fresh tears making their way down her cheeks.

"*Mistress*," Asi said in a tone that was far too hopeful for any outcome Saoirse could visualize, but she looked up anyway. "It seems the seamstress has included the remaining material in the package." Asi pulled a rustling swathe of material forth and smiled a small smile.

"But it's not far from sunrise. How can anything be done now?'

Asi's thin chest puffed out a little and she smiled "*Mistress*, my sewing skills are far from that of a seamstress, but my mother was one. She was the fastest to sew a garment in all of Ur and she taught me well. It would be a small work to change its shape to the proper one with the help of a needle if you... ouch!" She put her finger to her lips with an even wider smile, and Saoirse looked at her in confusion. "*Mistress*, here we have a fine, sharp bone needle! It seems that the seamstress may have suffered a crisis of conscience."

"Oh, Asi!" Fresh tears made their way down Saoirse's cheeks, and she only wished to embrace Asi to herself as she had embraced her friends at the inn not so many nights ago. Asi only bobbed her head and Saoirse thought she might have seen yet another blush to the girl's cheeks.

Arms full of fabric and everything else needed for the repair, Asi disappeared into the darkness while Saoirse hastily dressed in a different robe. The manservant accompanied Saoirse to the Temple for the cleansing ritual, to be followed soon by Kaylem and his own set of rituals. Gripping a small parcel of dates, nuts, and crumbling goat's cheese, also pressed into her hand by Asi, Saoirse nibbled as she walked, blessing her handservant for her thoughtfulness.

She prayed it was enough to avoid the nausea that still came over her like a wave if she did not eat early enough after waking. It would be catastrophic to hurl up the contents of her stomach in front of the entire population of Ur, or even worse, on the Sacred Steps. Saoirse pushed that thought away and focused on her steps and her chewing.

There was a small ripple of guilt as Saoirse remembered the instructions from the high priestess given very clearly—that she must fast all of today in honor of the sacredness of the occasion. Saoirse had nodded equally as seriously and agreed that she would, knowing it would be one promise she'd have to break. Given the lack of honor of the Temple elite, she didn't feel as bad as she might have for her lie.

The large maleservant walking behind Saoirse carried a large, smoking torch to guide them on their way through the dark city streets. The moon was shining almost like an eerie sun, peeking over one of the nearby buildings. It made more shadows than light, and she was glad of the accompanying servants, even

CHAPTER 26

though they were there in place of family.

At the thought of family, Saoirse almost stopped walking. She nearly collapsed onto her knees right there on the rough ground. It should have been her parents with her instead of servants, or at least a group of her friends. Maybe even a sibling would have been nice had her parents ever been wealthy enough to bring another child into the world. Forcing herself to block the tide of grief so strong she could hardly breathe, she compelled herself to keep moving. Kaylem would be her friend and family.

Once she could freely spend time with him, after tonight, things would be better, she told herself for the thousandth time. They reached the entry to the Temple complex and the guards, nobody she recognized, bowed deeply to her. She forced herself not to bow back. Some other guards emerged from the gloom and joined them, also bowing deeply. She would bow her head to nobody, aside from the high priestess and Anan, the temple leader, even though he far from deserved it. They turned aside to skirt the great base of the Temple and made their way behind the building to the flood-damaged priestesses' quarters.

Inside a large chamber whose walls were so scarred Saoirse worried they might fall down around her, lay the steaming vat of water that she would bathe in to begin her purification ritual. Flaming torches made the shadows dance, and more priestesses than she could count stood watching. The high priestess, in her meeting a few days earlier, had mentioned this would happen, but it did not settle the unease of completely disrobing in front of so many other women. All of them bowed as one, then stood, the front ones holding jars of various substances to anoint her with before they would leave her blessedly alone in the room.

Holding in the tiny protrusion of her belly as best she could, she removed her head scarf, her shawl, and then her robe. She stood shivering, feeling horribly exposed and not at all proud. Forcing her head high and her shoulders back, she walked toward the steaming vat of water, up a specially made ladder, and carefully lowered herself in.

The temperature was perfect, delightfully tingling on her cold skin, and it soothed the whole of her in its warm embrace. Saoirse hardly noticed the priestesses daubing various fragrant substances on her forehead, the parting of her hair, and her shoulders. Others sprinkled petals onto the surface, which floated around and clung, a little uncomfortably, to her skin.

The last remaining, most senior priestess, poured the fragrant water over her hair, massaging her scalp, and running a wooden comb through the now oiled strands. Over and over the comb glided across her scalp and downward, and Saoirse nearly fell asleep in the process. Saoirse secretly lapped up the attention. It felt so good to be fussed over after being so lonely for so long.

Once the final priestess finished, Saoirse sat alone with her thoughts. It was difficult not to think about what Ashira had done. Angry thoughts about Ashira and the dress raced around and around her mind as Saoirse glared at the candle directly in front of her, almost blinding herself in the process. Then she reminded herself that this was supposed to be a cleansing experience, to purify herself and present herself as cleansed before the Temple. Grumbling silently about the hypocrisy of such a practice compared to the rest of the elite, Saoirse decided she should at least make the effort.

The people of Ur deserved better. Kaylem deserved better. Since they had moved here, in the small moments they were permitted to be together, she had done nothing but complain about Maryam, Ashira and Kettel. But everyone around her seemed so hostile. Even at the desert compound when she was facing the prospect of working as a slave for the rest of her life, she had been surrounded by women who had cared for her.

Now, she had every luxury she could ever dream of, and had never felt so alone. She was apparently now in the highest echelon of society, but had never felt so restricted. She spared a moment to think of how miserable Kaylem's mother, the mistress, must have been in the years following her husband's untimely death. At the time Saoirse hadn't understood how loneliness and boredom could slowly erode even the most stable person's sanity away.

She made a promise to herself, as she sat there, to always look at a person with compassion, which might be somewhat difficult when it came to Ashira and Kettel, she thought with a grimace. But no matter what, she decided she would at least try to wonder what was happening under the surface to cause a person to behave in such a way. It was the only thing she could possibly think to do when she was about to face what could possibly be one of the most traumatic days of her life.

The fire having long been extinguished underneath the

enormous tub, the water was now beginning to cool, and Saoirse wondered how much time there was to go. The skin on her hands was completely wrinkled, and she wished she could be at her home, lying under her furs on her comfortable pallet, or eating a generous breakfast. Her eyes became heavy, and she couldn't stop herself dozing, nor her stomach from growling.

She hoped the nuts and dates of earlier would be enough to keep the nausea at bay. Not knowing when she could get out made the time stretch into forever. Rather than fret, she made herself lean her head against the uncomfortable rim of the vat, hoping that the underlying tiredness would allow her to rest for a little while. To her surprise, she woke with a start to a sound, her neck tense and aching.

"*Mistress*? It is now time to dress. I will help you out."

Saoirse was so glad to see Asi she had to stop herself from smiling and waving like a child greeting a loved one. Chilled to the bone, Saoirse stiffly climbed her way over the rim and down the now wet and slippery steps with weakened legs. Remembering what would come next sent her heart throwing itself around inside her chest again. She breathed deeply to try and calm herself down, remembering at the last instant to hold her belly in.

Asi and a junior priestess each had a soft cloth to dry Saoirse, who by this time was shivering so strongly she bit her tongue. They rubbed her numb skin back to life and wrapped her in a warm fur while Asi held up the ceremonial robe for her to inspect. Gulping back tears, Saoirse nodded and beamed at Asi with gratitude. The robe looked like it would sit perfectly, the extra panels Asi had magically added matching perfectly with the rest of the fabric. Asi's furious blush almost glowed in the gloom of the chamber. The priestess silently watched them with confusion written all over her face.

The robe slid over her body and even in her still simmering rage Saoirse could not help but sigh at the feeling of the silk gliding over her skin. Even so, visions of the beautiful, jewel encrusted robe she should have been wearing still haunted her. She told herself that Ashira must be a very unhappy person indeed if she needed to play such petty games, and battled to push the anger from her mind. This robe would be more than just adequate. It was stunning, and she knew the green would suit her perfectly.

Asi and the priestess applied charcoal mix to highlight her

eyes and piled her hair high on her head. For today, as the bride, she would not be wearing a headscarf, but a veil, matching that of her robe. Over the robe she would be wearing a white cape, to be shrugged away on the conclusion of the ceremony. The veil was also exquisitely sewn, maximizing the effect of the incredible figures painted on the silk. Asi and the priestess lowered it over her face and hair, with only her embellished eyes to be seen.

"Oh, *Mistress*. The gods themselves will be lining up to see you in all your glory."

The priestess ushered Saoirse over to a polished bronze mirror and she gasped at what she saw. The green of the fabric made her eyes shine through the gap in her veil. She hoped fleetingly that Ashira's robe was terribly heavy and uncomfortable, encrusted as it was with so many jewels and precious metals, and then she pushed it from her mind. For the first time that morning, she allowed herself a small smile. She couldn't wait for Kaylem to see her. This robe would have brought tears of joy without the memory of the other one she could have had.

It was time to begin her walk. Saoirse felt something being pushed into her hand. It was another small pouch of dates and nuts, and she sent Asi a silent blessing as they approached the huge gate, where she could already hear the crowd that awaited her. She chewed as inconspicuously as she could, glad for the veil. It would not do to be caught eating before the ceremony. She prayed that the gods would be merciful for the small heresy. Besides, she reasoned, this was only a repeat of the true ceremony which had already happened.

Stomach no longer growling quite so savagely, Saoirse readied herself by pausing just out of view of the closed gate. The crowd, permitted only as far as the gate, was even louder here. She reminded herself they were waiting for her; for their Oracle to appear. With a feeling as though she was about to jump from the top of the Temple, she blew out a breath, nodded to the guard who opened the gate, and came into view of the people.

The sound of the people momentarily faded into silence and then the people closest made gasping sounds, their eyes wide with what Saoirse hoped was awe rather than disgust. She acknowledged them with a small wave and the people at the front began to cheer. The cheer was taken up by those behind, and soon her ears felt like they would burst at the sound. Then the Temple

CHAPTER 26

guards escorted her toward the Sacred Steps so that she could begin her climb. Today would be practice for the entire thousand steps that she would climb next month on her consecration as Oracle.

Asi climbed on one side of Saoirse, the priestess who had helped her prepare on the other. Saoirse was dismayed to find that after only a few steps she was panting already. She slowed her gait slightly. Even after the hastily eaten pouch of food, nausea began to creep into her belly as the morning sun sent its first rays over the horizon. She forced the rising burn down and kept moving. The silk rustled softly against her body, its weave allowing her skin to breathe. Step by step, she inched herself closer to the midway.

After what seemed like forever, the sun's angle in the sky boring into one side of her face told her it was still quite early in the morning. Her throat ached with thirst, her legs weak. Saoirse kept going until it felt like she had never existed outside of this moment of eternal climbing. She allowed herself to look up just as the entrance to the Sanctum came into view, where the Temple elite were standing in the space outside it, awaiting her arrival. Despite her relief, she couldn't help but feel surprised that she had actually made it.

She had prepared herself as much as she could to see Ashira dressed in the glorious gem-encrusted robe. Yet nothing could have stopped Saoirse from gaping at the sight Ashira made, even from such a distance. The sun shone directly onto the group of elite waiting for Saoirse to finish her climb, and there stood Ashira, waving regally, almost impossible to lay eyes on as the light reflected from the magic fabric. Ashira dazzled, looking like one of the gods.

Saoirse narrowed her eyes and hoped her fisted hands weren't visible from where they stood. Her nails poked painfully into the skin of her palms. That incredible vision was supposed to be her own, shining and reflecting the sun's light, not Ashira. Saoirse suppressed the urge to run up the final steps and rip the incredible robe from Ashira's body. Instead, muttering curse after curse under her breath, she forced herself to finish the final climb.

Saoirse wasn't near enough to see Ashira's smug little smile, but she could very easily imagine it in her mind's eye. She sent her previous promise to be forgiving and compassionate to the underworld, where it thoroughly belonged whenever Ashira was concerned. In her mind an image appeared of Ashira gaping like a fish, just as the brothel owner had after Saoirse had stabbed him and blood was spurting from his body.

So shocked she almost stopped walking, Saoirse reminded herself to breathe and asked the gods to help her let go of her rage. It was only fabric, she told herself severely. It wasn't worth even losing her dignity over, let alone murdering someone. The gods themselves would bring justice to Ashira, Saoirse reassured herself as she forced her eyes downward to her feet and away from Ashira's imagined smirk.

A ghost of a breeze cooled her through the thin silk and she was grateful for its light softness. She wondered how Ashira's pale robe would look all stained with her sweat. She pictured Ashira baking in the blazing sun and hoped all those jewels were scratching her skin. Saoirse looked up again, unable to stop herself. The shimmering form of Ashira grew even closer, obscuring everything else in her vision. Saoirse growled and put her head back down. Instead, she made herself think about Kaylem, who would be waiting for her inside the middle Sanctum.

In her focus she nearly stumbled as the ground levelled. She righted herself, praying nobody noticed her slip, and forced herself to turn and face the assembled crowd. Ashira was there at the front of them all, of course, to greet her with open arms of exaggerated welcome.

"*Mistress*! What a terrible mistake. My servant sent the wrong package and I only discovered too late this morning. I am so filled with regret that this has occurred. I had the servant flogged for his error. There was nothing else I could have worn for such a stupendous occasion. Please, accept my apology. And yet you look absolutely radiant. The green is just extraordinary."

Wishing she could punch Ashira in the face, Saoirse forced her fisted hands to remain still and stiff beside her. A look in her eyes caused Ashira to take a step back, disquiet on her face.

"It is no matter, Ashira. This green brings out the color in my eyes perfectly, don't you think? The paler fabric might have made me look a little wan."

Ashira laughed nervously. This cheered Saoirse immensely and gave her the courage to remember they were not alone. She looked around at the rest of the faces before her for the first time. Everyone was standing and watching the exchange, listening

CHAPTER 26

intently. They seemed to be waiting for something. Saoirse watched them back, overwhelmed for a moment by the hostility she felt emanating from behind all the bland smiles, even though the colors around them were an equally bland mix of greens, pinks, and gentle oranges.

Surely she wasn't imagining the wave of hatred that almost knocked her over, and yet the colors around them should have been dark and jagged if that was the case. For a moment a surge of vertigo swept over her and she wondered if she was going mad, then nausea assailed her again and she put all her energy into forcing it down. Asi gently nudged her, bringing her out of her hesitation.

"*Mistress*, you must greet them," she murmured. "A wave will suffice."

Saoirse grimaced and raised her hand in a luke-warm wave, glad she was still hidden behind the veil. She reminded herself she would not cringe and feel afraid of these people who had made themselves so small and mean inside, and waved again, more vigorously this time.

"Many blessings mistress Ashira," she said loudly to Ashira now, who still stood at the front of the group. Something in Saoirse's voice once again caused Ashira to blink very quickly and hurry back to her companions. Saoirse straightened herself and forced herself to look more closely at them all.

There were many men she recognized intimately, and they were among the quickest to look away. The moments passed as each of the waiting elite ended up breaking her gaze, one by one. Not one of them held it aside from a woman she had never seen before, who looked back with open curiosity and even a true grin, instead of a hideous, bland smile.

Once she finished her scrutiny, Saoirse made her way toward the Sanctum, curious about the woman who had dared to hold her gaze. The group of people parted before her and she walked toward the entrance of the Sanctum, relieved that at least the first challenge was past. A waiting priestess motioned for Saoirse to enter the Sanctum's depths.

Inside, she found Kaylem waiting and she wanted to rush to him and be enfolded in his arms. Kaylem had sweaty patches darkening his robe and Saoirse wished one of them could have made a joke as they usually did to break the tension of the situation. Too late, Saoirse saw the high priestess who nodded. Saoirse nodded back, realizing that she should have greeted the high priestess first. She swallowed down a groan at the first of what was likely to be many social gaffes of the day.

Kaylem wore a head covering, and between that and his beard, there was little she could see of him aside from his eyes. She understood now why there was so much emphasis put on veiling, as it allowed one to focus exclusively on the eyes. Kaylem's gaze rested gently upon her, deep and quiet, and shining with love for her, Saoirse realized with a relieved sigh. At least someone in this group wanted to be in her presence. She focused more closely on Kaylem, unable to resist the urge to stare into him, instead of attending to the high priestess.

Kaylem's jaw dropped when Saoirse drew near enough that he could see her clearly in the gloom. Gathering himself, he bowed deeply and when he straightened, she could see the corner of his eyes crinkling in a smile. She crinkled her own eyes in return. The high priestess reached for Saoirse and joined her left hand to Kaylem's right, binding their wrists together with a soft cloth.

Beyond the crackling of flame and small murmurs of the high priestess, Saoirse could hear the elite making their way back down the Sacred Steps to await them in the newly-repaired Great Hall in the larger Temple complex. Saoirse's stomach growled and Kaylem winked at her. She stifled a giggle and crinkled her eyes again.

The high priestess began the Rite of Marriage in her sing-song voice. It was very different to the haunting marriage prayer uttered by master Hos, but still the soaring of her voice sent chills through Saoirse. She closed her eyes and allowed her heart to follow the rise and fall of the prayer, her chest expanding in ecstasy as she felt Kaylem so close. Kaylem caressed her wrist with his thumb. Opening her eyes, he was there to meet her gaze. They shared another smile with their eyes.

As they lost themselves in each other, the sudden silence drew Saoirse and Kaylem from their little world. The high priestess nodded at the small bowl of fragrant oil that lay on a nearby bench. Kaylem reverently lifted Saoirse's veil, applying the oil with a caress that made her want to grab him and run somewhere private to have their own special ceremony.

CHAPTER 26

They grinned at each other like crazed monkeys as she ran her own oiled finger down his forehead. Then they smashed a chalice of delicately carved clay under their feet in order to break down the old so that the blessing of the gods could enter the new marriage afresh. Saoirse was almost sorry to destroy such a thing of beauty.

The final stage was the exchange of pendants. Before Saoirse had entered the Sanctum, Asi had handed her the one Saoirse had picked for Kaylem long before. Now, Saoirse gently settled the lapis lazuli pendant over Kaylem's bowed head for the second time, and he did the same with a delicate, golden flower.

As they looked into each other's eyes, the sun chose that moment to send its rays into the Sanctum in a gentle swirl of color raining down around them both. Saoirse found herself smiling again. She looked upward for a moment toward the source of the colors, silently expressing her gratitude at the blessing so clearly bestowed on them from the gods.

Kaylem was the one to gently pull the veil back down over her face before they both bowed to the high priestess, who bowed back. As Saoirse and Kaylem exited the Sanctum followed by the high priestess, a tepid sounding cheer reached her ears from the elite gathered below as Saoirse threw off her white cape and lifted the veil from her face once again, leaving only her hair covered now.

She watched for a moment as the group, with Ashira's robe still dazzling in the sun, turned and made their way slowly into the Great Hall. Kaylem squeezed her hand and Saoirse wondered if he was thinking about the same thing she was—that they were the only ones in the Temple truly joyful for this occasion.

Saoirse imagined she could see Ashira's face in surprised outrage as the ceremonial robe, now exposed after the cape had been discarded, sat in exactly the way it should on her body, rather than clinging shamefully around her. Down the steps they walked as husband and wife, the cloth still binding their hands together which would remain until they sat for their meal.

CHAPTER 27

Approaching the entrance to the Great Hall, the delicious aroma of roasting meat wafted past. Her stomach growling like a ravening beast, Saoirse prayed the meal would come soon and taste as delicious as it smelled. The small pouch Asi had given her was well and truly empty and not nearly enough to stop her from feeling lightheaded.

Nausea would soon follow and then her stomach would do something beyond her control, likely right at the worst possible moment. Pausing at the entrance from where the rumble of the elite sounded within, Saoirse looked over at Kaylem if only to reassure herself that he was still there beside her. He smiled again, leaning in to brush first a hand over her cheek, and then her lips.

"It's done now, the Temple way," he murmured with his eyes full of amusement.

"Gods, I missed you, Kaylem," she answered into his ear, caressing it with her lips, making him shiver.

"By the way, you look as though you came straight from *D'ingir* and the gods themselves dressed you," he replied into her ear, sending delightful tingles all over her body.

She chuckled. "If you'd seen the mood I was in earlier when I found out Ashira stole my robe, it was probably more like the underworld."

"She looks ridiculous. It would have suited you much better." He tilted his head sideways. "But, on saying that, the green is bewitching and really brings out your eyes."

"That's exactly what I told her when she rushed over to gloat,"

CHAPTER 27

Saoirse said with a wink, which made Kaylem's eyes bulge. "But truly, that ceremony was beautiful. I'm just sorry that we have to now ruin this mood with those testicle-sacks in there."

Kaylem chose that moment to choke on something in his throat. Saoirse dipped her head toward the entrance to the Great Hall where the noise was already increasing.

"I'd rather be eating a simple meal at the crumbling old hall with the chanting group than anything to do with this lot." Kaylem's hand and voice were both soft as he stroked the firm, tiny roundness at her abdomen. She nodded, wishing, too, that she could expect to see the friendly faces of the chanting group inside the Hall instead of the elite.

Even though she had only briefly met Raya and Jivan, they had felt like true friends, and she suddenly yearned for their presence. Kaylem took her hand and reluctantly led her toward the opening, Saoirse feeling as though she was heading to the stoning pits instead.

Hoping nobody could hear the complaining of her stomach, they made their way into the Great Hall. If Saoirse waited too much longer the nausea would be her unwelcome accompaniment to the dinner. It would just be her bad luck to need to void her stomach into one of the tall, beautifully decorated urns standing at regular intervals along the walls, or onto one of the shining timber tables. For a moment she even imagined vomiting all over Ashira's robe and that made her feel a little better, if only for a short time, until she saw the group of women standing there in a tight knot on the other side of the Hall.

Unlike at the desert household, for this meal she would be expected to sit with the other Temple women for the first time, even though she barely knew any of them. Kaylem would be with the men, as was the way in formal occasions. As she looked closer, Saoirse saw that all of them were already enjoying glasses of ale and wine.

The roar of voices quieted as they noticed Saoirse and Kaylem. Everyone stopped to stare as the newlyweds made their way cautiously through the room. Saoirse dimly remembered hearing that it was customary for the wedding guests to wait for the bride and groom to appear before partaking in any food or drink, and to cheer their arrival to welcome them for the celebratory meal. It didn't look like anything like that would happen today, so Saoirse imagined it in her mind. For a moment she allowed her heart to overflow with the joy that she would have felt if everyone were genuinely celebrating their union.

Now was the time that Saoirse must separate from Kaylem, and the thought made that imagined joy shrivel up and die. The fabric binding them together dropped to the floor as Kaylem gently stroked it from their joined hands. Saoirse felt bereft as Kaylem nodded encouragingly to her and moved away. He headed bravely toward where the men stood, waiting to slap him patronisingly on the back too hard, and make a pretense of congratulating him.

Saoirse forced herself to step toward the awaiting women, who whispered and tittered as they stared. Not one of them nodded or came to greet her. Praying she wouldn't trip on a cushion, Saoirse forced away a wince as the one person she hoped wouldn't greet her, finally came to greet her. Ashira's face was flushed and Saoirse wondered if it was because of the empty looking cup of wine in her hand, or if she was angry. Ashira looked Saoirse up and down as though Saoirse was some kind of livestock.

"Here is our great Oracle!" Ashira called out to the room in a voice that sounded like she had a throat full of wasps. "Your beauty astounds us all, *Mistress*, and such a spectacular robe! I must congratulate the seamstress."

"Ah, yes. Your seamstress, dear Mistress Ashira. Your seamstress, of course, was measuring for you as I could hardly put this robe on. I did not imagine that you were quite as slender as that. It is especially fortunate one of my servants is magically gifted in the ways of sewing." Saoirse gave Ashira a simpering smile and shuddered to imagine what horrors the woman might inflict upon the seamstress if it was known that the woman had disobeyed Ashira's instructions.

"Ah… I did wonder at the quality of the stitching there..." Ashira examined a seam on Saoirse's robe critically. "This is not like my seamstress's work at all." Ashira beamed sympathetically at Saoirse for such a misfortune. "Come, *Mistress,* and meet your companions on this *new* journey of yours as a woman of our great Temple."

Saoirse heard the unspoken dig about her dubious origins that Ashira loudly proclaimed instead in the tone of her voice, the smug tilt of her smile, and the narrowing of her eyes. Saoirse nodded with a similar expression, which hurt her face, and

CHAPTER 27

allowed Ashira to lead her toward the group of women. All of them now crowded around Saoirse, gushing their welcomes in high-pitched voices which exuded superiority and amusement.

In the middle of the highly perfumed throng, Saoirse found herself close to fainting from the stuffiness of the surroundings, mixed with the food smells emanating from the hearths of the cookhouse just outside. Her stomach was threatening to mutiny and she begged it to wait just a little longer.

Forcing the smile back onto her face, she took in the seating arrangements behind where the women stood. A curtain would soon split the Hall in half once they were seated; one side for the men and the other for the women. Even though this was standard for any celebrations, Saoirse had always thought it ludicrous that in high society, men should not see women eat. She was certain it hadn't always been that way.

Saoirse dreaded the thought of not being able to see Kaylem, left instead with these women who spoke such venom in their sweet, sighing voices. Now that she had been welcomed, they all turned back to one another and continued with whatever they had been talking about before. It was like a different language to Saoirse, who had never heard the formal language used for conversation like this. It made her feel like a pile of dung, and she suspected that it was supposed to. She stood alone with a smile that felt more like a snarl, until a mumbling servant announced the time to be seated.

The curtain was pulled closed and with it disappeared her last glimpse of Kaylem. She knew he would also be dreading this meal. With a sigh she made her way to her seat next to Kettel. Ashira, her sparkling robe making gaudy reflections on the table surface, sat on the other side of Kettel.

An unknown older woman sat to the left of Saoirse in the next most senior seat. They nodded silently to acknowledge each other. Saoirse wondered who this other woman might be that she had never met before. She was apparently even more senior than Kettel and even the high priestess, who Saoirse did not see anywhere in the throng.

The maddening smell of food wafted through the room and Saoirse sat impatiently, craning her neck to try find a glimpse of servants bringing platters. The richly brocaded cushion she sat on was uncomfortable, its beaded surface protruding into her rear.

She would rather be sitting on a prickle bush watching the stars out under a desert sky.

She brought herself back to awareness of the huge, low wooden table with herself at its head at the front of the room. The floor was carpeted in delicately woven, vividly colored rugs. Ornate tapestries depicting the gods hung from the walls. Preoccupied with her desire for food, Saoirse didn't pay much attention to the general conversation until she heard her honorific being uttered.

"...do you not believe, *Mistress*?... *Mistress*?" The unknown woman beside her was talking.

"A thousand apologies, Mistress. What was it you were saying?"

"Do you not believe that the new dwellings are a vast improvement on the old ones? I was only saying to my beloved husband, bless his soul, days before the flood that we really should have our house rebuilt. He died after the flood. A delicate nature he had, and though the mourning period is over I cannot bring myself to wear anything but white."

"May he rest with the gods." muttered Saoirse and the woman nodded her thanks.

"We have not yet had the pleasure to meet. I am Emel, *Mistress*."

"A blessing to meet you Emel. Please, tell me as I have been fasting through the day, when is the meal to begin?"

"Yet that is strange as I have heard that Ashira instructed to hold the serving of any food, even small relishes, until after the speeches, at your request."

"I see..." She seethed inwardly while her heart sank into her feet. Ashira must know, then, that Saoirse was with child. It was the only reason she could think of that Ashira would do such a thing, knowing Saoirse would be even more ravenous than usual after a day of supposed fasting. "Tell me Mistress Emel, do you know, are there many set to speak?"

"The great Anan shall open the proceedings. There is the high priestess next, to bless the occasion. Then the high officials to give their good wishes to the newly married. We have many toasts to drink throughout the speeches, so there will be even more wine and ale then. Ashira thoughtfully arranged the high quality wine in order to put the guests into a celebratory mood, as she has

CHAPTER 27

spoken highly of your taste for fine wine."

"I see," Saoirse said, her teeth hurting from where she was grinding them into dust.

"As the guests of honor," continued Emel, "yourself and Kaylem will be partaking in many toasts. The feast begins, *Mistress*, at sundown." Emel did a little shoulder shrug of excitement and Saoirse couldn't help but feel that she was missing something else very important, and that everything was very, very wrong.

"I have seen brides quite intoxicated by the close of the night. It is strange, though, since usually the Oracle is required to drink small ale rather than wine. As the bride is usually quite famished, she is first to nibble upon dainties brought to all while the speeches occur. The liquor will be limited for your great self once the Oracle Initiation ceremony occurs next moon, hence you must enjoy it tonight for one of the last times, *Mistress*." She smiled mischievously, as though sharing a secret. "I myself have been anticipating this event purely for the delicious wine and food," Emel continued with hardly a breath taken.

Saoirse sat with a fixed smile on her face, seeking desperately around her for what could possibly be causing the urgent and ever rising tide of dread twisting her insides.

"Ashira has a reputation for providing only the best in festivities," Emel went on, "and when we discovered she was arranging the celebration we all felt so glad for you, that you have been so warmly welcomed into our modest group. It is such an honor to be seated next to you, *Mistress*. I do wish we can be calling on each other in the future."

Saoirse nodded absently to Emel as she forced herself to take a deep breath, even if Emel didn't seem to need to. "In fact, *Mistress*, I was only recently remarking to my dear departed husband that it must surely be time for the new Oracle to appear, and now here I am sitting beside her! I must say I was surprised when Ashira instructed me to sit by you, as my husband and I are by custom seated at the other end of the table far away from the senior elite, yet I figured you must have taken pity on the new widow in your infinite kindness."

Saoirse made herself nod. She was sure her smile was more of a rictus now and her lips felt stretched in all the wrong places. Emel had broken off with what started as a beatific smile, which changed to something more uncertain now. "I considered surrendering my seat, yet it was such an honor bestowed to myself and my family. Do you not think?"

Saoirse blinked at Emel in silent panic, forgetting to breathe. The high priestess, she noticed too late, was sitting with a furious expression at the lesser end of the table. Neither Ashira nor Kettel would be blamed for this utter disaster. She could see the mutterings and glances now. A couple of the women Saoirse had seen grouped around Ashira earlier even had the dubious decency to look slightly ashamed of themselves. A waft of deliciously spiced meat caressed her nostrils and teased her stomach, which twisted evilly.

There was no option but escape, Saoirse decided as she took in the full significance of the crisis that was quietly unfolding around her. The gods only knew whether other guests were similarly insulted, and it made her want to scream that she would not be aware of those. Excusing herself as politely as she could, she picked her way toward the exit and sought out the privy, silently cursing Ashira with every step.

Once away from the crowd, she found herself needing to lean a hand against the wall at regular intervals for support as the nausea decided it was time to make a full appearance. Cold sweat sprang out on her skin, drenching the thin material of the robes and causing her to shiver.

"*Mistress?*" Saoirse jumped and almost tripped over Asi.

"Oh, thank the gods it's you. What are you doing here?" Saoirse had never been so happy to see Asi in her life and wished she could hug the girl.

"I'm helping in the kitchens," she whispered back.

"Asi, your little bags of food saved so much more than just my dignity today. But if Ashira gets her way, I'll starve most of the night."

"*Mistress*, I'll bring you some meat."

Saoirse reached out and grabbed Asi's hands. "Thank you! Only if it doesn't put you in danger. I'll be waiting in the privy."

"But *Mistress*, isn't that blasphemy to eat where we—"

"Not this time, Asi. It's the only thing that will save me from inflicting worse blasphemy by throwing up all over Anan as he makes his speech."

Asi flinched, apparently terrified of even a mention of Anan. She turned and raced toward the kitchens. Saoirse slowly made her way to the tiny cubicle that housed the privy, which to her sensitized nose smelled worse than the servants' latrine at the household. Pulling the flimsy door shut, she convulsed into the hole in the floor, imagining the mess instead splattering all over Ashira. She wished she herself could make a speech to all the wedding guests, about how Ashira's husband had visited the inn of Ur on many occasions and made soft, sweet Sybel his favorite.

A large, quiet, and anxious mouse of a man, Ashira's husband had an insatiable hunger for wine and food. He had been one of the most loyal visitors to the inn before the flood. Saoirse couldn't imagine how much he would be missing it now. She leaned against the wall after watching the trickle of running water wash the mess down the mud-brick pipe, hoping nobody heard her retching.

She wondered how that trickle of water managed to make it up so high. Were servants bringing large vats from the river to fill a cistern somewhere in the wall? Then she tried to visualize the system of invisible pipes that would carry the contents of her stomach through the network of tiny canals that carried waste from the privies and kitchens, all the way back down to the river.

It was something she appreciated now that hardly a trace of her stomach contents remained, even though it would have been a special kind of torment for the workers who built it. Her thoughts were interrupted by a knock at the door. She cleared her throat to indicate the cubicle was occupied.

"*Mistress*, it is Asi."

She flipped the latch eagerly.

"It's not much, but hopefully it will keep you from sickness. The kitchen is in chaos, nobody saw me."

"A thousand blessings to you, Asi," she whispered. "I honestly don't know what I'd do without you."

Asi blushed for a moment and then looked at her curiously. "*Mistress*, may I also ask why the head cook has requested that you are to eat no flesh?"

Saoirse hit the wall, bruising her fist. "That gods damned stinking dog's arse," she snarled, or tried to through her mouthful which sprayed out unattractively in front of her.

"Oh, *Mistress*!" Asi breathed, her eyes popping.

Saoirse swallowed her mouthful. "My apologies, Asi. A daemon has taken on a body in the form of Ashira, who ruins me and my standing with the Temple elite in more ways than I can ever know," she whispered. "I am famished, with child, and the guest of honor, and she has now destroyed any iota of joy I might have taken in the occasion. This accursed woman has even caused a terrible insult to the high priestess, who currently sits at the back end of the table."

Saoirse's words came out indistinctly as she gnawed on another hunk of meat, sauce dribbling ecstatically down her chin. The smell of the privy had either disappeared, or she had become used to it. Either way, she no longer cared and had to suppress a hysterical giggle at the situation as the glorious meat made its way into her stomach.

Asi seemed to have understood at least some of what she was saying. Despite the tiny nook they were squashed into, Asi did not show even a glimmer of distaste for Saoirse's dreadful manners or their forced proximity. "No, *Mistress*! Not the high priestess!"

"I don't know what to do. It will be known by everyone that I insulted her in the worst possible way. She will treat me worse than a pile of refuse for the Initiation Ceremony next month."

Asi's eyes were wide, and she blinked up at Saoirse in sympathy. Both of them looked in alarm toward the door when they heard footsteps approach. Saoirse was still chewing on the meat, and she forced it down, swallowing with a loud gulp. With both of them on high alert for anyone approaching, Asi quickly helped Saoirse return to a semblance of respectability. After a deep breath, Saoirse opened the door, peeking around cautiously. The area was deserted. Saoirse breathed out in relief.

"Blessings, Asi," she whispered with a smile. Her heart still felt like it was clawing its way to her throat, but in that moment the beginnings of an idea began to form in her mind. It was easier to think now that she had something a little more solid lining her stomach. Asi bowed and disappeared back to the kitchens as Saoirse returned to the hall with a prayer to the gods that her plan might be successful.

As soon as Ashira spied Saoirse, she approached in a very officious manner. "*Mistress*, we have been awaiting you with great anticipation. The speeches are to begin!" Ashira clapped her hands as though this was the most exciting thing in the known world. "You may wish to... er..." Ashira's eyes narrowed, and Saoirse felt her stomach drop to her toes. "There is a morsel in your teeth, *Mistress*."

CHAPTER 27

Saoirse wiped her mouth as discretely as possible, wanting to disappear into the floor. Ashira had spoken in a voice loud enough for many of the people close by to hear. Saoirse wished she could slap Ashira's pale cheek. Instead, she spent a moment clenching and unclenching her fists under the sleeves of her robe, taking the time to survey the lower end of the table, while Ashira hovered beside her still talking. Saoirse nodded her head now and then, eyes glued to her next destination.

Beside the formidable frame of the high priestess now sat an empty cushion, whose occupant had just recently stood to mingle with some of the other women. Saoirse sent up a small prayer of thanks to the gods for allowing such fortunate circumstances. Before she could persuade herself to do otherwise, Saoirse turned rudely away from a still-talking Ashira.

As she approached the back end of the table, Saoirse heard gasps of astonishment and whispers. Suppressing the urge to look back to see what Ashira's expression might hold at such an insult, she instead stood right next to the high priestess and bowed deeply. The entire group of women became silent.

"Honorable high priestess," Saoirse said in a voice loud enough to carry through the entire space. "It seems there has been a grave mistake with the seating arrangements. If you would be so kind hearted as to allow me to offer my regret and sit by you for the remainder of the night, I would wish to correct this most disastrous error." In front of Saoirse sat a tiny stone carved with the name of one of the other lesser elite women she had never heard of. She wished she could throw it at Ashira's stunned face.

"Very well then." The high priestess's face flushed and then softened somewhat into what Saoirse hoped was understanding. Saoirse acknowledged the nod the high priestess returned and sat as dexterously as her agitated body would allow. At the other end of the table, Saoirse noticed the others had resumed their whispering and giggling. Emel prattled joyfully and obliviously across Kettel's silent form at Ashira. Saoirse smiled sweetly over at Ashira and held up a mug she found in front of her as a toast.

"*Mistress*," said the woman on the other side of Saoirse with a voice loaded in such irony it might have bordered on rude had Saoirse not looked over and caught the mischievous twist to the woman's mouth. Saoirse saw that it was the very woman who had been the only one to return Saoirse's gaze after the ceremony.

Indeed, even now, the woman's entire expression promised a refreshing detour from the usual gossipy vapidness of the others.

"Such an honor it is to be in your exalted presence, great *Oracle*," said Yana with just the correct amount of simpering laced with an irony that made Saoirse's own mouth twist in amusement.

"I am surprised you find the courage to converse with myself so openly in the presence of such esteemed company," Saoirse simpered back, batting her eyes rapidly.

"I am named Yana, *Mistress*, and I hail from a line of great Temple scribes, I'll have you know," gushed Yana with a swoon that made Saoirse snort.

"The gods be with you, Mistress Yana. I have not met you before."

"I've been away in Erech." Yana spat the words with disgust.

"I know Erech and feel quite the same way."

"It's the back end of the world, as far as I'm concerned." Saoirse felt both shocked and relieved that Yana was so quick to dismiss the formal speech. "By the way, *Mistress*, I have to commend your latest move to overcome Ashira's plotting. I've been on the wrong end of her games too many times, but what she's done to you so far has really been impressive. Too much power and not enough to do to occupy her time..."

Saoirse nodded ruefully and Yana shrugged. "I'm still trying to work out where her vulnerabilities are. They have to exist somewhere. She is human after all... I think." Both of them shared a laugh. Saoirse looked back to the other end of the table and found to her gratification that Ashira and Emel were both in the same position as before. Ashira was refilling her cup, looking a little slack-mouthed, while Emel's mouth never stopped moving. Kettel sat serenely between them.

Yana chuckled at the sight. "Much to my father's chagrin I refuse to hold my tongue when it's so obvious something's just not right. He gets upset every time I talk about it, poor man, because he worries for my safety." Yana's gaze became intently fixed on hers. "Watch out for all of them, don't trust anyone. They are little better than a nest of evil widow spiders, although even those hideous creatures are in accordance with the goddess."

"I wish I could disagree. Having experienced it for myself it's like watching the flood all over again but in slow motion. Why is it that you see it so clearly when everyone else, aside from

Kaylem, doesn't want to know?"

"I've known these women since I was born, unfortunately," Yana murmured. "My mother, bless her soul, warned me to stay clear of them wherever possible. She saw it in them too. When she lived, we went everywhere around the known world and nowhere else seems to be quite as affected by whatever's going on here. I love getting away whenever I can."

Saoirse couldn't agree more.

"But now my father's getting old and I'll be left alone with these monsters..."

"But surely there are others who can see through them?"

"I'm sure there are, too, but everyone is too scared to say anything so we all just silently go along with it..." Yana sat up straight all of a sudden, her attention toward the front. "Oh, the speeches are starting, how utterly *thrilling*," Yana said in a deadpan tone. "Make sure you get comfortable, *Mistress*, because you're in for a very long evening."

"Oh Yana," Saoirse whispered, "everything you've told me fills me with dread, but I'm so glad to have met you."

They giggled silently, scowled upon ferociously from afar by Ashira. The curtain was pulled back enough to expose the front of the room. Anan made his way to the area which allowed him to be seen by everyone. He greeted first the high priestess, then Kaylem and Saoirse with a cheeky smile and wink. Saoirse was certain the order was wrong as the audience began muttering and nudging each other. She was tempted to send Anan a scowl in return, but instead she nodded in the way expected of her.

He spoke at first in obscure riddles that brought guffaws from the men as well as some of the women in the room, too. Beside her, Yana made a sound of disgust. "You don't want to know what that was about," she whispered. "They have all these awful inside jokes and really, they're just a bunch of brutes wearing expensive cloth and oils."

Saoirse shrugged. "I think I'm glad I don't know."

"The richer the robe, the crasser the conduct." Yana nodded knowingly.

Soon the jokes mercifully finished and then Anan spoke at length regarding the importance of worship and respect for the authority of the Temple. Saoirse and Yana exchanged grimaces at his hypocrisy. A toast was then drunk in honor of the happy couple. Saoirse only had the smallest of sips of her wine, knowing how many more toasts that lay ahead. One of the servants rushed over to fill her cup with what smelled like such potent wine, even the smell made her head spin. The minute the cup touched the table, a servant raced over to try fill it up again.

Next to talk was the high priestess, who creaked to standing from beside Saoirse and made her way to the front. Saoirse could not help but notice the look the high priestess bestowed onto Ashira as she walked past. It was the only sign that the high priestess was upset. Without another word, the high priestess led the guests in a prayer to the goddess Inanna. That was the only nice part of the ceremony, Saoirse thought. She bowed her head in acknowledgement as the high priestess returned to her seat.

Many officials spoke after. Saoirse was horrified to recognize a man from the lesser elite, who thanked her profusely for asking Ashira to include him in the speeches. Saoirse, feeling very unsophisticated, rolled her eyes at Yana who was looking at the man in a very confused way.

"Why would they ever invite Duri to speak, of all people? There's something very disturbing about him," Yana whispered.

"I'm sure you know my history," Saoirse whispered back. "That man was the most frequent Temple worker to visit the inn." Yana almost spat her wine on the table, and Saoirse patted Yana's back as she brought herself back under control. The man did two toasts, and Saoirse only tipped the cup to her lips instead of drinking. Ironically, she was parched with thirst and would have loved a small ale. She resigned herself to endure what she was certain were many more embarrassments that Ashira had prepared for the evening ahead.

Another servant rushed his way over to try fill Saoirse's cup, but it was already almost overflowing. Yana tugged on the servant's clothing and held out her own, but the servant seemed single minded in his intent to focus only on Saoirse. He ignored Yana's request and walked away. Yana snarled at the man. Another servant came along not long after and mockingly poured small ale into Yana's cup.

"Who do I have to kill around here to get a real drink?" muttered Yana over the drone of the latest official.

Saoirse smiled joyfully. "How about we swap?"

Yana batted her eyelashes at Saoirse and nudged her cup

closer. Saoirse moved hers toward Yana. "This is going to be fun I think." Saoirse drained her cup at the same time as Yana and then the servant rushed over again to fill it.

The smell of food was affecting more than just Saoirse by the time the lesser officials were finally finished with their speeches. Many were fidgeting in their seats, and stomachs all around were growling. Saoirse noticed a couple of older women had fallen asleep resting on their folded arms on the table. She subtly pointed them out to Yana who had by then imbibed three large cups of wine and laughed too loudly at them.

Nobody seemed to care, and Saoirse noticed many of the others were laughing too loudly as well. The speeches continued, even though nobody was really listening any more and the hum of conversation was far louder than anyone at the front could project their voice. It seemed not to matter though, since the ones who were left were the lowest of them all and had nothing much to say.

The sun was long set by the time the first platters began to make their way from the kitchen, and even then, the man still droning at the front of the room broke off what he was trying to say to follow the platters eagerly with his eyes. Saoirse also watched very closely as the servants dished liberal portions to those at the head of the table.

From a distance, she could see that the meat looked to be dry and tough from so long being kept warm by the cooking staff. She stifled a bitter chuckle. The meat had been perfect when she had eaten her share in the privy, and she wished she could have shared that little joke with Yana. The friendship was too new to let that secret go.

"It's likely there won't be much left by the time it reaches us. I do pray that you enjoy lentils, *Mistress*. It's such a shame, for your wedding feast to be so marred. But at the same time, it gives me great pleasure to see Ashira's face right now as she tries to chew that overcooked leather."

"I cannot tell you how pleased I feel to hear that. I'm ready to consume the carpets!"

True to Yana's prediction, a bowl of lentils and a hunk of flat bread eventually appeared in front of Saoirse. Despite its humble nature, the sauce was delicately spiced and the bread was baked to perfection. She ate slowly, unwilling to cause any shock to her delicate stomach, savoring every mouthful. There would be no stealing her enjoyment of the food itself despite the mockeries of the evening.

Chalice after chalice of fine wine were lined up in front of Saoirse as she and Kaylem, the guests of honor, were required to partake in many toasts. She pretended to become ever more inebriated with each one while discreetly swapping with Yana, whose voice became progressively louder.

It seemed not to matter though as it matched the rest of the conversations flowing and ebbing around the Hall, even if Yana did say things that were less and less appropriate, even to Saoirse's seasoned ears. Even the small ale began to affect Saoirse despite the meal, and she found that she was light headed and giggly, dissolving into hysterics every time Yana pointed out violent undulations in the curtain as a man on the other side acted the fool. Uproarious laughter from beyond the curtain followed.

Music began to play. Saoirse looked up in surprise, but it was also on the other side of the curtain, and she couldn't see a thing. More roars from the men's side suggested that they were enjoying watching dancers in very provocative attire. She and Yana blinked at each other silently, eyes wide. Were there no lows that Ashira would not stoop to?

All sense of polite modesty gone, inebriated women began to leave their seats and run around like children. Saoirse could hear what sounded like a fight now on the other side of the curtain, with crashing of crockery and shouts of aggression, as well as cheering. Looking around, Saoirse noticed many plates of food were left untouched, the strips of meat looking more like the tough salted jerky the merchants carried with them to travel.

Both Saoirse and Yana jumped at a loud ripping sound. They watched in horror as a group of women proceeded to tear down the curtain that screened the men's side. A sudden silence filled the Hall as men and women blinked at each other. Saoirse only had eyes for the performers standing still now at the front of the room. Forcing herself to breathe, she made herself remain where she was despite the prickling rush making her body feel like it was on fire.

"What in the name of the gods…" she heard Yana say as though she was a great distance away.

Saoirse squeezed her fists so hard her nails pierced the skin of her palms. Her chest felt suddenly hollow, and she wished she could burrow under the table, curl up into a ball, and sob. Zara and Sybel stood at the front of the men's section, wearing nothing but shimmering, gauzy scarves. Their faces were pale and drawn as they both now gazed over at her. Sybel shook her head sadly and Zara just stood and stared at Saoirse, her eyes empty.

"Dance, whores, dance!" roared one of the men, breaking the silence.

"Dance, whores!" echoed another.

"*Whores?*" shrieked a staggering, inebriated woman Saoirse did not know, her face twisted and purple with anger.

"Dance you gods forsaken sluts!" yelled another man.

"Dance, whores, dance! Dance, whores, dance! Dance, whores, dance!" An entire group of men took up the command and it became a chant. The music resumed and the girls, hesitant at first with the women watching on, resumed their dance, faces drawn and tight, mouths set in straight lines.

Ashira sat smirking at the now empty table, watching Saoirse with a half smile that Saoirse wished she could carve out of her face. Instead, she tried to see where Kaylem might be in the mayhem. It was difficult to see who anyone was from where she sat as most people were now up and moving around.

She focused her attention on one of the beautiful tapestries hanging from the wall, numbly wondering how she might find Kaylem and sneak from the room before anyone could notice them. Surely, they were all too intoxicated to care anymore. Even Ashira's head seemed to wobble on her alarmingly slender neck, in the corner of Saoirse's vision.

Yana, looking slightly green, mumbled something unintelligible and staggered off, leaving Saoirse and Ashira sitting at opposite ends of the otherwise empty table. Saoirse stared at Ashira with what she hoped was an expressionless face. She would bring them all down, Saoirse promised to herself in that moment. If it was the last thing she did, she would put an end to this disgusting dung heap once and for all.

Sensing a pull in the direction of the men's side, Saoirse turned away from Ashira, who looked like she might soon collapse. Craning her head, Saoirse finally found Kaylem, also still sitting in what looked to be his originally allocated spot, a heavy scowl on his face. He was turned toward the back wall, away from the dancing girls, and Saoirse could not have loved him any more than she did at that moment.

Their eyes met and as one they stood. Saoirse strode toward him through the crowd, pushing people out of the way as they fell into her path. Hands finally clasped together, they picked their way to the exit. As they stood at the door to see if anyone would notice their departure, Saoirse looked one last time at Sybel and Zara, who were once again gyrating their bodies to the music. A group of both women and men were now shrieking and dancing in a similar way at the front of the room.

With a hand over her heart and tears running down her cheeks, Saoirse sent a silent apology to the girls, who looked back at her. She bowed her head to them and both sent small, sharp nods back her way. The dance continued, the crowd now shrieking demands for Sybel and Zara to remove more scarves from their already barely covered bodies.

Saoirse allowed Kaylem to lead her from the room. They emerged into the cool stillness, the sounds of the crowd now in the background as the night insects filled their ears with soothing noises. With the moon high above to light their way, Saoirse and Kaylem wandered back to their dwelling in silence under the dazzling night sky.

Once home, they tiptoed through the dark, empty dwelling and onto the rooftop where they lay together on a fur. Tracing each other's features with gentle fingertips, there was no need for words. Kaylem tenderly kissed her tears, which glittered in the light of the moon. It was a bittersweet reunion as they found comfort and joy in each other's embrace, confident in the knowledge that all they had to trust was each other.

CHAPTER 28

The water was hotter this time, almost uncomfortably so. Saoirse reminded herself how cold she had been in the last cleansing before the wedding, so she tried to enjoy it. Still, her heart raced and she felt giddy as the heat infiltrated her body, similar to when she suffered from a mild fever. Thoughts came and went, such as how grateful she was to have Yana as a friend now. They had searched the markets together for the perfect robe to wear for today's ceremony. It was waiting safely in its package in one corner, and if she craned her neck, she could actually see it sitting there.

After it arrived the day before, she had run her hands over the beautifully made garment again and again just to reassure herself it was really all hers, and Ashira would not have the chance to ruin it. She had even slept with it sitting beside her pallet just to make sure. This particular robe was a light scarlet color encrusted with tiny silver and gold beads—the perfect material when climbing the entire thousand Sacred Steps in the late spring heat.

She had deliberately chosen silk again, given how wonderfully cool the material had been for the wedding. She scowled into the gloom. That was twice now that she'd thought of the wedding day since getting into the water, which was a shame because it was a day that she preferred not to touch on in her thoughts ever again. After all, her true wedding day with Kaylem at the desert household was where the beautiful memories lay.

The heat threatened to overwhelm her again, making her pulse throb in an alarming way against her eardrums. Lifting her upper body and arms out of the steaming water to cool herself, she couldn't help but feel a little guilty. She was certain she heard someone say that she must stay fully immersed, but she worried about the tiny, secret lives growing deep within her. Also forbidden was the large morning meal of eggs, dates, bread, and yogurt. Nobody knew aside from Asi, who had risen well before anybody else to prepare the food. It had not been easy forcing herself to eat at such an early hour, but she was grateful, even if a little repentant, to be facing this day—her initiation into becoming Oracle—on a full belly.

Worried someone might discover her hanging various body parts out of the water, she sank back down again. Thoughts of Ashira and Kettel intruded on her peace and she tried her best to push them away, knowing that the calmer she was, the better she would cope with what was to come. It would have been easier trying to push away clouds in the sky. Saoirse had not heard from either Ashira or Kettel since that disastrous day. She had thoroughly enjoyed every minute of her relative freedom, aside from the moments when Maryam needed putting in her place. Luckily, those had been few and far between in the past weeks as well.

Saoirse's thoughts churned around the woman who had caused so much damage. Ashira was unused to being under the authority of anyone, aside from Kettel, who quietly exerted her power in a way that only a truly compelling leader could. Once the Initiation Ceremony was finished later today, both Ashira and Kettel would, apparently, be expected to acknowledge Saoirse as their superior. She allowed herself an ironic chuckle at the thought, knowing that the reality would be very different.

The two most senior women of the Temple would never give Saoirse even a glimmer of loyalty, let alone allow her power over them, despite her obvious lack of ambition. If only they would just leave her alone to do whatever was expected of her as Oracle, then everyone could just get on with their lives. But the coming inauguration was ripe with possibilities for Ashira and Kettel to destroy her even more than they already had, and beyond that stretched an eternity of opportunities more numerous than the Sacred Steps. She would rather climb those steps a thousand times, than endure what Ashira likely had planned for her today.

Would Ashira sabotage the musicians Yana had hired to

entertain the guests tonight? What about the meal? While Saoirse had done her best to keep tabs on every part of the preparations, she couldn't control everything. And then after today was over? There would be a lifetime of social occasions and official meetings where she'd be dealing with the Temple elite on a regular basis. Was she truly supposed to live from now on in this state of constant vigilance?

Thoughts spun through her mind in a whirl of increasing intensity until she felt her breath locking up in her chest. Her heart threw itself around inside her ribs, the heat of the water making her feel like she was going to suffocate. She pulled herself out of the vat once again, water streaming over the side. Despite the tightness of her chest, she forced herself to breathe deeply, over and over again.

Already Saoirse felt exhausted and the main event of the day was yet to even begin. After lying awake most of the night before, tormenting herself with every possibility of how things could go wrong, she had somehow found a few restless hours of sleep. When Asi came in to wake her only a couple of short hours ago, her eyelids and body felt like they were trapped under a mound of desert sand. It had been like climbing a mountain just to rise from her pallet. Taking in more breaths, Saoirse sent a silent plea to the gods to give her the strength she would need to get through the day ahead.

For a long time, nothing happened. She winced as her heart still raced and gasped for breath. Deciding it wasn't helping to think too much about how stressed her body was, she pulled her attention away from the urgent but pointless messages, reminding herself she wasn't actually, truly going to suffocate to death right there on the spot. Rolling her eyes at herself, she made herself listen instead to the sound of the air hissing in and out of her lungs, the water lapping around her body and the spitting of the candles on the walls.

As her body finally cooled down, her breaths gradually loosened and an image came to her of the desert sky at night. Instantly, her body started to soften, and she could feel the tension draining out of her like the water dripping from her skin. The vision was so vivid she could almost reach out and touch the spread of stars, and she could have sworn she could hear the chirp of the night crickets and the sigh of wind over the dunes.

After a while, she found herself shivering, and lowered herself back into the water. She began to think about Kaylem and how blissful the past moon had been. Maryam had left them alone for the most part, and they had spent hours making love in private corners of the dwelling, and wandering aimlessly through the markets.

There had even been one incredible day when she had talked Kaylem into disguising themselves as servants and wandering along the river. She smiled at the memory. Afterward, they had slept on the roof, watching the stars and worshipping each other until the sky was gray with predawn. As the water cooled to a more comfortable temperature, Saoirse's eyelids began to feel impossibly heavy, and she leaned her head against the wall of the bath. As she tumbled into sleep, she found herself floating through the desert sky, higher and higher, until the air thinned to nothing and the light of the stars became brighter.

Eventually the brightness became blinding, and she felt the substance of herself being unraveled. Instead of feeling afraid, the process was an ecstatic undoing, almost like disrobing and freeing herself of constrictive clothing. Underneath the fabric of herself was a sense of bliss so strong it sent tears running down her face, and the light was so bright it obliterated everything else. She might have allowed the light to completely swallow her up had a noise not awoken her and brought her back to her body floating in the now almost cold water.

Opening her eyes, Saoirse creaked her stiff neck around enough to see Asi reaching for her, with a group of priestesses standing behind. Her body felt like a lifeless stone. She made her limbs move, squeezing her hands and wriggling her toes to bring them back to life. Stiffly picking her way out of the water with Asi's help, a memory jabbed into her, of when she was small and had parents who cared for her and treated her with love. She pushed the memory away and received the cloth that would rub the feeling back into her limbs and dry her off.

As she was dressing, she looked downward to see the small swelling that must still be hidden until at least the next month. The robe, as Asi helped bring it down over her body, brushed delicately against her chilled skin. Then she sat still while they fitted the headdress over her plaited hair. She was now relatively calm and as ready as she would ever be for what lay ahead.

CHAPTER 28

She pushed aside remnants of her previous worry over the coming feast, replacing it with the memory of her dream, the echoes of its beauty still reverberating inside her. Silently, she sent thanks to the gods for their blessing. The dream reminded her that she was more than her skin. Her deeper essence would always endure, no matter what insults the elite threw at her body and mind.

There was nothing more she could do at this moment but stand next to Asi, and as she waited to begin the climb, she focused her energy inward. An image of Inanna formed itself within the glow left from the dream and she welcomed the vision with a brilliant smile. This time, she would climb alone, with only the gods to accompany her.

As she approached the Sacred Steps, the sound of the people of Ur swelled as she drew nearer. As she rounded a corner, she began to hear their words. Many voices were raised in hope, telling of a golden age to come. One man called out a blessing that the gods would gift the new Oracle with the power to bring Ur to glory.

She smiled at the man as he came into view, belatedly remembering that he wouldn't have been able to see her face beneath the headdress. The man's eyes bulged when he caught sight of her, and he reached his arms out, gabbling excitedly. She nodded to him, which she realized a second later was an enormous honor. The man roared in triumph and raised his arms to the sky, babbling an incoherent prayer. The people around him grumbled good naturedly as the man jostled them all.

She turned her head toward the Sacred Steps, which were blurry through the veil of the headdress. Still feeling weak from the long soak, she wondered for the thousandth time how she would reach all the way to the top. "Don't look at the top," she muttered to herself. "Just don't look at the top." The crowd cheered as she set her foot upon the first step, and she allowed their noise to fade into the background. She looked at the top and swore softly. The steps stretched into the distance, into eternity.

"Just look at your rutting feet," she gritted out to herself, forcing her head down and her legs to climb. Soon she forgot about everything but the next step. Her ascent was slow and steady. She kept her eyes focused downward, watching nothing but her feet, becoming hypnotized by the movements, by her breath moving in and out of her body.

As she climbed, Saoirse noticed other pairs of feet to the sides of her. She allowed herself to look up enough to glimpse who stood there—the priests and priestesses lining the steps on the way up. The most junior of them stood lower down, and the high priestess would be the one to greet her on the top step of her climb.

At the Great Hall below, the Temple elite would be gathering to grudgingly welcome their new Oracle once the Initiation Ceremony was complete, Kaylem among them. He was really the only one she wanted to see, as well as Yana. She wished the three of them could just have a quiet meal on the rooftop of their abode to celebrate, instead of all this.

Saoirse's body grew heavy. She noticed that whenever she thought about the elite and their malice, her energy sapped away from her and left her weak. She forced herself from those thoughts, to instead contemplate the intense blue of the sky and a couple of eagles swooping overhead. A part of her flew with them for a moment, which gave her the energy to push her body up a few more steps.

The coolness of early morning was nothing but a memory now, the sun's blast becoming more intense with each passing minute. Sweat began to run down her body, which was quickly wicked away by the delicate silk. Soon, her head began to thump, and her body felt like it was full of mud-brick instead of flesh.

There was no option but to keep climbing. This part of the climb was familiar to her after the previous moon, and she found herself going into a trance-like state as she climbed. The entrance to the mid-way Sanctum was dark and cool as she approached, and Saoirse heard chanting emanating from within. She turned her awareness back to her feet and continued her climb.

Trudging with legs that felt like jelly, Saoirse cursed whoever made the rule that forbade her to leave her home unless properly accompanied. If only she could have walked around the city more often, she would have been fitter and more able to cope now. A wave of nausea rose up in her and she swallowed it down with a gulp. It would just not do, to lose the illegal breakfast she should never have eaten in front of the eminent members of the priestcraft. She swallowed and her aching throat clicked dryly.

She passed the mid-way Sanctum, the chanting disappearing

CHAPTER 28

into the whirr of the wind. Now, even her eyeballs were baking in the hot blasts of desert air, and it was becoming painful to breathe. The heat reminded Saoirse of her days in the full sun looking for firewood. Back then she always felt hungry, and Marsi and Deni would click their tongues at her and shake their heads as she scrounged around always looking for extra morsels to eat.

Now, she reminded herself, she only had to ask the servants and it was provided for her. She was healthy and rested, for the most part, despite the many nights spent hiding from Maryam and enjoying Kaylem's touch. The thought of seeing Kaylem soon lifted her energy and helped the nausea pass. It was only a matter of time before she could gaze into his eyes again.

Just as that burst of enthusiasm began to fade, a slight breeze chilled the sweat gobbled up by the fabric of her robe and gave her another boost. Looking to the side, she saw one of the most senior priests and nodded in acknowledgment. A laugh huffed out of her as she recognized his face from a night when he came to visit the inn. He looked up at her with narrowed eyes. Smirking under her veil, she moved her gaze back down to her own feet once again, only allowing herself to look up when she noticed another robed set of legs.

A senior priestess nodded now, looking hot and bothered by the wait. Saoirse nodded back. She was going to make it, and a sensation like the silver water from the well bubbled up inside of her at the realization. She smiled at the priestess from behind her veil, stifling an urge to pat the woman's cheek like a mother would pat a small, cranky child. The priestess looked taken aback, possibly expecting Saoirse to be exhausted and lifeless. This lifted Saoirse's spirits even more and her body surged up the final steps.

The top step surprised her, and she nearly stumbled into the arms of the high priestess, who looked down at her with her usual expressionless face. To Saoirse's left was the small chamber where Milar's poppy still hid. She pushed away all the memories of the time after the flood. Right now, she would need all her wits about her.

Anan stood beside the high priestess, she saw now, giving her a knowing grin, his eyes sparkling merrily, although she couldn't help but notice a certain tension in the way he stood and a redness to his eyes. Had he already used all the poppy from the first package? Would he be approaching her for another batch soon? She reminded herself to formally acknowledge him before she turned back to the high priestess, pushing her thoughts away from what likely lurked within them both.

She allowed herself, for a moment, to look around her and as she did, she gasped in awe. Anan and the high priestess were like two small blobs of darkness surrounded by a stunning sky, which almost blinded her in its brightness. Colors danced in the air like living things, and she found herself swamped for a moment with life, with the fullness and power of it. She became aware of an enormous, ancient presence, sparkling with intelligence and amusement, infinitely greater than the tiny awareness within her that she identified as herself.

Her own tiny awareness suddenly expanded outward until she became one, for just a thrilling, but terrifying instant, with that greater presence animating it all from within. She found herself part of the wind, part of the eagle in the sky, and part of the mountains she could just make out in the distance. Then, she *was* the sky, the yellow-brown earth, the silver streak of water snaking past the great city of Ur, the verdant green strips running along each side of that river, and the thousands upon thousands of other tiny living things making up the scene before her.

Before she ended up fragmenting into her surroundings, she shook herself and did her best to contain her essence back into the confines of her body. It was like trying to thread an entire herd of oxen through the eye of a bone needle. She gave up, instead just trying to find the center of herself, where her own tiny spark radiated from.

"Let the living blessing be invoked today," Saoirse gasped to the sky, the air, and the *life* thrumming around her. She turned to the still expressionless high priestess and took her hands in her own. "This is the day I take my rightful place as Oracle. I will give all I have to the people of Ur." The priestess's hands sat limply and awkwardly in hers and she released them with a twinge of disappointment. The high priestess had not shared the incredible moment with Saoirse at all.

"Yes, *Mistress,*" the high priestess answered in an almost bored tone. Saoirse looked more closely at the high priestess and a dark weight pushed her down for a moment. A servant passed Saoirse a mug of small-ale, distracting her from her scrutiny of the high priestess. She was so thirsty she almost choked on the cool liquid as she swallowed it down. Stifling a small burp, she looked out over the known world again, wonder and joy bubbling up out of her despite her worries. The breeze toyed with her headdress and she wished she could rip it from her head and allow her hair to fly with the wind.

"We are so close to the gods up here!" she called to the high priestess, whose body she now noticed with surprise, emanated a soft green which gradually merged with the glowing space around her. Saoirse sighed deeply and something released inside of her. It was the first time she had ever seen any kind of colors around the high priestess and now it looked like the woman seemed to be free of the Ushum infesting everyone else.

Dimly, Saoirse wondered how that could be, given the high priestess's position, but the coolness of the ale was now coursing through her parched body, and the beautiful colors in the sky tugged Saoirse's back to them. The life around her sang. She reached under her veil to wipe the last dregs of ale from her mouth, completely forgetting her manners. Then, she held her arms out wide and smiled, tears coursing down her cheeks.

"I didn't sense their presence during the storm, but today the gods are celebrating. Can't you sense them, high priestess? Isn't it glorious? Can you see the colors?" Saoirse turned in a circle until she was overcome by a bout of dizziness and knew no more.

CHAPTER 29

Saoirse awoke to cool darkness. There were people whispering and muttering around her. Someone was fanning her and sprinkling water on her face.

"If only you could see the colors," she mumbled. If only the people could perceive the blessings that were always there just waiting to be noticed... Then there would be no more despair, no more hatred. If everyone could see the colors, they would rejoice and know that they were all in the embrace of the gods. "The colors..."

"*Mistress!*"

Saoirse could feel small hands urging her up.

"*Mistress*, it is time. You must awaken. The high priestess is waiting. The sun is making its way across the sky."

"Just a little longer, Asi," she mumbled and turned herself away from the insistent nudging. The pallet she was lying on was cushioned and very comfortable. Her body was so heavy and she was so tired. Behind her eyelids, a dazzling show of lights and colors still played and the dizziness returned when she moved.

"*Mistress!*" Asi's nudging became prodding and Saoirse frowned at her rudeness. "It is time for the Oracle Initiation Ceremony. Everyone awaits you." Saoirse stiffened and there was a small pause, as though maybe Asi realized what she had done. Then Saoirse felt a hand softly rubbing her back, normally forbidden by anybody aside from Kaylem himself or a consecrated priestesses of high stature in the Temple hierarchy. The touch was nurturing, simple, and tentative. It sent tingles up her spine and she lay still, enjoying the rare caress, not wanting to ruin the moment by looking around.

It reminded Saoirse of when she was a small child and her mother would rub her back when she was upset. A surge of grief suddenly raged through her and lodged in her throat. She choked, noticing she was no longer wearing her headdress. Her grief would be plain for all to see on her face.

She blinked back tears that would only embarrass her and smudge the black on her eyes, allowing herself to enjoy it just for a moment longer, relishing the soft, stroking, anonymous hand. She wanted to stay under its caring stroke forever, all worries banished by the comforting movement. After a moment it stopped and the hand rested on her shoulder.

"*Mistress*, you must come now." The voice belonged to someone else. She cracked open an eye and saw one of the other highly ranked priestesses now standing above her. Asi was nowhere to be seen.

Many hands helped Saoirse rise and she was filled with gratitude for their tenderness. More tears tried to leak from her eyes, and she took a large breath in and out, trying to calm herself. A warm hand was held out to her and she grasped it like a child. The hand was small with work-roughened skin and then she saw Asi at the other end of it. Asi, she saw now, was loyal and had not left her side since the darkness of the early hours.

As Saoirse stood and looked around her, leaning on Asi, she saw that they were in the chamber where she had confronted Anan on the day of the flood. Gibil and Kusu both grimaced at her from their places on the wall and she suppressed a shudder. She turned her attention away from the memory and allowed Asi to tug her gently toward the brightness of the opening.

Asi's hand led her into the sun, and she blinked, unwilling to let Asi go. She reminded herself that many would be watching and it would not do to be seen holding a servant's hand. Reluctantly, she loosened her fingers. Alone, she composed herself, drawing up to her full height, which was more formidable than that of some of the men. Entering the tiny innermost Sanctum standing at the very pinnacle of the Temple, she waited until her eyes became accustomed to the gloom.

Her gaze was drawn first to the Sacred Flame, kept burning for eternity to signify the everlasting life of the gods. It was impossible not to think of Milar's blasphemous parcel of poppy still hidden under a brick behind the altar, no matter how much she fought to keep her mind clear.

But Milar was dead, and she was not a prostitute any more, she reminded herself over and over, blocking out the memories of the night he had tried to kill her. She had killed him instead and she had survived. She stopped for a moment, wondering if she truly deserved the honor about to be bestowed upon her. She had killed two men. It had been to defend herself and others both times, and yet...

A throat clearing noise interrupted her thoughts. Saoirse noticed the high priestess standing beside the Sacred Flame, almost tapping her foot in impatience. Struggling to hold the dwindling sense of connection she had felt so strongly earlier, she murmured an apology and approached the altar.

As she stared into the glow of the flame, Saoirse listened to the high priestess rushing through the chants. The words were beautiful. Why wasn't the high priestess lifted by the utterance of the sacred words in her mouth, the sense of them falling into the quiet of the Sanctuary like cleansing water through a waterway? The high priestess's face was expressionless as always and Saoirse saw with a shock that the words were actually meaningless to the high priestess. The woman was not actually capable of sensing the shifting, wonderful energies imbued into each word.

No wonder the Temple was corrupt, Saoirse realized with a rush of despair. The consequence of such blindness was a lack of passion for their work, leading to boredom. Even if Saoirse had been capable of holding the energy from her previous state of euphoria, there was little chance the high priestess would even have noticed, she saw now. Even so, the high priestess's voice was resonant and beautiful, and a glimmer of light showed around her at times throughout the chant.

Saoirse watched the high priestess more closely. There were dark streaks in the colors around the high priestess that reminded Saoirse of dried blood. The pretty green was gone. The words and tone of the chanting, she noticed now, were gradually changing from the usual honoring of the gods to something strange and different. Here and there was a word that clanged as it was uttered in a tuneless almost-shriek. Saoirse could sense the words somehow weakening something within her own body, as though it was poison.

After her exultant state of earlier, Saoirse was still feeling vulnerable and wide open. Losing the thread of the chant, she noticed that the streaks around the high priestess matched some dark puddles and streaks that lay around the altar. With a shudder, she realized that there was a coppery smell in the room, redolent with the unmistakable tang of blood, and she wondered why she hadn't noticed it as soon as she had walked in.

A set of images formed in her mind which made her want to scream and run from the Sanctum. She saw a young girl, screaming as a lesser priestess and one of the Temple men held her down, and another priestess holding a knife to her throat. In her vision, the sun was only just gracing the horizon and Saoirse realized she must be seeing what happened before her arrival. Her inner eye showed the silhouette of the high priestess looming in the light streaming into the entryway. Saoirse struggled to draw in a breath and she sagged onto the closest wall, her inner hearing filled with the luckless girl's screams.

A shard of black ice grew in the shuddering pit of Saoirse's stomach. Its chill made its way outward until her teeth chattered and every hair on her skin stood on end. The priestess's voice droned on and on, nothing like the beginning of the chant which had been filled with beauty. Saoirse broke her gaze with the high priestess, whose eyes had begun to flicker in the most terrifying and, unfortunately, familiar reptilian way. She wondered how the high priestess could have hidden even the colors around her so well, now that what must be the true ones were out for Saoirse to see.

The colors reminded her now of those around Milar when he had been trying to kill her and the brothel owner, Salik. Something inside of her sank further in the knowledge that whatever had been inside those men, and whatever was inside the high priestess, was now likely to be very angry at her.

Saoirse fought the panic that threatened to turn her insides to water. Even looking away from the high priestess didn't help the sense that something was trying to bore into her, as though a sharp spear was being drilled into her stomach. A pressure grew from her insides, which were being squeezed aside by something else.

Shadows in the corners of the ceiling began to expand toward her and whisper. The whispers bored into her despite jamming her hands over her ears, because the whispers were now inside of her.

You are not wanted here. You will lose this battle and your unborn children will pay the price. Your visions are worthless, there is nothing you could offer as an Oracle. You are arrogant and deluded to even imagine you could ever change anything here. You are weak and we are all- powerful. We will overcome your pathetic will and use you as a mindless tool of the Temple. Do not fight, there is no use, just surrender to the shadows and then you will no longer be weak, but strong and able to do all that you desire. We are here to offer you the world, yet you must surrender... just surrender...there is no more you can do, it is over...

Dark shapes oozed from the corners of the ceiling and stretched poisonous tentacles toward her. Saoirse could feel a scream growing in her throat, but she was paralyzed, and the scream stayed stuck inside. Trembles shuddered through the deepest parts of her. There was nothing she could do to fight them off.

She was weak, just as the shadows said. She was just a scared and lonely child all alone with no family, no friends, and nobody loved her. Kaylem was only after her power as the Oracle. She was nothing but an orphan, still a slave, just with fancier robes. The shadows whispered that only with them would she find true freedom and the power she needed to wreak her revenge against the ones who hurt her.

Saoirse felt herself slipping under, as though she was drowning. With the final dregs of her strength, she flung out a plea, a blind call for help. Not expecting much, she did her best to hold herself above the blackness that reached to swarm into the deepest parts of her, reaching into her will to turn her into a mindless puppet...

CHAPTER 30

Instantly, a blinding flash of light swelled from the center of her chest and filled the chamber. She glimpsed the essence of what looked to be master Hos making furious swatting gestures at the shadows, his eyes filled with thunder and his mouth open in a roar. It brought a small smile to her face and her heart filled with gratitude. She sent a small wisp of thanks after his retreating form as he nodded at her and disappeared. The shadows fled instantly, leaving Saoirse standing alone and blinking in front of the high priestess.

Saoirse's ears rang. The high priestess watched her expectantly, all sign of the sinister flickering gone. Saoirse narrowed her eyes back at the high priestess who, she was certain now, had tried to somehow infest Saoirse with an Ushum. The high priestess made a sound like a grunt of frustration and shook her head, as though disappointed.

"You must light this. I have finished," the high priestess told her in a dead voice, almost throwing a small, unlit torch at her.

I would rather serve a nest of evil widow spiders than this gods-damned Temple, Saoirse stopped herself from saying.

Another, quieter voice told her to keep her mouth shut as she was their only hope for change. It sounded suspiciously like master Hos, which gave her a tiny glow of comfort through the shock of what she had just been through. *Light the flame,* the voice told her. *Fire is pure, just light the flame.*

She reached the small torch toward the Sacred Flame and watched as a tiny sliver of fire first nuzzled, then licked, at the oiled fiber. This would be carried back down the Sacred Steps to light a larger ceremonial torch which would remain lit during the celebration feast.

Numbly holding the flame, she joined the rest of the small group of priestcraft who had been waiting outside the Sanctum. Together, in silence, they took the thousand steps back downward toward the Great Hall. Someone, probably Asi, had reinstated her headdress, which she had hardly noticed at the time. Somehow, despite her knees threatening to collapse, she found herself stepping down the last of the Sacred Steps. Now as she approached the rest of the elite, she was filled with a shaky relief.

The smell of cooking food wafted past in the gentle breeze, growing stronger as they drew nearer. Under normal circumstances it would have caused her mouth to water, but any hunger she might have had shriveled within her. Her stomach lurched along with her steps, and she swallowed the bile back down as well as she could, along with flashbacks of what had just happened in the inner Sanctum.

The journey toward the rest of the elite seemed to take forever and end far too quickly. Her knees trembled as much as her body. Had those things truly just happened in the inner Sanctum with the high priestess? The murmurs and laughter of the people waiting for her sounded so normal as she approached them. She shook her head to try and clear it. Were the shadows just nightmares because of her jangled nerves? A strong gust flicked the veil and sent a burst of air to her face. She heard the cry of an eagle echo in the cloudless infinity of the sky and did her best to return to her body in order to face the next part of the trial.

The Temple elite stood chattering in small groups outside the Great Hall at the bottom of the steps. Saoirse wondered what work these people actually did. The priests and priestesses, along with the scribes, seemed to do the lion's share of the actual worship and recording of that worship. So, what was left over for the elite? If Anan was before her, he might say that he ruled the Temple, which was a position of very high responsibility. But what, exactly, did that mean? Saoirse suspected it was actually very little.

Rage filled her, a searing wave of fury that threatened to pour out of her at how these hateful parasites had somehow managed to find themselves in the position of dictating the rules of life.

CHAPTER 30

What gave them the right to say whether one person and not another had any value? What gave them the power of life and death over the people of Ur? How dare they so callously bring so much evil, especially in the most sacred spaces dedicated to the worship of *life*?

As she came closer, Saoirse held in her shrieks of accusation at the ones she recognized from her gruesome vision of this morning's sacrifice. The priestess who had so casually cut the young girl's throat was standing talking to the man who had held the poor girl down. Saoirse would have emptied the contents of her stomach right there in front of them if she hadn't been so forcefully clenching her entire being.

Wishing she could just run away from them all, Saoirse sighed and forced herself to approach the waiting throng. A vision of Kaylem filled her mind and she yearned to see his face among them. Extravagantly dressed women tittered and cooed at each other, while the men slapped each other on the back, roaring with laughter. Were they really all filled with the same darkness that had just tried to fill her?

It looked to Saoirse like they were in an especially festive mood. Were they celebrating what they thought was her demise to an Ushum? She couldn't bring herself to meet any of their eyes, even though she noticed the ones closest to her were now peering at her in a curious, almost rude way.

Servants walked among them offering small morsels of food and mugs of ale. Saoirse noticed the high priestess whispering to Ashira and Kettel, then turning and walking away, leaving the two women rigid in their bearing. Saoirse suppressed a shudder, dreading what revolting scheme they would devise next. The horrors of the Sanctum made their petty schemes pale in comparison. Ashira and Kettel had not noticed her yet, which filled her with utter relief. They stood whispering intently to each other as she saw Kaylem break through the crowd to rush toward her. After that, she only had eyes for him.

"Shaji! I've been standing here like a man starving to death, wishing only to see your face." He lifted her veil, raking his eyes over her face, up and down. "But you're so pale! Did the ceremony go well?"

"The ceremony..." Kaylem's face fell as he took in the haunted look in her eyes.

"We'll talk about it later," he murmured, moving to her side to take her arm. Saoirse wished she could fall into his arms and sob, but instead she clung to him silently, forcing her feet to move her forward toward the Hall. As the two of them approached the entrance, she noticed the silence around them. The group was already disappearing inside, despite it being customary for them to wait until Saoirse had entered first as the honored guest. Saoirse hesitated a moment, taking a last breath of the clear air, the chirring of insects sweet in her ears. The eagle called again, and she wished she could be soaring with it instead.

"Shall we?" Kaylem asked, looking at her with concern as he removed her veil. Saoirse reminded herself to breathe again before moving, feeling too exposed with her face uncovered for all to see.

As they entered, Saoirse almost walked past Yana, who called out to her. She embraced her friend cautiously. Was Yana also affected by the darkness like the others? Would her eyes flicker in the same way? Was Yana, whose colors around her were also a deep green, hiding something uglier? Saoirse reminded herself that Yana couldn't stand the Temple ways and the other elite. Yana regularly met her eyes and Saoirse had never detected even a hint of anything else there but warmth. She hugged her friend back a little more strongly. Yana released her first and held Saoirse at arm's length, her eyes filled with friendliness and maybe also a flicker of worry.

"I've done my best to make sure there are no nasty surprises. Let's get this over and done with."

Saoirse squeezed Yana's arm in relief as Yana stepped aside for them to move further into the Hall. The stifling heat inside made Saoirse feel faint again, but she tightened her grip on Kaylem's arm and almost hung from his strength, stepping with him more deeply into the relative gloom. As they noticed her arrival, the guests slowly stopped their chatter, and everyone stood staring at her with the same air of expectation that the high priestess had earlier.

Did all of them know what the high priestess had attempted? Had they met together beforehand to plan how they would plant the Ushum inside of her as well? She took a moment to swallow down a bray of hysterical laughter before noticing Ashira standing nearby. Ashira's eyes were fixed onto her with an unreadable

CHAPTER 30

expression. Kettel stood benignly beside Ashira and gave a nod.

Saoirse turned away from them and made her way slowly to the head of the women's table, feeling as though she was walking to her doom in the stoning pits. Although, she thought as her feet automatically dodged around cushions and servants, she decided the stoning pits would have been preferable to literally being taken over by a daemon from the underworld.

The newly repaired curtain, she now noticed, sat open in anticipation of the speeches. It would close once the banquet began, and Saoirse hoped there would be no naked dancing girls tonight. Saoirse could see Kaylem standing uncomfortably among the group of still laughing men who took turns to slap his back so hard he almost fell over. She watched him and nobody else, glad to be left alone. He found her gaze and held it gently.

The high priestess groaned as she dropped onto her cushion beside Saoirse. Saoirse jumped and forced herself not to look over. Instead, she stared at her own hands as they wrung themselves into tortured shapes in front of her. There was a flurry toward the front of the Hall and Saoirse saw that the speeches were about to begin. Everyone else rushed to sit down.

The knowledge that Saoirse was surrounded by Ushum infested daemons caused her hands to writhe even more vigorously, to the point of pain, as she considered what was to come next. Yana had warned her that as the newly consecrated Oracle, she would be called up to deliver her first ever prediction to the Temple elite. Even worse, the high priestess would introduce her.

Saoirse forced a sip of small ale down to prevent herself from hyperventilating into a swoon. The speeches of the lesser elite would come first, according to Yana and Kaylem, then she herself would be the last to speak. In previous times, everyone would be anticipating the moment when the Oracle held the floor, but she couldn't imagine many would be keen to hear anything that came from her mouth tonight.

She looked around the Hall, trying to catch a glimpse of anyone else who might also be unaffected by the Ushum, and who she might feel even a glimmer of support from in a room full of dangerous enemies. She hoped for the thousandth time that when it came time for her prediction, everyone would be too inebriated to even notice. The guests were still talking and laughing among themselves, and Saoirse wondered who would be the first to start, feeling almost a little sorry for the one deemed the lowest official of the elite.

The high priestess grunted suddenly beside Saoirse as she unfolded herself from her cushion, causing Saoirse to jump again and give a little squeak. As the high priestess rose and made her way to the front of the Hall, more and more people fell quiet. Silence blanketed the room for a moment and then everyone fell to hushed whispering. Saoirse saw Ashira and Kettel nodding to one another in satisfaction.

"Oh Saoirse," whispered Yana, who had crept up beside her. "I can't believe this. The speeches were meant to start with Tumar! They've completely reversed the order of things. This is not what I planned. It was meant to happen at the end, before your first reading of the omens."

Saoirse almost cried in relief and felt her entire body let go of its tension.

"This is to prevent you from speaking, Saoirse. They're doing this to discredit you before you even take your place—"

For the first time since the blighted ceremony at the Sanctum, Saoirse felt like she could draw a full breath and she almost smiled at Yana. "Would they honestly have listened? It's for the best."

Kaylem's eyes were full of questions as he turned to her across the Hall. Saoirse shrugged her shoulders at him and turned back to the high priestess who was beginning a chant with a carefully blank face. The chant blessed the new Oracle and prayed for the Truth to fall like raindrops into Saoirse's heart in order to bring the message from the gods to all.

The melody was lovely and should have been stirring and mysterious, but the intention was utterly empty. Saoirse noticed that the high priestess was now openly glaring at her. So were many of the others around her, she noticed with a prickle. She looked down at the snarl of her hands still tangled on the table. If only the high priestess had meant even a word of the blessing.

Anan then rose to speak with a smarmy smile on his face, his words full of innuendo. He didn't seem to care that whatever they had planned for her had failed. She guessed they would try again sometime soon and keep trying until they succeeded.

She made herself take a breath and to savor the small victory of earlier, instead of panicking about when the next time might be. Anan's speech brought roars and foot stomping from the

CHAPTER 30

men which pulled Saoirse out of her reverie. There were delicate giggles from the women. She watched the table in front of her and sipped on her small ale in silence.

By the time the next blessing had begun by a lesser priestess, conversation once again flowed in time with the clink of mugs against each other. The odd order of speakers was already forgotten now that the people had finished their second and third drinks. Each and every lesser priest and priestess took their turn to give blessings and speak empty platitudes of the golden age to come. The audience fidgeted and continued their conversations, which became louder as time progressed. They motioned regularly for the servants to refill wine and ale.

The last and youngest speaker to mumble through her blessings was completely drowned out as a group of men in the lower corner of their table began loud demands for the feast and music to begin. Her speech cut short, the blushing priestess left to quietly return to her seat as the servants pulled the curtain shut and brought out the first platters of food.

The small group of musicians chosen by Yana began to play, far from the lilting drinking tunes chosen by Ashira for Saoirse's wedding. This music was haunting, almost in a similar strain to the blessing earlier by the high priestess. Saoirse nodded at Yana in appreciation. The curtain was pulled closed, signalling the start of the meal. Everyone craned their necks in anticipation.

When the food finally arrived, Saoirse's stomach turned again, threatening to violently rebel. She toyed with her meat stew that would have been delicious under different circumstances, but the cloying spices only made her yearn for the freshness of the night outside. Conversation hummed in the air, making her head hurt. The high priestess, back turned rudely toward Saoirse, discussed something in a serious tone with the woman seated on the other side. Yana, who had insisted on sitting where she belonged at the other end of the table, met her eye encouragingly now and then. Saoirse raised her mug and drank as Yana downed yet another wine.

At first the people ate in a relative state of decorum until Saoirse heard the men becoming rowdier, having already finished their meals. A group of men began bullying the musicians into playing more raucous tunes. After a pause, the head musician started a lively, well-known ballad played regularly at inns across the land.

Yana looked at Saoirse with her eyebrows raised. The musicians had been told to try and prevent the group from getting rowdy. Saoirse gave another resigned shrug. The noise inside the Hall reached a roar. Saoirse noticed Ashira and Kettel talking intently, regularly glancing at her. The time passed agonizingly, and Saoirse wished she could just get up and walk out. Yana joined the women dancing to the music. She beckoned to Saoirse and whooped as the musicians started another popular tune. Saoirse wondered how her friend could so easily dance with these murderers and held in her scowl.

There was movement beside her and Saoirse looked up to see Ashira plop herself down onto the empty cushion on the other side of the high priestess. Ashira was flushed and there was a slight wobble to her head. The revelry in the background faded as the two women stared at each other without speaking. Saoirse dreaded to look too closely into Ashira's eyes.

"What is it you desire, *Mistress*?" Ashira spat the honorific as though forcefully ejecting something unpleasant from her mouth. Saoirse blinked at Ashira for a long time.

"Desire?"

"You, a common, filthy whore and your conniving husband now have all the coin and possessions you could possibly wish for. A fortunate turn of events has afforded you the greatest opportunity you could possibly have conceived in your sordid little lives." Ashira clutched Saoirse's arm and Saoirse pulled it away, trying not to retch at the smell of Ashira's breath. "How did you know about the storm? A refugee from farther up the river, perhaps? A *true* wise woman you overheard?"

Saoirse almost screamed as Ashira's eyes flickered. The same reptilian glimmer filled them as that of the high priestess earlier and Saoirse shrank her body as far away from Ashira as possible, wondering if she should silently call for master Hos again. Nasty black and brown colors jerked around Ashira, and her mouth twisted until her lips were pale with fury. Saoirse tried to move herself back as Ashira brought her face too close. "And yet you still seek to continue this pretense in the face of all of us openly despising you. Why do you not collect your riches and leave?"

Saoirse looked away and forcefully held onto her bile. The last thing she wanted was to see even more of the terrible

CHAPTER 30

presence squatting inside Ashira's body. She wondered what kind of person Ashira might have been before the Ushum had taken over. Should she feel sorry for what might be left of Ashira locked away in the depths? Or was there nothing left of the true Ashira but her empty flesh?

The thought of the true Ashira trapped somewhere inside gave Saoirse the courage to look her in the eye, trying to find even a glimmer of someone human. Ashira's mouth worked for a moment before she continued, her eyes still glimmering and glinting in a way that made Saoirse want to throw her drink at Ashira's face and run.

"...you now possess more than enough to start your lives elsewhere, and you can hire a nurse for your babe once it arrives." Saoirse realized she had missed a whole lot of what Ashira had been saying, but at the mention of the babe, Saoirse tried not to gasp in shock. Somehow Ashira knew!

Saoirse did her best to keep her face neutral but couldn't help the blink of surprise. "Oh yes, *Girl*," Ashira spat with a smirk. "Do not underestimate me. Had I known of your ambition, a mere mention to Kettel and you would have been put to death after murdering poor Milar. Only the gods themselves know what other blood lies unseen on your hands."

"Blood? On *my* hands?" Saoirse laughed in Ashira's face.

"How dare you laugh at me..." Ashira grabbed Saoirse roughly around the shoulders as the words almost exploded out of her, in time with each shake. Saoirse barely noticed as a vision erupted from the touch and she sank her own hands into Ashira's.

"Your husband! He is missing, Ashira." Ashira tried to draw back, a mix of disgust and horror upon her quickly sobering face. Yet Saoirse held Ashira steady, preventing her from escaping her touch. "I know where you buried him after poisoning him with the oleand juice. Oh, yes, Ashira. I also do not miss much. I can see it now..."

It was Saoirse's turn to curl her lip in disgust as her fingers drove dents into Ashira's ashen skin. "How you flogged that unfortunate servant boy to dig such a large hole in the mud so it would fit your husband's body. Then you sent the boy to his death as well. How could you do such a thing? Oh, and now I can see before that. Your husband is coming home from the inn, his favorite prostitute's scarf mistakenly remaining in his pocket.

You suspected, but it was never something you truly wished to discover. Kettel is the only one who knows." Saoirse's eyes narrowed as she slowly returned to the present. "Did your beloved husband call out to you for mercy before he died? Blood on your hands, indeed."

Ashira's eyes had grown to saucers, the whites of her eyes showing as the eyes themselves rolled around in their sockets. Saoirse wondered what kind of battle the true Ashira, if she was still in existence, fought to regain control, both of her own emotions and the conversation.

"You..." Ashira pointed a shaking finger at Saoirse and the reptilian glint returned. "You are an abomination of nature who should have been put to death at birth. It's a wonder you even survived to become the fraud you now are, preying on all around you with your so-called *talents*." Ashira spat, narrowly missing the feet of a cowering serving boy. "To see into the darkness of others hearts can hardly be called a *gift*."

Saoirse fought a hysterical giggle trying to force its way up past her constricted throat. She decided to stay quiet instead of pointing out Ashira's glaring hypocrisy. Ashira twisted her mouth into a sneer and her unnatural gaze bored into Saoirse, who felt momentarily paralyzed by its venom.

"I cannot believe that the Temple once saw such a grotesque ability as sacred. It's fortunate we move into a time that is no longer so ignorant and we can recognize you for the accursed daemon you are."

Ashira's accusation broke the spell. "Me, a daemon? Ashira, I think you need to go look into the mirror before flinging baseless accusations like that."

Ashira's eyes flickered furiously again. "It is a curse you carry, *Girl*. Not merely in your abilities but where your life will ever lead you. You can be nothing but cursed. Cursed and hated by all!" Ashira cawed with a mad laugh and gulped her wine, spilling much of it down her front in the process and choking on a mis-swallow.

"Choking on your hoarded spite, Ashira, or whoever you are in there? Or are you still feeling the wrath of the spirits of all those you've murdered?"

Ashira clumsily wiped her face with her robe. "You should be terrified of me, whore-Oracle, for you have far worse to fear of me, than I of you. Tell everyone here my secrets and see if it makes a grain of difference. Kettel and I are the ones who lead the Temple. The men bluster and fluff their cock's feathers, putting on a show of power. Yet it is the women who ultimately lead Ur, and you are deluded if you think to bring us down."

Saoirse shook her head in wonder. "You are very presumptuous, Ashira. I had no intention of bringing you down, nor any interest in your pitiful games of power. Actually, until seeing the scope of your depravity, I didn't even imagine someone could stoop so low as you have done lately in so many ways. It's almost the behavior of a terrified child."

Ashira's eyes narrowed. "What is it then that you desire from us?"

"I desire nothing but to live my life alongside my family. I desire to live in the light of truth and all that is good, and to pass as much of that goodness as I can to the citizens of Ur. Is that why I am such a threat to you, Ashira? Do I hold the power to bring you to nothing due to my preference for what lies at the heart of truth? No matter how many dirty little secrets you hide, I'd rather just get on with the work I'm here to do. Just leave me alone and I'll be more than happy to stay as far as I can get from you."

Ashira gave a simpering smile laced with bitterness. "My heart bleeds for your sincerity and I do not doubt that the gods are applauding up there in their little home." Ashira's eyes became hard and glittering again, and the round pupils turned to vertical slits. "You and Kaylem should leave Ur at sunrise tomorrow. Pack that elaborate new coach of yours and all your many bags of coin."

Saoirse made to stand up, but Ashira held her in place. "Nobody here even wants an Oracle these days. The people no longer believe in such superstition, and you'll find you are wasting your... talents... on petty squalls between neighbors. How can this be helping the city of Ur? Leave, or your lives will become far worse than they already are."

Ashira leveled a hard stare at Saoirse for a moment and then abruptly stood, knocking over the servant she had nearly spat on earlier. Steadying herself against the wall, Ashira stalked away, seating herself back beside Kettel who had moved away from Saoirse at the first opportunity she could. The music and dancing took preference once again in Saoirse's consciousness, swelling suddenly in her ears, and she looked around in surprise.

Saoirse was sure those reptilian eyes would haunt her dreams for the rest of her life. She told herself, with a dash of bravado, that it was only one more thing on the list that would wake her screaming at night as there were plenty of other memories already doing the same. This latest one could get in line. She wandered her gaze around the Hall, taking in the depravity surrounding her.

Greasy remnants of food were smeared all over the delicately woven rugs only recently cleaned after the wedding celebration. Works of art that would leave many open mouthed with their beauty were knocked from their place and destroyed in wild bouts of dancing and the occasional fight. Splashes of wine and ale could be seen marring areas not stained by food spills.

Even the tapestries lining the walls weren't immune from the destruction, one of them stained red after a mug of wine was carelessly thrown away by one of the dancing women. It reminded her of the puddles of blood marring the altar. Saoirse abruptly stood and made her way to the curtain. She peeked out into the men's section to find Kaylem, who was yawning and looked just as she felt. He gave her a small smile. A noise behind her brought her attention toward the nearest corner where she noticed a young priestess vomiting into a painstakingly decorated urn.

Returning her gaze back to Kaylem, she noticed that he was slowly standing and turning his body toward the exit. He looked back at her with a shrug, gesturing at everyone around them who wouldn't even notice their departure. Saoirse nodded eagerly and made her way along the rear wall where she met Kaylem at the door. They stepped outside without a backward glance. A blast of cold night air made her shiver, even though she took in huge, grateful gulps of it.

Kaylem tucked his thick shawl around her, and she leaned into him, desperate to feel his solidity, and warmth, and goodness. The quiet outside filled their ears and they stopped for a moment to take in the stars faded by the light of the full moon at its zenith. As they headed homeward, there were no words to speak. The city lay still and dark, awaiting the new dawn that many of the citizens of Ur were hoping would somehow be different now that the new Oracle was officially consecrated. Saoirse pushed away the dread of her coming role and she looked at Kaylem as they arrived at their abode.

CHAPTER 30

Kaylem opened the door for her, and they stood in utter darkness. The servants had not expected them to be back at such an early hour, so they were completely and wonderfully alone. Taking her hand, he led Saoirse slowly up the stairs to his chamber where he stood before her, stroking her face in soft caresses that drew tingles down the softness of her skin. Saoirse breathed out in a sigh and cupped his hand with her own, wanting only to be in the moment and forget everything about the day.

She drew his hand down to her heart, which spoke out a message just for him. With his other hand, Kalyem untied the loose knot of her headscarf, tossing it to the floor. She shook her head and allowed her hair to fall freely around her shoulders. Next to be discarded was his turban, and with shared breaths they raked gentle fingers through each other's hair, massaging tight scalps and running lines of tingling coolness down eager flesh.

Saoirse pulled Kaylem's robe away and smoothed her palms down his chest. The whisper of her skin on his awoke a deep ache in her. Suddenly impatient to be rid of the final evidence of her ordeals, she pulled the silken robe from her own body, with a half-formed thought that she might burn the thing later on.

There was nothing she wished for in that moment but for the whole of her to be as close to him as possible. His warmth radiated around her like a small sun, and she basked in its glow as she leaned into his embrace. His hand found her abdomen and circled the swollen mound; one, two, three times, then moved gently lower. Saoirse leaned her hips toward his hand, which worked into the core of her and intensified the ache until the whole of her throbbed. She moaned, putting her own hands to use as their lips joined, moving of their own accord in a slow dance.

As Kaylem's gentle workings caused her to arch and draw her breath in an ecstatic hiss, they moved to a low bench where Kaylem gently sat her down and parted her, kneeling to kiss her warmth deeper inside. The air around them hummed, then began to shimmer. Saoirse breathed out in a groan as Kaylem's tongue coaxed her to climb, higher and higher. Just as she thought she had neared the peak, yet another rise appeared for her to climb and soon the tension within was screaming to be broken.

Grabbing his shoulders, Saoirse nudged him backward until he lay, stretched out for her on the pallet like an offering. She eased the length of him into her until she straddled him and they were gloriously joined, breathing in deep gasps. Their eyes locked together as she noticed from the corner of her vision that the colors danced around them like a celebration. The pulse deep within her made her entire body throb and she undulated with him in time to its beat.

Faster and faster it pulsed and both kept its time as it drew them up into a delirious spiral. Breaths heaving as one, they allowed the spiral to pull them into its apex where a shattering caused the colors to break into a cascade of rapturous sparks. Their cries shattered the stillness of the night. Their tears of joy and grief mingled as they lay, entwined in each other's limbs to watch the fragments of colors dance their way across the ceiling, eventually dissipating to join the glittering stars above.

CHAPTER 31

Saoirse sat nervously in a very uncomfortable chair that she was certain was designed by a craftsman who had never imagined having to sit in it himself. She could picture someone very important sitting in it for important meetings, such as the king. Ashira might have liked it, too. It was ornate to the point of gaudiness. It would have been nice to even have a cushion to sit on, but the hardness of the bare timber already made her rear ache.

She surreptitiously ran a hand along one of the armrests, decorated with gold embossed carvings of various scenes of rich people over-eating and drinking. A similar scene lined the other armrest, but depicted sexual conquests that would have been impossible in real life. Behind her, on what should have been the back rest but was mercilessly brutal if she leaned on it, two snakes were entwined together, one red and one black.

A line of priests and priestesses stood along the side walls of the narrow Oracle's Chamber in obvious resentment of having been chosen for this task. It made her want to slap them for having so little faith in her, despite spending most of the night in fits of worry that she might need to invent prophecies if nothing came to her today.

Worse, she was terrified that her unenthusiastic attendants would know and report back to their various superiors. She tried to remind herself of how well the spontaneous reading had gone at the markets with the merchant and she wondered how the man was faring. She hadn't seen Abdul at the markets since.

Despite eating sparingly of goat's cheese on flat bread before her arrival, the meager meal felt as though it had turned into hot ash and threatened to crawl its way back to burn her throat. Forcing herself to swallow a mouthful of ale with an uncomfortable click, the liquid made her stomach feel stretched to the point of wanting to eject its contents all over the beautiful rug at her feet.

There were no wall vents at all in this part of the Temple complex. It was set in an area deep in the inmost workings of the main building, somewhere behind the Sacred Steps. To Saoirse it felt like a dungeon, albeit an overly sweet-scented one, but the fragrant oils only made the space feel even smaller. They would have been cloying in their intensity even had she not been of delicate stomach already. The rich decorations further served to clutter the room, and she yearned to be out in the fresh air and sunlight. Even the abode that she had so desperately wished to escape began to hold more appeal.

Her ceremonial headdress sat uncomfortably and made her head feel so heavy she wondered how she would keep it upright for much longer. Along with the ancient lapis lazuli gemstone lying against her forehead that had been reverently lowered over her, the entire thing now threatened to give her nothing more than a thumping headache. It was all, apparently, supposed to represent the Sacred Sight.

She told herself not to be so negative. This piece had been worn by previous Oracles since before writing existed to record such things, and from the moment the stone had touched her forehead, she had jolted in recognition of their presence. The previous Oracles would have been real Oracles, accepted and celebrated by the temple, and she could sense how much of their power the stone had retained after their deaths. Saoirse wasn't certain what she was exactly, but she couldn't quite entirely block out the echoes of Ashira's vitriol from the Oracle Initiation ceremony only a mere few nights before.

Doing her best to avoid imagining those past Oracles looking down on her with disapproval for her lack of training and custom, she tried to force herself into at least looking like she was calmly and eagerly anticipating what was to come. Apparently, soon she would begin some of the classes all priestesses usually undertook before their consecration. The thought of sitting in a room together with a bunch of sniggering children as they learned the basics made her shiver even more with dread.

And yet she wondered how there would be time to ever learn anything now that she was here sitting in this chair. There had been so long between Oracles the citizens of Ur had apparently become desperate enough to line up around the corner of the Sacred Steps. As she had passed them, hidden by her many shawls and scarves on her way to the Oracle Chamber, she had almost torn herself away from her entourage and fled. It had only been her long talk with Kaylem the night before on their rooftop refuge, outlining how the process would work, that kept the shock at bay. The reality, though, was far more intimidating than his descriptions.

The richly brocaded curtain blocking her vision to the outside world twitched. With a barely suppressed tremor, Saoirse watched to see who had paid the most silver to be the first. It drew back jerkily, and a man strutted in who looked and felt far too big for the room. Her claustrophobia worsened. She wished for a fan, certain that if she demanded one it would be brought, but she didn't wish to come across as a needy shrew on her first ever session. The strong smell of the man's sweat mixed with some oil he was wearing, plus the medley of incompatible other fragrances in the airless space, made her stomach rebel yet again.

The way he looked and the air he exuded destroyed her hopes of starting gently. Saoirse guessed he was a gentleman farmer who overlooked many peasants, not required to lift a finger in working the land himself. He seemed accustomed to barking commands and she could see he was struggling with his desire to bark rudely at her. Instead, he appraised her like she was a farm animal.

The man fiddled with his gleaming moustache, unleashing even more fragrance into her space. She could feel her mouth twisting in repulsion and forced herself into a more neutral facial expression. He stood smugly upright, not performing the customary sweeping bow that would have been performed without fail in previous times. Kaylem had told her that all of the people seeking her advice should make obeisance to her while in front of her like this man was.

Saoirse reluctantly allowed it to pass, unsure what she should even say. The clergy lining the walls smirked at each other on seeing the man's rudeness and Saoirse's lack of assertiveness. She forced her attention back to the new arrival, flat and heavy in the knowledge that she had already lost the respect of all in the room with her inability to demand the proper customs. The opportunity to say something passed when the man lifted his head, allowed his eyes to flutter self-importantly, and took a breath to speak.

"*Mistress*," the man announced, as though he was berating her. She frowned at him, and he smiled and winked. She wished she could throw a bunch of creative insults at him like she used to be able to do at the inn of Ur when a customer became too rowdy in the main room. Back then, there were a couple of strong men who worked for the inn waiting to back her up. She mentally shook herself away from pining after a past filled with horrors that she had literally prayed every day to be free of, bringing herself back to the present.

"Many blessings and may you live in wisdom, wise Oracle," the man added in a voice that inferred she was far less great than he was. "I am called Siro and I come to beg a great favor." His words were exactly in accordance with what Kaylem told her should be said, although his voice dripped with scornful insincerity. She held her head high and looked down her nose at him, despite the sneer on his face at his petty victory.

"What is it you wish to know?" The reply came out in a voice that was, infuriatingly, too small and, to her great disgust, held a slight tremble. One of the priestcraft actually sniggered. Siro raised an eyebrow at the noise, but then turned back to Saoirse with a sigh.

"It is my wife." In that instant, his entire expression hardened even more. "I work hard, bring her all the riches she could possibly desire. She possesses the best of everything, yet do I receive gratitude for my toils?"

Siro scuffed his foot and shrugged, clearing his throat loudly. "I think not, and it makes me wild with fury that she treats me so. I am a very important man with much to accomplish and do not possess the time to waste on such insolence. I am of a mind to turn her out if she continues to hold her blatant disregard for my efforts."

The look in his eyes was almost pleading now, and she could see how he struggled with any kind of humbling emotion. "I do my utmost to give her my regard, even allowing many servants to the care of herself and the children. I suspect that she has committed the ultimate of unrighteousness by lying with another. There are

CHAPTER 31

times I wish to beat her, my passions run so high at her disrespect and disregard. I must know. Does she lie with another?"

Saoirse attempted to arrange her face in a neutral expression, not entirely sure what to say for a moment. For all his obvious feeling for his wife, the man exuded violence from every pore of his skin. It was difficult for her to concentrate past the cloud of his seething emotion, not to mention his overwhelming fragrance which continued to assault her from every angle. She wished she could demand the man be forcibly removed from the room and thrown down the Sacred Steps.

"Have you a possession very much valued by your wife?" she asked instead.

"I took the liberty of bringing her marriage pendant." He handed Saoirse the piece and she took it, unsure what to do next. The chair became even more uncomfortable, and she shifted on the seat in irritation, thinking longingly of the many cushions along the low table where her and Kaylem sat for meals, or the mound of lovely soft furnishings of their rooftop escape. This entire charade was likely to end up being a waste of time, both for the man before her as well as all the attendants and, most of all, for herself.

Nobody wanted her to be here. She fantasized handing back the marriage pendant and just walking away. But now in her distraction, something was happening to her. The chair's discomfort became far less obvious. The man's presence faded and then a blankness filled her being. A tiny part of her sat in the world of the living, in a place full of color and sound, not to mention smell. The rest was in a gray place of nothingness devoid of any vitality. She fought against it. This hadn't happened in the markets with the merchant. She hadn't even really seen anything much there. It was more just knowing what words to say, more than anything.

As the scene before her became farther and farther away, she numbly wondered if somehow she had died. Maybe Siro had struck her and she was lying dead on the floor. Her inner essence observed the waiting man with detachment. It was certainly an improvement on the terror she had felt earlier, and she noticed now, that essence had somehow expanded to fill the space in a way that made her more able to breathe. She would gladly have stayed there forever to escape the tension in the room, although the worry of botching her first sitting caused her to hold a tiny part of herself back.

There was no sense of anything at all lying on the other side of this blankness aside from more of the same, and she had the feeling that if she expanded her awareness, it would stretch out forever. Forgetting her earlier relief to escape from the chamber, she now struggled to retreat from the nothingness, wondering if she would welcome the overpowering cloy of the room if she was to find her way out of this trance.

Even though she could see the man tapping his foot vigorously, Saoirse could not even hear the noise of its collisions with the floor. After recognizing that her struggle would only cause more waiting for those around her, she eventually gave up and surrendered into the strange sensation, completely at the mercy of whatever process was occurring.

Tap tap tap tap tap tap tap.

The sound of something alive boomed its way into her hearing through the nothingness. She used the sound as a beacon to guide her consciousness back into the room.

Tap tap tap tap tap tap tap.

The sound was comforting in its familiarity, yet unsettling in its urgency. The impatience of the noise pulled at her and she felt herself being jerked uncomfortably back into her body, the sensations in the room now harsh in their intensity. The room was even smaller somehow and her throat closed over, forcing her breath to whistle in and out.

Now Siro had red darts flying every which way from the dark soup of colors surrounding him. Saoirse could see that he was very close to walking out of the room, but she was now beyond caring whether he stayed or departed. Saoirse changed the grip on his wife's pendant in order to return it to him and suddenly her tongue was tied with shock as the woman's terror hit her like a bludgeon. A gap opened in her consciousness, like curtains being drawn apart, which brought forth a vision.

Blood flowed freely down Siro's wife's face, mingling with her tears, as she cowered from his onslaught. It was not uncommon for a man to forcibly lie with and beat a woman, although Saoirse found it impossible not to feel revolted, especially with the brutality Siro brought to his actions. Another vision came, of Siro roaring obscenities while his wife shielded the children with her body. A mug of ale in his meaty hand splashed its contents in time with every inebriated, bellowed oath. Saoirse sat for a moment trying to separate herself from the woman's emotions, as well as from her own anger toward the farmer who was now boiling over with ferocity.

"Well, what can you see?" He growled.

"Silence! I am not yet ready to speak." A surge of power flashed through her. This man and his petty rages would not be getting the better of her. She had been somewhere else this morning in her trance, maybe even to the underworlds, and returned unscathed. Her fear for this man paled in comparison, and she saw that his true need was to be brought kicking and screaming to a more lasting humility.

Saoirse heard him splutter in reaction to her command and imagined him almost purple faced in his fury. She wanted to laugh, but instead forced herself to keep her eyes closed, unwilling to look at him quite yet. The moments passed and Saoirse felt the man's nerves screaming. She was glad of the attendants now, even though she could feel their impatience for this to be over with. Siro would not be going anywhere now and, knowing he had lost ground in his domination over her, he was ready to fight to the death. She forced herself into a semblance of calm, finally opening her eyes and focusing on a statuette of Inanna placed in a notch of the wall.

"I can see where the heart of your dilemma lies." She now allowed herself for the first time to look directly at the man, whose rage scattered momentarily into confusion in the face of her cold glare. Within that glare she could now sense the past Oracles contributing their disapproval, not upon her anymore, but straight at Siro, whose bluster evaporated into genuine fear.

She and the past Oracles glared at him until he broke the gaze and looked downward. She could see that tears formed in his eyes, which he jerkily and savagely flicked away. Her heart beat a tremulous victory dance within her chest. Her lips twitched with a force she was almost incapable of holding within the physical limits of her body. She loomed over the man who stood with his head bowed for the first time since entering.

"What do you see, *Mistress*?" he mumbled through clenched teeth, unable now to look up at her. Saoirse sensed that the attendants lining the walls were now watching with interest, but it no longer mattered as she fought to gain control of the awesome power surging through her. She understood that she must translate the surge into something this man would understand, putting it into words he could not deny. The harshness in her voice covered up her overwhelmed tremble as she allowed the power to use her tongue.

"Your wife is a gentle soul is she not, Siro? She yearns for harmony and wishes not to feel terrified of her husband anymore. Only then may it be possible for her to cherish you in the way you desire… that is, if it is not too late. A dog that is kicked and roared at, instead of petted, will become filled with hostility and fear toward the one assailing it." Siro now looked up at her in indignation, opening his mouth in denial.

"Silence, shameful wife beater!" Saoirse roared and the man once again uttered a strangled splutter. Even the clergy blinked up at her now, their eyes wide in their faces. The surge was now impossible to hold with her conscious control and it found its way out of her any way it could. She felt it streaming from her eyes and mouth as she addressed the now cowering man. She listened to the words coming out of her own mouth with fascination, admiring their sagacity.

"Do you wish for your children to learn the ways of violence, or devotion? So far, they have been infected with your fear and hatred, like they are diseased. You must from now on be gentle with your family. It is time for you to learn patience, otherwise you will die alone, unloved."

She breathed in and out, an enormous breath that felt as though she breathed the entire scene around her. "Nobody will discover your body, Siro, which will lie rotting on the straw until it is mere bones, your flesh withered by moons of time. Nobody will even care until tax collectors come to take all your riches that you worked so hard to gain. Your coin will spend years uselessly gathering dust in the Temple coffers and your spirit will twist in torment in the netherworlds for your evils."

The man now twitched at her feet she noticed, much to her satisfaction. She suppressed a desire to kick him as he was so close, his nose pressed to the floor as he should have done all along.

"You have forgotten to honor the gods who nourish us all. You have forsaken their great riches of the heart. Instead, you have replaced that for love of the coin. It is of great danger to spurn abundance of the spirit. Your own spirit is now shrunken and mean, and you seek to reach in and destroy the souls of those around you because you begrudge any spark of joy they still hold."

Siro's shoulders shook convulsively and Saoirse almost smiled before she caught herself. It wouldn't look good to be celebrating such an important man's suffering.

"In order to be happy, Siro, you must do the very thing you dread. Turn your rage into devotion for the gods, as well as for your wife and children. Tame your temper. It is you who have done them wrong, and you must honestly seek their forgiveness if you do not want to lose them. For they love you despite the way you treat them, even though they will not tolerate your treatment of them for much longer."

Saoirse shook her head in disappointment. "As it is, they would rather live a poor life away from you, than continue with you and your riches. And if you continue the way you are, your sons will go on to become just as angry as you. Is that what you truly want in your heart, Siro?"

The farmer looked at his bare feet, shuffling them on the rug so hard Saoirse imagined their friction would cause the rug to smoulder. She could see from his colors that his rage had increased a thousand fold, and he was desperately controlling his desire to roar vile obscenities at her in the same way he did at his wife and children.

Never would a woman have spoken to him in such a way since his mother, and Saoirse suspected his mother may not even have chastised him when necessary. The man clenched and unclenched his jaw many times in the buzzing silence that followed. Saoirse could not avoid feeling a slight tinge of unease at her outburst, as this man was very influential within his circle and could possibly arrange an unpleasant end for her if he so chose.

"What do you suppose I would die of in the safety of my own home?" he growled.

"Accidents and illnesses occur when least expected, and without our loved ones to care for us, our bodies become vulnerable to perish in isolation."

Siro looked at his feet mauling the carpet for a while longer, his breaths coming in heaving gusts.

"*Mistress*, you did not answer my original question," he snarled, "does she lie with another?" He addressed the rug instead of her face. The question brought forth a new surge of power and once again she opened her mouth to speak, unsure of what words would issue from the strange, unknowable depths within her being this time.

"Do you really want to be asking this question given the indiscretions your own behavior has been full of? I would say that you only feel insecure because of your own infidelities." The indrawn breaths of both Siro and the attendants distracted her for a moment, and she looked down to see her hands massaging the gold inlays.

She could see dates hanging from intricately shaped palm trees, and plates of what looked like olives. She took the opportunity to look up again and pierce Siro with her own fury. "You do not deserve such a kind and loyal woman who has always waited patiently for your return, while you lie with prostitutes and anyone else who will lift her robes on your travels."

She didn't mention that the poor woman had been terrified of stepping a foot out of line even in Siro's absence in case he discovered any excuse to punish her further. Saoirse sneered openly at him now.

"Be humble from now on, Siro. Claim your inadequacies as your own and maybe you stand a chance of saving your marriage. You might yearn for respect and adulation, yet how can you honestly expect that when you treat those around you in such a way? You have created for yourself your own prison of fear and anger."

She sat straighter and took a breath, wanting this to be over. "One more thing; do not *ever* force your wife to lie with you again without her accord, otherwise you will rue the day you ever touched her with violence in your heart. This audience is now concluded. Begone!"

She flicked her wrist at him dismissively, throwing his wife's marriage pendant at him. Siro turned on his heel and stalked from the room without even a farewell, almost tearing the curtain down in his exit. As he left, Saoirse could see the firestorm of rage around him, and she ruefully thought of how there was now yet another who despised her.

The priests and priestesses lining the wall, whom Saoirse had momentarily forgotten, stared at her open mouthed. One priestess who nodded and smiled was glared into neutrality by the priest beside her. Saoirse allowed herself a moment of satisfaction, as well as a subtle blink of gratitude directed at the wayward priestess who blinked back in acknowledgment with a twinkle in her eye. Elation filled her and she resisted the urge to stand and dance around the tiny room, instead forcing herself to sit in silence for the small break between seekers. Her body twitched restlessly, a residue of power seeking its way out via some kind of physical activity.

Next to enter was a heavily pregnant woman. Unlike the rage filled man, her demeanor was timid and full of nervous humility. She performed the sweeping bow with awkward exaggeration. Saoirse stifled a giggle. She noticed that some of the attendants were twisting their mouths in an attempt not to also laugh.

"*Mistress*, oh Highborn One." Saoirse almost burst out laughing at the honorific and imagined some of the priestcraft lining the walls might be inwardly sniggering as well. "I am so grateful to seek your advice. I am named Dalia. My dilemma is distressing, and I have sold many of our precious goats to listen to your words. The babe in my womb will be born before the next moon and there is a terrible question to be asked that I cannot even put to words, it is of such a shameful nature."

Tears began rolling down Dalia's cheeks and she dramatically handed Saoirse her marriage pendant. Saoirse sat in silence for a moment in confusion, waiting for the woman's question. As the silence stretched on, she replayed the woman's introductory words and then realized that she was even expected to somehow intuit the question, as well as its answer. She spent a further moment grumbling to herself in disbelief at the woman's nerve.

Saoirse looked at the Inanna statuette in the wall niche. It stood silently, gracefully, refusing to share any secrets. So, there would be no assistance from the goddess. Saoirse looked down at the pendant in her hands, for want of anything better to do. It was a handsome piece of carnelian embedded in a silver casing. It, too, was silent, unwilling to reveal what troubled the woman so strongly. Then the blankness began stealing into her again and for a moment she panicked, suppressing the urge to throw the pendant back at the woman and run from the airless room.

The terrible silence enfolded itself around her like a cloak.

Caught between worlds, she sat in the midst of the endless nothingness, wondering how much time had passed and whether her body would soon shrivel and die, trapped in such a state. Her mind was also taken over by the blankness and it wasn't until she surrendered into the oblivion, that something opened beyond it.

The agony of returning to her body brought her crashing back into herself with a shock. Her senses, painfully acute all of a sudden, brought back the shuffling and fidgeting of the many impatient people waiting for her. Her hearing became so sensitive that a mere brush of a hand against a robe became unbearable. A priest cleared his throat and it caused an explosion inside her head.

The walls moved in on her and sweat sprang out coldly all over her body. She had expected this process to be difficult, although if she was required to suffer like this each time a new seeker of her advice entered the room, she would surely perish by the end of the day. Squinting from the light of the torch which now seared her eyes, she wondered idly how previous Oracles endured such suffering day after day.

Before this strange, torturous state had come over her, the room had been too dim; now she could barely see from the glare. Her breath once again whistled in a throat that had become a clenched fist and she readied herself to faint. As her body became limp, her throat thankfully opened and a new vision pounded its way into her consciousness.

In the vision the swollen woman standing anxiously in front of her was slim and lithe, embarrassingly naked, and lying together with a man who was tall, handsome, and muscular. Their surroundings were humble, suggesting that the man was a peasant. Once they finished their writhing, Dalia rose, dressed, and regretfully took her leave. Walking a short distance to a richly appointed abode, she looked back at the peasant hovel, a single tear making its way down her cheek.

Once inside, she washed, donned a different robe, and joined a small, impeccably dressed, rat-like man for their evening meal. The vision changed to show Dalia once again disrobed, this time in the company of her husband. Unlike her passion with the peasant man, she lay under her husband dully, a faraway look in her eyes. Once this scene passed, the vision faded, and Saoirse was left with the knowledge that the babe was not of the woman's

CHAPTER 31

husband, who was sterile. The words fell into Saoirse's mind like rain and then moved to her throat, making it almost impossible not to speak them.

"It will be of concern when your son grows to be the image of his father. You will have a few years before the resemblance becomes so strong, they will look as two peas in a pod if they stand side by side."

Saoirse stopped for a moment and took a breath, hoping she hadn't said anything too incriminating. From the confused looks on the faces of her attendants she figured she hadn't been too indiscrete. It would have been devastating to share the woman's indiscretions in front of such witnesses, especially since Dalia's husband would likely be known by them. Dalia's eyes became saucers.

"I want to tell you a truth about your... neighbor..." Saoirse gave the woman a meaningful look with eyebrows raised. "You think your neighbor means you well, but actually this person is only using what you give as a convenience." Dalia's eyes grew, if such a thing was even possible, even wider and then tears began to form. She started to sob.

"It is best if you somehow convince your husband that this neighbor has committed a dishonesty severe enough for dismissal, yet mild enough to restart their life elsewhere. If this happens in a timely way, all will be well. If the neighbor remains, there will be trouble. Do not explain, merely grant the person some silver as they leave."

Saoirse stared at Dalia whose sobs only became more violent, unwilling to allow anything else from her mouth that might permit the attendants to discern what wasn't being said. The seconds ticked by until Dalia gathered herself.

"May I request that we converse in privacy?" Her breath hitched and she swallowed loudly. "With the predicament I find myself in, I feel uncomfortable in the presence of so many."

"They are here to protect me and take records of the readings, although I suspect that a lady so advanced in her pregnancy may not be of such a threat." Saoirse looked around at the goggling attendants. "Surely there are circumstances in previous times where an Oracle authorizes a reading to occur without the presence of the clergy?" A pause ensued, where they nodded soundlessly to each other and slowly filed out of the room. Dalia immediately collapsed again into a fit of sobbing.

"You will find a different kind of happiness once you are past your mourning for this man who cannot provide for you. He truly doesn't love you. What you have done, while deceitful, has become a blessing to your husband who will think he has fathered this fine son of yours. He will love you all the more, as well as love the boy who will become his son in everything but seed."

"But *Mistress*, I cannot imagine my life without Hakim. We talked about running away—"

"Then, Dalia, you truly are a fool if you think this way. This man sees you as an amusement. It is your husband who is devoted to you and will care for you and the babe. Running away with this man, or absurdly announcing your infatuation, will find you without a home, your babe perished from hunger and disease. This Hakim will abandon you. You will rue every day of the rest of your life, which will be severely shortened by hardship."

"You cannot truly mean such cruelties," sobbed Dalia.

"Allowing this man to stay on will also bring you heartache as you look at him every day, which will bring your regard ever further away from your husband. And, as the child grows he will resemble this man so closely, to have them side by side will do far worse than anything you could ever wish upon your worst enemy."

Dalia responded with a sob.

"You have been given the chance of a wonderful life and this farm laborer will do very well finding work elsewhere."

Dalia sniffed loudly, dragging her robe across her face as her eyes burned into Saoirse, who wanted to growl in frustration. "You *will* find happiness, Dalia, even though you yearn for passion. It will come with time. Turn your back on this man. Don't be foolish. You will be rewarded for your loyalty to your husband and for providing him with a son."

Dalia's face was a reddened mess of anguish. "*Mistress*, the words you utter are far crueller than anything I could possibly have imagined. Do you seek to wound me to the core?"

"You senseless girl!" Saoirse hissed in frustration. "I say this not to wound you but to ensure your life is harmonious and content. Your lover himself would say the same were it not for his selfish desire to keep his pretty little plaything. Although, isn't it true, that he has avoided you since your belly began to swell?"

CHAPTER 31

Dalia was breathing heavily and Saoirse swore she could almost hear the woman snarl.

"Those feelings you have, you think they're so strong, but they'll fade with time, and you'll one day look on the memory and smile with relief that you listened to me. Your husband will see that smile and know that you are finally, truly content. Especially so when you look at your son, who will grow healthy and strong with all the benefits of such caring parents. How are these words cruel? It is the truth and if you do not heed my advice, your life will become full of misery."

"I cannot accept that he doesn't love me." She hiccupped and wailed again.

"Ask him yourself before giving him the pouch of silver, after which you will tell your husband that his best worker stole your finest alabaster jar."

Face set with determination, the woman stood as abruptly as her belly allowed and, turning on her heel, took her leave with a toss of her head. Saoirse huffed and wished she had never wasted her energy trying to convince the woman of anything. People didn't want to hear the truth, she realized. They only wanted pretty lies.

Taking advantage of the moment of solitude before the attendants returned, she closed her eyes and leaned against the back of her chair despite its uncomfortable terrain, wishing she could lie down on her comfortable pallet in her chamber at home and sleep. She made a note to bring a couple of cushions next time for her back, which already drew, and ached, and felt cold and stiff on the hard surface. No matter how much gold and fancy designing the chair boasted, she would much rather have reclined on a simple rug on the floor of their rooftop sanctuary with a couple of cushions. And maybe an ale.

Had she known it would be so tiresome, she thought irritably, she might have taken Ashira's advice. Or, maybe she would have postponed the start of her work until after her babes were born, although she suspected even today's torment would be preferable to the priestess classes which she would have had to attend instead. She wished she had come to do this in a previous time, when the dying Oracle would find her successor before passing on and give guidance, or when the people had more respect for her words.

CHAPTER 32

A loud throat clearing brought her attention back with a start and she realized she had dozed off. Her mouth tasted sour and her head felt thick, as though she had drunk too much ale. The clergy were back at their original positions and a woman stood blinking up at her.

"May I have small ale please?" she asked one of the attendants and to her surprise he nodded, springing from his place at the wall and racing away as though he didn't wish to miss anything. Saoirse bit her lip at the irony that bubbled up in her and turned to the woman in front of her, nodding for her to rise from her deep bow and to begin.

"*Mistress*, I am called Nara and I come to seek your wisdom."

"Do so at your discretion, Nara. The first two seekers have left this room in a fury as I did not tell them words they wished to hear. I would only warn that you must be prepared to hear truths that oppose any impossible desires you may be attached to. I tire already of advising those who refuse to listen."

"*Mistress*, I have come not for myself, but for my mother, Bahira. The healer has visited and says she is dying, that there is no hope, yet I feel that surely there must be a way..." The rest of what Nara was planning on saying was lost in sobs.

"Nara, did you bring something dear of your mother's that I can hold?" The woman wordlessly handed over a scarf, a delicate piece interwoven with silver thread.

"My mother was married wearing this." Nara paused as she fought for control over her grief. "My father passed last winter in

CHAPTER 32

the flood and my mother has been grieving since. She wishes to join him, yet I tell her it is not her time. I must not lose both of my parents. There is a babe to come in five moon's time and my husband works the field. I have nobody else to help me. She is the only one in the known world who I can truly trust. Please..."

Nara collapsed onto the floor at Saoirse's feet and hid her face in her hands, her shoulders shaking silently. The scarf sat lifelessly across Saoirse's palms, and this time she didn't have the will or the energy to fight the blank, dead layer of gray that settled over her. To her surprise, it made the transition far easier this time. The closure of her throat was only slight, and she pulled her attention away from the stifling smallness of the room to the suddenly vibrant, dynamic feel of the scarf in her hands.

Saorise saw a wedding full of joy. Theirs was a rare marriage, where both Bahira and her husband had joined in love rather than duty. Even rarer was that both families agreed to the union, and everyone was celebrating noisily. Saoirse could not help but compare the genuine celebratory air of the occasion to the debacle of her own recent wedding.

The vision faded and Saoirse now saw the same woman shriveled and gray, lying lifelessly on a pallet in the gloom. The sun shone outside, and she showed no interest in allowing its rays in through the closed wall vents. A previously cherished neighbor came to visit, and Bahira turned away to face the wall. Bahira wanted to die and there was nothing to stop her, aside from Bahira's husband Raafiq, who was now leaning his spirit form over Bahira and attempting to talk to her and rouse her from her stupor.

"Nara, your father. He has not properly passed. Were you and your mother unable to perform the customary rites? He does not know he has lost his body. This is why your mother is so drawn to die. She can hear his whispers from the limbo worlds, and he is unable to move onward. There are many spirits still trapped like Raafiq after the flood, deprived as they were of ceremonies." At her words, Nara's sobbing renewed, and Saoirse watched her gulp the emotion down in order to speak.

"He never made it up the Sacred Steps in time. We searched for him, calling out in the fields, and out over the river, and we were almost swept away in the flood trying to find him. We only just made it before they closed the gates, and we never saw him again."

"Nara, your father found death in the river, but it was before the flood that his life was taken. It was an unfortunate accident. I see him stumbling, falling, and hitting his head on a river rock, and he has no memory of it happening as it was so sudden. This is why you never found him. Telling your mother this may give her some peace. But to free your mother, you must perform a ceremony to lead him onward. It will no longer do to chant the ordinary Death Rites, as he is too trapped. I will send ones to you who will free your father from his vigil."

Nara's eyes rounded and she nodded vigorously in gratitude.

"He imagines he is helping her by whispering encouragement in her ear. He tells her that the sun shines outside and the children play. He expresses his undying love and begs her not to leave her body. Yet it is his very presence that draws your mother away from her body. She feels his closeness and can't bring herself to turn away from it. She also pulls him back from moving on with her need. But your mother won't listen if you try to tell her. She'll try to stop the ceremony once she discovers that her husband's essence is fading, but once he is gone, she will be able to grieve and finally let him go."

Saoirse smiled as Nara stood before her, now radiant, and for the first time, serene. It was so joyful for her words to be received with such gratitude. Here was the culmination of her gift. It wasn't to seek out the sordid details of people's lives and rub their faces in their shame to try make them change their ways. There was another way that she could do this with love. Saoirse and Nara smiled at each other in the glow of shared wonder, that if Nara succeeded, a life would not only be saved, but her mother would also be given another chance to feel the wonder of being alive once again.

Saoirse knew just the people for the task of guiding Raafiq to where he was meant to be going. Once her day was over she would find a small street messenger, and she thought of how Raya and Jivan from the chanting group would be glad to accompany Raafiq on his final journey and help with his wife's bereavement. The attendants looked at her in confusion, and a little bit of disapproval, when she and Nara embraced and said fond farewells.

Saoirse sipped on her ale with a nod of appreciation for the

CHAPTER 32

clergy. She hoped that the next seekers would divert the clergy's thoughts away from how the ceremony for Raafiq would not be sanctioned by the Temple. She was sure the family didn't have the coin to pay for an official Temple ceremony, and knew that Raya and Jivan from the chanting group would have far more ability to help Nara's mother, anyway.

Thoughts about the chanting group made her forget for a moment who might be waiting outside the gold curtain to come in next. She wondered how the rebuilding of the small hall might be faring, and how often they met up, and whether her and Kaylem might be able to sneak themselves in some time soon. Kaylem had managed to sneak them some coin to help with the rebuilding.

Thinking about being seated with master Hos again, and the chanting group, and under the shade at the desert household, filled her with yearning. It had been so long since she had seen him. Now that she was part of the Temple, it would be even more of a heresy to be caught with the chanting group. She tried to imagine an entire lifetime unable to see master Hos, or take part in the chanting, and it filled her eyes with tears. Another seeker came to kneel at her feet, and she knuckled her eyes and turned to the man with a sigh. Compared to her life these days, she had had more freedoms as a prostitute at the inn of Ur than she ever would as the Oracle.

Soon the morning was lost in a whole procession of seekers. Some were genuinely wishing for the truth, while others wanted an easy escape from a difficult situation. Each time a much-loved possession was placed in her hands, Saoirse found that the transition became easier. The nothingness was even beginning to feel almost friendly. She noticed that some visions appeared straight away, while others took their time.

She sternly lectured men who quietly fumed like Siro had done. There were gentle words to grieving mothers about lost children. Saoirse noticed that even the attendants were shedding tears when she found herself reluctantly telling one young mother-to-be that the babe in her belly had died the eve before and she would pass its body at sunrise. Despite the difficult words she had to tell so many people, Saoirse felt the awesome power sustaining her throughout the day. The words coming from her mouth never failed to surprise even her as there was always something new to say.

Eventually, though, even such power could not bring her through another minute. Saoirse declared the day over, the pounding of a headache descending over her. As she stood, she swayed on her feet, and she was gratified to note that almost all the attendants rushed forward to support her. Swathed in scarves and hidden from the large line of those still sweltering in the merciless sun, she decided she didn't feel too sorry for them now that she knew that most of them wouldn't even bother listening to what she had to say, anyway. It would do them good to wait a little longer, as it may give them some time to meditate on their stubbornness.

And besides, after the long day she could barely walk and had to lean on one of the taller priests as he escorted her back to her abode. She wondered how many seekers the Oracles of old saw in a day and decided it must have been far less than what she had done, judging by how wilted she now felt. She worried for what it might have done to her babes to have pushed things so far.

The clergy had also fallen out of line with relief, having stood silently for most of the day with only a small break for the midday meal, which she had spent alone in the stifling room out of reluctance to face the rest of the elite. And Kaylem would be eating in the men's section, on the other side of the kitchen to the women's, which was forbidden for her to even enter.

The priest whose arm she clung to bowed deeply to her as he handed her over to Asi, who met them at the front entrance. The other pair of priests who had accompanied them also bowed in farewell. Saoirse nodded in acknowledgement, surprised by the turnaround in their attitudes compared with this morning.

She clung to Asi with relief, suddenly unsure if she could even keep her eyes open for another second, and the last thing she saw was Kaylem swooping to support her as her legs gave way beneath her.

CHAPTER 33

Saoirse was aware that she lay on a pallet somewhere that felt like it could maybe be home as familiar smells were around her. Someone had covered her with a fur, which was a little too warm in the late afternoon heat, but all the same, its weight was comforting. She vaguely heard Kaylem and felt him gently wringing her hand with both of his as he talked to Asi who, by the sound of her rustlings, was on the other side of the room.

Yet even those sounds and sensations were muted to Saoirse. There was only a vague sense of her essence having been pushed too far beyond the confines of her body, as though it was water leaking from a jar full of holes. Those holes were a problem, she was certain of that, but couldn't remember why. Her essence, she now noticed, was suddenly filling the entire room, and she could possibly even dissolve even more outward through its walls, maybe even spy on the nasty old servant whose name she couldn't remember for some reason. The woman had certainly done enough spying on her, that was for sure.

The upper corners of the ceiling were beginning to darken. She remembered this happening at some stage before, but she couldn't place why it made her suddenly feel so scared, and weak, and vulnerable. The shadows began to whisper. She wasn't quite sure what they were saying, but she shied her essence away as though the shadows were crawling with evil widow spiders. Those whispers were familiar, even though they were under the threshold of her hearing.

Her body was on the floor, she noticed now, lying on a pallet a long way below her. She couldn't remember what the blanket felt like. She tried to force herself to sink fully back into her flesh, but her essence had dissipated too far, and she wasn't quite sure how to bring herself back. Kaylem, she could see now, crouched beside her, and looked like he was wringing her hand far too strongly. It would possibly bruise, but she couldn't feel it. All she could sense were the shadowy shapes that started to crowd in around her. She was weak, they would take her over and there was nothing she could do. They had her this time. She should just give up and surrender to them. Then she would taste true power and finally know victory over her enemies.

There was something off about what they told her, but her mind wasn't working like it should. All she knew was that there was a terrible sense of danger which was growing, moment by moment, as the shadows clotted even more around her. Confusion set in. Was she dreaming? She tried to move away from the shadowy shapes, but they responded by crowding in even closer.

She noticed that her hand had the ghost of an ache and she turned to Kaylem, so far below. Somehow, focusing on his presence made the shadows retreat just a little. He called her name, talking so rapidly she couldn't make out all the words. There was something he told her to remember. Saoirse focused more closely. He was talking about the stars at night and what they had shared sitting out in the courtyard at the desert household. She watched an echo of a smile flit over her face as a sense of happiness filled her at the memory. The shadows retreated even more.

Then he spoke about the well, and how he would watch her peer down it and he would wonder what she was looking for. As he mentioned the well, Saoirse found that she could picture it vividly, exactly as it had been last time she saw it. From the outside it was nothing special—just a round, raised stone wall around the deep shaft penetrating into the depths of the desert floor. It was only when she could see the water at the bottom that the sacred nature of the well occasionally showed itself. Those had been the rare times when she could see other beings reflected there.

A sudden yearning filled her, so strong she almost completely forgot about the shadows, and even Kaylem. To just know who those beings actually were, that had shown their reflections in the silver water...If only she could know, she could then let go in

CHAPTER 33

peace. She pictured what she had seen of the beings. They were so bright that when she caught a glimpse of them, she could only just barely see a shape and occasionally a flash of color, but they seemed to have had wings.

As if to picture the well was enough, she found herself suddenly hovering over the courtyard where the well itself sat near the yellow-brown wall. Its stones were crumbling a little more than she remembered, baking in the merciless heat. She floated toward the well until she was above it, then found herself traveling down its shaft, which reminded her of the tunnel to the underworld. Was she dying? It certainly didn't feel terrifying now that the shadows had gone.

At the bottom of the well the water was so bright it threatened to blind her. At first she fought for breath as she plummeted into its depths, but soon found it warm and filled with life force that she could draw from all around her. Soon, she sank so deep that she found the bottom. It should have been solid, but her feet sank through even that. The mud sucked at her essence, and she did her best to push her way along, until she popped out the other side, which was so dark at first after the brightness of the courtyard, she couldn't see a thing.

When she was finally able to make out what lay ahead, she blinked in confusion. She was floating in a sea of stars. Before her, also floating, was a colossal, spherical rock, larger than anything she could ever imagine, surrounded by thick clouds. She drifted closer and the enormous rock filled her vision. Even closer she drifted until all there was was dead looking rock and great angry mountains belching smoke. She huffed in confusion. This didn't look at all like she imagined the underworld to be. It was all wrong.

There was a rumbling sound that came from far away and yet filled her entire being. She sensed that it was the thread holding the fabric of her essence together, and if it ever fell silent, she would fritter away to nothing. Everything would fritter away to nothing. It was ancient, irresistible, and interspersed with a kind of music. The music tugged at her, urging her to dance, and filling her with a sense that she could, just with a wave of her hand, create anything she could imagine.

A movement on the surface of the rock pulled her awareness down to the rock's surface. She drifted closer. With a gasp,

Saoirse saw the beings, this time not at the bottom of the well, but dispersed around the vast stretch of rock, making all kinds of movements. They were far larger than what she had ever imagined, shining just as they had at the bottom of the well. Their wings stretched far beyond their bodies in different and glorious colors that she wouldn't have even been able to name. Her heart lurched. There were seven pairs and all of them, to her surprise, were dancing.

It was a joy to watch as they moved as though in a trance. There was something familiar about the dance. One of them, the one with the blueish looking wings, seemed to be leaving trails of steam all over the place. Another, gusts of wind. Then a more ponderous being, with russet colors swirling in its wings, made movements which did something to the dead looking rock; making it look more like earth than rock. Yet another being, this one more of a green color, brought a tiny touch of budding growth to the new patch of earth.

Saoirse wanted to shout as her entire essence jumped in excitement. This was the Dance of Creation! The beings were gods, dancing the Dance of Creation and bringing life to the rock. A flash caught her eye and she saw yet another being with great wings of fire. She couldn't help but stare at the being, which danced its own dance of awakening and destruction in equal measure. It stopped what it was doing for a moment that felt like an eternity and stared right back at her. Her essence shivered right to her core and she was struck down by vertigo, as though time through the endless ages had looped and overlapped.

She couldn't help but stare back, drawn deeper and deeper into the being's essence. The tug within her grew stronger and she drifted even closer. It was like looking into a mirror, coming across a fragment of herself in those eyes made of nothing but flames. The being *was* fire. *She* was fire.

This was why she came into a situation and couldn't help but stir everything up. Fire was warm and wonderful to sit around when the night was cold. Fire was useful when at the beck and call of humans. This was far different. This was pure fire, untamed and wild. It spoke of nothing but power in all its great and terrible potential. Fire could annihilate and it could also inspire. Fire drew the gaze of all and inspired fear and awe in equal measure.

Fire moved ever upward toward *D'ingir*, the home of the

gods, and she suddenly understood that all she needed to do was to follow the fire within herself in order to find her way there. She could go there right now if she chose. That was what the being conveyed with a gesture so small she almost missed it.

There was something pulling her back away from the scene before her, even though somehow this scene felt far more like home than anything else she had ever encountered before. An echo of a vow she had made long ago tickled at the very edges of her memory. To Kaylem perhaps? The being shook itself to negate her question and she could have sworn it conveyed exasperation.

The pulling sensation grew, and she saw herself lying on her pallet for an instant, felt for just a moment Kaylem's hand, his voice drawing her back. Her essence almost split into two with the force of the pull between the two directions. *D'ingir*, the home of the gods—all that she had been yearning for, lay closer than it had ever been. And yet there was something unfinished, something she must go back for. An ancient vow.

She met the being's gaze once again and saw something like devastation as it flicked one of its limbs at her and blew a giant breath, sending her flying back through the star-flecked darkness. She shot out of the well and found herself stuffed roughly back into her body, which closed around her and made her feel like she was suffocating. Her body stank of sweat and death. The fur was too heavy, too hot. Kaylem's tears fell on her face, his breath acrid in her nose from his grief.

She squirmed, trying to push off the fur which was stiff against her throat, and she felt like she couldn't breathe. Kaylem fell silent for a moment, then gasped.

"Shaji?"

Saoirse grunted and managed, with Kaylem's help, to kick off the stifling fur. She marveled at the sensation of sweat cooling on her now exposed body, the sense of breath entering and leaving her chest. She even managed a weak smile in return to Kaylem's worried gaze, aware of the warm skin of his hand over hers. And somewhere, deep within her, she sensed a flame sputter to life and knew that all was exactly as it should be.

ABOUT THE AUTHOR

Penny lives with her three children and Sid the failed farm dog on the northern beaches of Sydney. In an ideal world, Penny would have infinite amounts of time to indulge her obsessions which include delving into the hidden magic of ancient civilisations, exploring the subtleties of the healing arts and contemplating the deeper esoteric realities. Of course, reading from an endless and eclectic supply of books while lying in the bath sipping on kombucha would have to be a regular occurrence as well.

Other Books by Ozark Mountain Publishing, Inc.

Dolores Cannon
A Soul Remembers Hiroshima
Between Death and Life
Conversations with Nostradamus, Volume I, II, III
The Convoluted Universe -Book One, Two, Three, Four, Five
The Custodians
Five Lives Remembered
Horns of the Goddess
Jesus and the Essenes
Keepers of the Garden
Legacy from the Stars
The Legend of Starcrash
The Search for Hidden Sacred Knowledge
They Walked with Jesus
The Three Waves of Volunteers and the New Earth
A Very Special Friend
Aron Abrahamsen
Holiday in Heaven
James Ream Adams
Little Steps
Justine Alessi & M. E. McMillan
Rebirth of the Oracle
Kathryn Andries
Time: The Second Secret
Will Alexander
Call Me Jonah
Cat Baldwin
Divine Gifts of Healing
The Forgiveness Workshop
Penny Barron
The Oracle of UR
The Oracle of UR, Book 2
P.E. Berg & Amanda Hemmingsen
The Birthmark Scar
Dan Bird
Finding Your Way in the Spiritual Age
Waking Up in the Spiritual Age
Julia Cannon
Soul Speak – The Language of Your Body
Jack Cauley
Journey for Life
Ronald Chapman
Seeing True
Jack Churchward
Lifting the Veil on the Lost
Continent of Mu
The Stone Tablets of Mu
Carolyn Greer Daly
Opening to Fullness of Spirit
Patrick De Haan
The Alien Handbook
Paulinne Delcour-Min
Divine Fire
Holly Ice
Spiritual Gold
Anthony DeNino
The Power of Giving and Gratitude
Joanne DiMaggio
Edgar Cayce and the Unfulfilled Destiny of Thomas Jefferson Reborn
Paul Fisher
Like a River to the Sea
Anita Holmes
Twidders
Aaron Hoopes
Reconnecting to the Earth
Edin Huskovic
God is a Woman
Patricia Irvine
In Light and In Shade
Kevin Killen
Ghosts and Me
Susan Linville
Blessings from Agnes
Donna Lynn
From Fear to Love
Curt Melliger
Heaven Here on Earth
Where the Weeds Grow
Henry Michaelson
And Jesus Said – A Conversation
Andy Myers
Not Your Average Angel Book
Holly Nadler
The Hobo Diaries
Guy Needler
The Anne Dialogues
Avoiding Karma
Beyond the Source – Book 1, Book 2
The Curators
The History of God
The OM
The Origin Speaks

For more information about any of the above titles, soon to be released titles, or other items in our catalog, write, phone or visit our website:
PO Box 754, Huntsville, AR 72740|479-738-2348/800-935-0045|www.ozarkmt.com

Other Books by Ozark Mountain Publishing, Inc.

Psycho Spiritual Healing
James Nussbaumer
And Then I Knew My Abundance
Each of You
Living Your Dram, Not Someone Else's
The Master of Everything
Mastering Your Own Spiritual Freedom
Sherry O'Brian
Peaks and Valley's
Gabrielle Orr
Akashic Records: One True Love
Let Miracles Happen
Nick Osborne
A Ronin's Tale
Nikki Pattillo
Children of the Stars
A Golden Compass
Victoria Pendragon
Being In A Body
Sleep Magic
The Sleeping Phoenix
Alexander Quinn
Starseeds What's It All About
Debra Rayburn
Let's Get Natural with Herbs
Charmian Redwood
A New Earth Rising
Coming Home to Lemuria
David Rousseau
Beyond Our World, Book 1
Beyond Our World, Book 2
Richard Rowe
Exploring the Divine Library
Imagining the Unimaginable
Garnet Schulhauser
Dance of Eternal Rapture
Dance of Heavenly Bliss
Dancing Forever with Spirit
Dancing on a Stamp
Dancing with Angels in Heaven
Annie Stillwater Gray
The Dawn Book
Education of a Guardian Angel
Joys of a Guardian Angel

Work of a Guardian Angel
Manuella Stoerzer
Headless Chicken
Blair Styra
Don't Change the Channel
Who Catharted
Natalie Sudman
Application of Impossible Things
L.R. Sumpter
Judy's Story
The Old is New
We Are the Creators
Artur Tradevosyan
Croton
Croton II
Jim Thomas
Tales from the Trance
Jolene and Jason Tierney
A Quest of Transcendence
Paul Travers
Dancing with the Mountains
Nicholas Vesey
Living the Life-Force
Dennis Wheatley/ Maria Wheatley
The Essential Dowsing Guide
Maria Wheatley
Druidic Soul Star Astrology
Sherry Wilde
The Forgotten Promise
Lyn Willmott
A Small Book of Comfort
Beyond all Boundaries Book 1
Beyond all Boundaries Book 2
Beyond all Boundaries Book 3
D. Arthur Wilson
You Selfish Bastard
Stuart Wilson & Joanna Prentis
Atlantis and the New Consciousness
Beyond Limitations
The Essenes -Children of the Light
The Magdalene Version
Power of the Magdalene
Sally Wolf
Life of a Military Psychologist

For more information about any of the above titles, soon to be released titles,
or other items in our catalog, write, phone or visit our website:
PO Box 754, Huntsville, AR 72740|479-738-2348|800-935-0045|www.ozarkmt.com